MURPHY'S RESCUE

A Sweet, Small Town, Second Chance Romance

CLOCKTOWER ROMANCE
BOOK 9

BECKE TURNER

SUNBERRY, NORTH CAROLINA

A place to call home.

Welcome to fictitious Sunberry, North Carolina. Settle back, put your feet up and prepare to enjoy a basketful of southern hospitality. With a population of twenty thousand diverse residents, Sunberry is the small city Americans dream of calling home. This slice of southern comfort offers a four-year college, an historic opera house complete with second-level entertainment, and a full-service hospital. No need to feel like a stranger. Sunberry residents mingle with new inhabitants, especially service members returning to civilian life.

If you're a veteran from nearby Camp Lejeune, a local rancher breeding organic cattle along the river, or a dog trainer developing new puppies to assist the disabled, you're bound to find a happily ever after in Sunberry. After all, doesn't everyone crave a home?

I want more Becke Info!

MURPHY GENERATIONAL LIST

Dear Reader,

I hope you enjoy MURPHY'S RESCUE, a continuation of the Murphy family following events in MURPHY'S STANDOFF. To refresh your memory of the family members, I've provided a character list with a brief description below:

- Murphy Matriarch: Stella Murphy (83)
- Marital Status: Widow
- **Son: Ryan Murphy (56)**
- Marital status: Married Ava Robey, widow (54)
- **Son 1: Kyle, oncologist (33)**
- Married: Dana, nurse, single mother (28)
- Daughter: Samantha (Sam) 7 years
- **Son 2: Whit Murphy (32)**
- Married: Talley, teacher (32)
- Daughter: Ellie 2 years
- **Son 3: Nate Murphy, builder (30)**
- Married: Chaz, restaurant and salon owner (27)

- **Daughter 1: Hope, U of SC student (25)**
- Single

CHAPTER ONE

11:30 AM

Freedom beckoned—once she tracked down her blasted car keys.

Hope Murphy's heart raced as she rummaged through her cramped pantry-turned-bedroom. She didn't have time for this. Her thirty-day countdown was already ticking, each second amplifying her dread. She swallowed hard, trying to dislodge the knot of fear tightening in her throat. She couldn't afford another failure. Not with everything on the line and a debt collector breathing down her neck.

"Think!" She pressed her fists against her temples, struggling to silence the relentless deadline flashing in her brain. Pay today or face a huge penalty and deeper debt to that horrible man.

Frantic, she jerked the faded quilt from her cot. When her missing key fob clanged to the floor, she snatched it and raced to the door.

Outside, a bleak winter day mirrored her dreary thoughts. March 8. Another year wasted, no closer to success. Her planned Thanksgiving announcement? A colossal flop.

The headlights on her Subaru flashed and she slipped inside the safety of her car. The engine started with a soft hum, reminding her of her brother Whit's generosity—and her fragile independence. With the doors locked, she blew on her numb fingers.

"Murphy up." Dad named her Hope for a reason.

On the sidewalk to her right, a woman, bundled in a hoodie and mittens, walked her dog along the narrow streets studded with overgrown skeletal trees. Along the row of rundown rentals, no one else stirred. Her classmates were still in bed or already on campus. Which is where she would be— in her previous life.

11:40 AM displayed on her car's touchscreen.

Everything she owned jostled for space behind her. On the passenger seat a manila envelope bulging with cash peeked from her backpack's zippered pocket. Hope touched the envelope. In twenty minutes her nightmare would end.

Stay focused. No distractions.

Once she completed the payment to Sleaze, the label she'd attached to the shifty-eyed payday lender, she'd lay out her next steps. She could salvage the situation—if she got to the meeting on time.

The opening bars of her favorite song, Nate's call indicator, blasted the silence.

"No!" She didn't have time to talk to the youngest of her three older brothers. Holding tight to her focus, she turned the wheel and the car lurched from too much accelerator pressure. Her phone continued to play the tune and Nate's smiling image lit up the phone's screen.

"I'm kind of busy right now," she answered, biting back a snarky response.

She loved her gentle teddy bear of a brother, but she had to get to her appointment.

Nate's voice crackled through the phone, a warm anchor

to home and a reminder of why she couldn't afford to fail. "It's good to hear from you too," he said.

Thank goodness his deep voice held no criticism, just the familiar comfort that increased her ache for home. Heavens, she loved her steady youngest brother because few things riled him. That's why brushing him off cut so deep.

"Sorry." She turned onto Assembly Street. "I'm running a little late for class." Which was a total lie. She'd dropped out of school last semester due to insufficient funds.

"Are you driving?"

"Just got in the car. It's freezing here. I'm so ready for spring." *And to get the debt off my back.*

"I won't hold you up long," Nate said. "We're planning a surprise party for Mom on March 19. It's during your spring break, so no excuses about classes. And Hope, it would mean the world to her. You know how much she misses you."

A lump built in her throat, the raw reminder of how much she missed Mom's comforting embrace. But if she didn't make her loan payment, she'd never be able to come home. "I can't talk right now. Call me later."

"Five minutes," Nate said. "You owe your family that much."

"Fine. You've got five minutes," she said. "But I've got to pay attention to the road. Columbia's a little bigger than Sunberry, you know."

While Nate provided the details to the planned party, she navigated the Columbia streets.

11:50AM

"That's it," Nate said. "Just promise to add the date to your calendar."

A car swerved from the curb in front of her, and Hope slammed on the brakes, heart pounding.

"Thanks for the signal," she muttered.

"Hope?" Nate said, concern edging his voice.

"Hold on." She checked her rearview, the reflection of her anxious features staring back, searching for a way out. "A parking spot just opened."

Hope pulled into the vacant space, her hands trembling with regret. She'd give anything to drive to Sunberry. Just the thought of the comfort of the family home calmed the jitters shaking her shoulders. It had been too long since she'd felt on track.

When she could trust her voice she said, "Entering the date now—with notifications."

"Great. Please don't disappoint Mom again," he said, softening his voice.

His gentle reminder resurrected the burn in Hope's throat. Blinking hard, she removed the cap from the plastic antacid bottle nestled in the cupholder and swallowed the chalky liquid, grimacing from the taste. The mild chewables tasted better, but they'd stopped working after Sean stole their app. And the woman who strived for honesty? She wiped her lips with the back of her hand. Replaced by a gal who drank antacid like Kool-Aid.

"So you're coming?" Nate said.

"I'll be there. But I've got to go."

On the sidewalk three women in dress slacks and heels entered the restaurant where she'd scheduled the meeting. The constriction in her chest eased. Safety in numbers. She turned off the heater.

"Jack Cline's coming too," Nate said, forcing her thoughts to return to her family.

She glared at her phone. "Your five minutes are up!"

"Just wanted you to know so there's no... unnecessary drama."

The emphasis on his final words straightened her spine. That's exactly what she was trying to do—end the drama.

She snatched her backpack and scrambled out of the car,

her heart pounding with fear and determination. Once she paid off Sleaze, she'd prove it.

"I'm 25," she said, feeding the meter. "An adult. Jack and I are ancient history." And she didn't have time to think about the guy she'd dumped because he was going nowhere. Embarrassment pinched her shoulders. She'd won the grand championship for career disaster. And it ended now!

"Hope?"

Nate's tone made her hesitate on the cracked sidewalk.

"Sorry, Bro. When you repeat the lecture, my brain turns off."

"The 19th is two weeks away." Nate said. "This is important. Just come."

Right now, she'd give anything for him to come inside the restaurant with her. But she didn't speak the ridiculous thought. Still, she'd loved to see Sleaze's expression if her burly brother accompanied her today. Her tremulous grin faded. Murphys always cleaned their messes. She had to do this one alone. It wasn't her fault, but it was still on her plate. Problem was? It terrified her.

CHAPTER TWO

Jack Cline reloaded his nail gun, the scent of freshly cut wood sharp in his nostrils. The familiar task offered a brief comfort against the anxiety gnawing at him with each darkening cloud. The Martinez add-on was coming along under deadline. But they couldn't slack off. Supplies were unreliable, and early spring in North Carolina often brought unpredictable weather patterns. They had to finish framing today. But he needed an extra hand and Nate Murphy, his friend and boss, continued to grip his phone.

Ominous clouds gathered in the southern sky, promising an imminent storm.

"Come on," Jack muttered.

Rain guaranteed a delay and this job meant profit. He'd busted his chops over the last two years and earned a chance at a partnership with Murphy Baker Construction (MBC).

Nate's stiff posture and clenched fist shouted just how much the caller, Nate's sister Hope, was tying him in knots. Jack eyed the next wall, anxious to start but stuck waiting for Nate to finish.

Jack's finger hovered over the trigger, his mind racing. All he wanted was to get on with the job. He didn't want to think about Hope or the pain she'd caused him, nor the fact those memories remained raw despite the years. He for danged sure didn't want to overhear her latest drama with his boss. Although he'd never been the sharpest nail in the cartridge, he wasn't dumb enough to give Hope Murphy another shot at his heart. One romance trial had been enough for him. Now, he only engaged in casual relationships.

His cheek stretched into a grin. However, he could get into seeing her face when she learned he was in line for partnership in a successful construction business. She'd never be able to hide her shock. Not with the big brown eyes she'd inherited from her mother. Which was another problem. He liked the Murphy family, and nothing wrecked a friendship and partnership faster than romance.

He snatched his cap from his head and hair fell over his eyes. "Are you stupid Cline?" he muttered. "Cut the thoughts about Hope!"

Five minutes later Nate ended the call.

Jack lowered his voice, worry lines etching on his forehead as he watched his friend struggle. "Are you okay, man?"

"It's Hope again." Nate exhaled, the weight of his frustration clear. "Something's always up with her."

Jack snorted, trying to lighten the mood. "Calm doesn't exist in your sister's vocabulary."

"Do you mind if we break early for lunch?" Nate asked, glancing at his watch. "I need something to chew besides my insides."

He minded—a lot! But Jack swallowed his objection by grinding his back molars to sawdust. They had a chance to finish a week early. A week! That translated into more complimentary reviews, more business, and his *partnership*. Instead, he focused on the pavement and followed Nate to the truck.

Couldn't his partner see the storm brewing in the East? If

that sucker hit, a push was out of the question. Like Nate could concentrate with his sister hijacking his thoughts. For now, Nate was still the boss—until he got that partnership. Then, he'd speak his mind.

From his seat on the tailgate, Jack squirted spicy mustard on his turkey sub. "Family has a way of messing with us." Like Dad always messed with him.

"Chaz keeps saying, 'Give Hope time.'" Nate peeled back his sandwich wrapper with a snap. "She's been in school for freaking-ever and still hasn't graduated. Now..."

"Did she change her major again?"

"She didn't say, but something seemed off about her." Nate gulped his soft drink. "Hope's usually all over the party details—decorations, guest list, food, you name it. This time? Nothing."

Jack swallowed a bite of his favorite lunch without tasting it. "Seems weird. Hope's never pressed for something to say. She's busted my chops more than once."

"Tell me about it!" Nate snorted. "Have you ever played basketball with her?"

Jack's groan merged with the distant thunder, both sounds echoing his frustration. "Only once. She totally humiliated me."

"That's my sister. She's beat all of us at one time or another. Too bad she hasn't put the same effort into her career."

"She'll work it out," Jack said. "We all did."

Nate's gaze drifted toward the half-finished wall, though Jack knew his mind was elsewhere, lost in thoughts about Hope.

"If I hadn't fallen for Chaz, I might still be working it out." Nate exhaled like Hope had already beaten him again. "That's why I'm lenient with her. But Kyle? Little Sis makes him a nutcase. That's why my brothers elected me to call her."

"Sucks being the youngest brother sometimes." Jack unwrapped a candy bar. "Unlike most of us, Kyle never had a hiccup about where he was headed."

"My brother was born thinking he has all the answers."

Jack's laugh burst out before he could stop it. Good thing Kyle wasn't around. Nate's older brother was a good guy and a great physician, but he was a know-it-all. Jack figured all smart guys were like that. Since they could figure out complex problems, they probably did think they had the answers. For all he knew, they did.

"Kyle won't let it go—keeps hammering on how we're enabling her," Nate muttered.

"Enabling?" Jack straightened. "You mean like she's got a substance problem?"

"More like an accountability problem. And if you breathe a word of this to anyone, we will have serious problems."

Jack raised his hands. "No worries. This conversation is over my head. My adopted brother has ten years on me so I missed the sibling drama."

"I think it's a little sister hazard. Kyle, Whit, and I always watched out for her." Nate tossed chips in his mouth and wadded his trash into a tight wad. "Not in basketball, but other things. Kyle said she needed to suffer natural consequences. But it never seemed right. I wouldn't let a wasp sting her without a warning. I sure wouldn't let her twist in the wind if I could help her."

"Has she ever listened to you?"

"Heck no!"

Jack ducked his head to hide his grin. Nate was a great boss and a great guy, but a soft heart could take a guy down. "So Kyle thinks no pain, no gain?"

Nate nodded. "Pretty much."

"I floundered for a while," Jack said. "And I didn't find the answer in a book."

"You had a job to ground you. Hope switches tracks, and Whit funnels cash into her account. He never complains, but Kyle does. He swears Whit's money is wrecking Hope's life."

"And Kyle's not her dad," Jack said. "What do your parents think?"

Nate shook his head. "You know about their second honeymoon?"

Jack nodded and stood, hoping Nate would get the hint. A raindrop hit his cheek.

"Hope is the reason they took it. I just pray the party doesn't turn into a family intervention."

"With Hope?"

Nate squinted at the darkening sky. "I dunno. I just got a weird vibe from her today. I wish she would graduate with something and start her life."

"She'll work it out." He did—if Nate's family drama didn't jack up his partnership.

Jack tossed his lunch trash in the bed of his truck. Why was he defending Hope? Because he got it, or at least her situation. Since he'd graduated high school, his adopted dad had criticized everything he'd done. But now he wondered if Dad had just been worrying about him like Nate and his family worried about Hope.

"I'd be floundering like a fish on the shore if you hadn't given me a chance."

"You've earned it." Nate squeezed his shoulder and Jack stood taller. "You know, I completed Art's buyout at the first of the year. Talley's working on the numbers, but if they go the way I think... important changes could be coming our way."

Jack buckled his toolbelt to keep from jumping up in the air and shaking his fist at the sky. He'd done it! Jack Cline, total high school screwup, was going to be a business owner with a say in the next projects. Oh man, did he have a sweet deal in mind. He just had to keep his head on work and avoid Nate's sister. She might be hot, but she was trouble. He didn't need problems with his new partner.

Thunder rumbled.

"We better pack it in," Nate said.

"No lightning yet." Jack shot three nails into the plate. "We can finish this wall before it breaks. It would be worth the risk if we came in early and underbudget on this project."

A lightning bolt flashed across the sky followed by another crack of thunder. Giant rain drops splattered on the brim of Jack's hat.

"That's it for today," Nate shouted over a gust of frigid air.

Another flash streaked across the sky.

Jack hefted his tools with a grunt and sprinted after Nate, rain drenching him. He was so freaking close. Too close to turn loose of his dream. But darned if he could turn off the feeling of a far worse storm looming ahead.

CHAPTER THREE

11:59AM

Hope hesitated at the entrance to the restaurant, her knuckles white from her grip on her tattered backpack. Her instincts screamed at her to retreat to the safety of the Subaru. But inside the car, with its connection to her family, came deeper guilt.

She squared her shoulders. "Murphy up," she whispered, trying to steady her voice. "Focus. Pay off Sleaze."

After she'd put the unpleasant experience behind her, she'd rerail her life. Her part-time jobs weren't great, but she could save money. Scheduling could be dicey because she'd negotiated the use of her car in exchange for a place to live. Still, if she kept working, she could repay the college fund Whit had set up for her.

That was a must. If she had to work three jobs for the rest of her life, she'd pay back every dime. With a little luck, she'd manage that feat before Whit or her family learned what she'd done. Not that Whit would complain. The disappointment in his blue gaze would knock her on her butt. She'd confess—someday.

A woman's bawdy laugh interrupted her thoughts.

12:00PM

Move.

Although she hadn't seen Sleaze enter the restaurant, he could've come earlier or entered through the back door. With a man like him, anything was possible and probable. She'd have to stay sharp, get in, make the payment, and get out.

After that? She rolled her lips and blinked back tears. She just wanted to go home, breathe. But she couldn't tell her family what she'd done—not yet. And the lies? The lump in her throat resisted her efforts to clear it. Never in a million years had she dreamed she'd lie to her family. Never.

"Move! This won't fix itself."

Despite the busy interior, the darkened restaurant located in Columbia's popular Vista creeped her out. Sean swore Sleaze was a legitimate, nonviolent lender. But Sean had also stolen her app.

Besides, she was up to her eyeballs in risky behavior. After today, she would calculate every move. Like avoiding a meeting in an isolated office with nine thousand in cash stuffed in her backpack. She'd chosen a busy restaurant in the middle of the day. Smart move. And the nine thousand? Not so smart, especially when handing it over would leave her with twenty dollars to her name. She refused to focus on the irony of the situation.

When it was her turn to be seated, a young man dressed in black slacks and a t-shirt smiled. "Hope Murphy?"

Hope moistened her lips, her heart pounding harder. So Sleaze was here, waiting for her. Since her mouth had dried and glued her lips together, she nodded and hoped her face didn't reveal the fear gurgling in her gut.

After a steadying breath, she marched forward—like she was heading to a firing squad.

No fear, she silently chanted.

Surrounding her, diners talked and laughed. It would be okay. He wouldn't try anything in a crowded restaurant. She was caving to fear. In less than an hour, she'd be on her way to move in with her new roommate. Debt-free. Humiliated with her failure, but at least she'd sever her ties with Sleaze.

A black shifty gaze met hers and her step faltered. Sleaze's eyes narrowed at her approach—like that was even possible. Although she didn't expect him to stand, the motion of his hand toward the seat across from him annoyed her. She tightened her grip on her backpack and slid into the booth facing him.

"You're late," Sleaze said. "I've already ordered."

The screen on her phone displayed. She'd entered the restaurant at precisely 12:00PM, right on time. Besides, she would not cower to a man wearing a pink-and-green bowtie, regardless of his snake eyes. Her fingers tingled, clutching the backpack like it were a lifeline.

A cute guy dressed in the restaurant's black t-shirt saved her from responding to Sleaze. "What can I get you?"

Out of here. Hope forced a feeble smile. "Just water. I won't be staying long."

The waiter grinned and a dimple appeared as his eyes sparkled with interest. Heavens, what she wouldn't give to go to lunch and flirt with a cute guy. Anything, just to be normal.

Sleaze's snort returned her attention. She shifted her gaze to his, trying to assume a bored, degrading stare. Her face felt like Jell-O, refusing to obey her attempts to appear calm.

"This place has awesome burgers." He removed his dark-framed glasses and polished them with his napkin. The jerk was enjoying her misery.

"The lending business has been good," he said. "Going out for lunch is a rare break for me."

Yeah, well humans at his level were rare for her too, thank you very much.

When she failed to respond, he lifted his bony shoulder. No doubt she outweighed the man. But that didn't make her feel any better. Although she wanted to clasp her hands on the table to give the impression of a calm businesswoman, she couldn't make her fingers release the strap to her bookbag. Nine thousand dollars! Money she could've used to graduate as a medic. Money Whit had risked his life on the gridiron for. But she couldn't back up time. If she didn't pay Sleaze, she'd never be free.

With stiff, resistant fingers she slid open the zipper and retrieved the bulky envelope. "I want a receipt."

He held out a fleshy palm. "Of course. After I count it."

Her grip tightened on the envelope. "The receipt first."

He didn't move.

Fear raced beneath her flesh, but she held fast. After Sean's thievery and her contract with Sleaze, naïve Hope had matured. She'd ended up on the losing side this time, but that didn't mean she'd repeat her mistakes.

The server approached with a platter laden with a huge burger, fries, and cole slaw. The aroma of the seasoned meat and hot oil curdled her stomach. She didn't flinch. Didn't release her grip on the envelope.

Sleaze sniffed the air like he didn't have a care in the world. Then, he turned in his seat and produced a document. Hope hesitated, not wanting to reach toward him.

When his lip twitched, she snatched the receipt, careful to avoid touching his hand, but never releasing her hold on the cash. The urge to wipe that smile from his face surged through her. She'd never hit someone, but she'd seen her brothers in a few scuffles. If he made one move toward her cash, she'd make her brothers proud. Her determination must have shown in her expression because Sleaze turned his attention to his plate. Although a struggle, she managed to read and keep an eye on him.

A croak erupted from her. *What the—!*

"Problem?" Bain Vill, aka Sleaze, sipped his beverage.

Hope opened her mouth. No words came forth. Not a sound. She swallowed and jabbed her finger at the paper. "I borrowed four thousand plus interest." She inhaled a steadying breath. "At twenty percent four thousand is—"

"Fifteen thousand and change." Bain wiped ketchup from his mouth. "Just like the paper says. Because you haven't made any payment yet, the interest on a $4,000 loan at 300% Annual Percentage Rate (APR) is $15,258.79, plus late fees. I waived the $150 origination fee since you and Sean are friends. See? It's crossed off right there."

"You told me $5,000." Hope took another sip, but the chilled water didn't ease the rasp in her throat."

"That's right." Bain leaned forward. "If you'd coughed up the weekly amount. I'm a payday lender. That means the loan extends from one payday to the next. You didn't pay so late fees apply."

"But—"

Her hand shifted from his quick jerk on the cash envelope. She glanced down, but he'd already opened the envelope and thumbed through the cash.

"Nine thousand?" His smile evaporated, his voice flat. "Is this a joke? You're seven thousand short."

The server refilled their glasses. This couldn't be right. She'd earned top grades in math. Developed an amazing basketball app to track students' stats, scores, games, and practices, plus help parents find carpools and share videos of games. It was fantastic and basketball parents would love it.

She resisted the urge to chug her water. But she didn't know squat about lending practices and had trusted her thieving partner.

"This is a scam." Her intended hiss sounded more like a death rattle.

Bain slapped another document on the table and pulled out a pen. "No. It's a contract you failed to meet." She couldn't tell if he was mad or glad she was short. "But I'm successful because I'm flexible."

This was a nightmare. She had the right amount. He'd been clear about the parameters the first time. She remembered it.

But he kept filling out the form. Worse, lines were completed with her personal information already filled in.

"About one in five. That's how many don't pay on time." He looked up and she swore if he smiled one more time, she'd dump her water over his head. Except she'd drained her glass, again.

"Surprising, isn't it? I never figured you'd be one of them." Thank goodness he didn't smile. "But I do my homework. You have a famous brother."

Hope stiffened. "My loan has nothing to do with my family."

Bain signed the new document and turned it toward her. "Wrong again. Your family connections are why I made the loan to you."

Hope's fingers tingled. *Stay calm. Think!*

But her brain couldn't fire a single synapse with his gravelly voice humming in her ears. She licked her cracked lips. Could he do this? She didn't have time to find out. No matter what, she couldn't drag her family into this mess.

"Every dime I have is in that envelope," she said, cringing at her mistake to give him additional information. She had to think. Be smart. This was not the time to fall apart, but she couldn't stop shaking.

Bain shook his head. "That's too bad. Makes me wonder if I should trust you with a rollover loan. However,... NFL players make big bucks."

"No!" Hope winced and glanced around to see if anyone had noticed her outburst.

"I'm a businessman." Bain placed her cash into his briefcase. "How're you going to pay the seven thousand plus interest you owe me?"

"I'll work for it." She snapped her jaw shut to stop its trembling. "The same way I made this payment."

Bain canted his chin to the side. "The same way you ignored your weekly payments and got so far behind?"

They hadn't discussed weekly payments. She'd signed up for a loan payable in six months. At least that's the agreement she remembered.

"What else do you have of value?"

What else? Was he serious? He'd taken everything she had. Humiliated her. What else was there?

"Nothing you're going to get," she said, but her words sounded faint. "I only have a few belongings in my car."

Bain brightened. "What kind of car?"

Not her car. Whit gave her the Subaru. Just like he'd deposited the money into her college fund—which was also gone.

"You aren't getting my car," she said, praying the desperation clawing at her gut wasn't evident in her shaky voice.

"Says the woman who owes seven thousand dollars." Bain held out his hand. "Year and model?"

The leather booth closed around her. She thought she gave him the information, but she couldn't hear the sound of her voice over the pulsing in her ears. What would she do without a car? No car. No place to stay. No car. No way to work. No car. No way home.

"Hello?" He waved his palm in front of her face.

A popping sound echoed in her ears. Hope blinked. Across from her Bain had raised his hands like he'd won a prize.

"Since I like repeat customers, especially women with rich brothers, I'll make a deal on your Subaru." He grinned. "I checked it out while you were processing the shock and awe of your predicament."

What?

He held up her car keys and laid them on the table in front of her hand. What was happening to her? She'd stressed out. Of course she had. How many times did a woman go through an experience like this? She couldn't believe it and she was living it.

"I'll take the car and its contents. You've got a nice laptop on the front seat." He marked through the nine thousand. "I'll knock your principal down to four thousand."

He drew a slash through the monthly fee. "Here's your weekly payment or in your case the final amount due at the end of the month and a bill of sale for the car." He underlined $5,006.71 and held out the pen. "Sign here or keep your car and I'll call your brother for the outstanding amount. You choose."

He was *not* calling Whit. Sure, her brother would pay, but at what cost? A moan died at the back of her throat. She was an intelligent person. How had she missed the enormous risk?

The pen felt warm compared to her cold hand. She couldn't let him call Whit. Her family couldn't know how far down she'd fallen. Her signature resembled a caterpillar trail through a raindrop.

"That's a wrap!" Bain exchanged her keys with the customer copy. "See you in thirty days."

The table between them shifted and his voice moved above her. However, her muscles seemed frozen in place.

He slid the restaurant check in front of her. "Thanks for lunch. It was delicious!"

Hope's gaze slid to the check. The blurry type focused: $13.95. Her mother's loving gaze filled her memory and she yearned for the warmth of her arms. But she was a grown woman in a giant mess. Mom was too smart to get involved with a payday lender. But Mom had instructed Hope to always keep an emergency stash. For once she'd listened to her mother and hidden a twenty-dollar bill in the bottom pocket of her backpack. She'd planned to use it for gas. Except her car was gone along with her means of transportation. With numb fingers she retrieved the wrinkled twenty and placed it on top of the check, kissing her chance at freedom goodbye.

CHAPTER FOUR

6:55AM

Eager for a productive day Saturday morning, Jack navigated the pothole-riddled entrance to the Sunberry Farm Store. Although Nate didn't work weekends, Jack did.

His coffee-brown Chevy Silverado belched an exhaust plume into the frigid March morning. Jack zipped his hoodie.

"Come on, Mother Nature," Jack muttered. "Spring's late."

He needed a weather break so he could get a jump-start on his special project—right after Nate gave him the partnership.

After shutting off the engine, he stepped onto the graveled lot. Movement to his right halted his step. As he turned, the blue tarp covering the pickup's bed moved and then something dark emerged.

A person crawled over the side of the truck and stood. Holy! That was Cody Barnfield's truck. His breath hitched in his chest. Was that...Hope Murphy?

The figure straightened and extracted a small backpack

from the pickup bed, and then replaced the tarp and turned toward him.

"What are you doing?" Jack said.

Hope froze, her eyes wide, her mouth slightly ajar.

Jack blinked. Up to no good, just like in high school. But they were a long way from high school.

She moistened her lips, no doubt framing an explanation. Some things never changed.

Her glance darted around the shadows of the lot like she expected a boogie man to jump out. "Don't sneak up on me like that," she said in a whispered hiss.

"I'm a customer here." Jack grinned. "No sneaking involved. You're the one crawling out from under a tarp. Cody would've let you ride in the cab."

"I don't want anyone to know I'm in town."

Moving closer, the hair at the nape of his neck lifted. She was not the red-carpet diva he'd dated in high school. Hay protruded from her hair and stuck to her clothes. A faint animal odor prickled his nostrils. Black smudges circled her dark eyes, giving her a haunted appearance.

"Why are you whispering?" he said. "And why are you dressed like that?" Not that he cared about the way a person dressed. Shoot, his everyday uniform consisted of jeans and a Carhart hoodie.

When she shivered, he shrugged out of his sweatshirt, draping it around her shoulders. "Come on. Get in my truck."

His thoughts spun for traction while he settled her in the passenger side, slid behind the wheel, and cranked the engine and the heater. This didn't make sense. The Murphys were a prominent Sunberry family. Why was Hope slinking around the feed store like a homeless person? And where were her wheels? She used to drive one of those small, foreign SUVs.

He opened the thermos sitting in the cupholder and filled the cap. "This should help warm you."

She cupped the container with trembling hands. "Thanks."

Jack directed the vent toward her, the warm air matching the unexpected tenderness he felt. He plucked a stick from her hair. "You've got something in your hair."

"Hay." Hope rubbed her scalp. "It's itchy, but it kept me warm."

"Why—"

"I needed a place to sleep last night," she said, like it was common for her to have hay in her hair and smell strange. Not to mention he'd found her sneaking from Cody's truck with no luggage, no car, and no coat.

Jack adjusted his cap, the answer clearing his confusion. "You slept in Cody's barn?"

He braced for her to lose her mind and dress him down for suggesting such a thing.

Silence.

Holy.... He was right.

"I got in around three AM and I didn't want to wake anyone." She sipped at her coffee. "I was hoping Lil would come down to feed the horses. I figured I could borrow clean clothes from her and then work out a plan. But Cody fed them this morning. Par for the course considering my luck over the past forty-eight hours. But I got here okay. It's a wonder considering that truck driver."

Jack slapped his hand to his temple. No. Just no. He hadn't heard right.

"Repeat that story." He pumped his hands like he was testing a new mattress. "I didn't sleep well last night so I'm a little fuzzy."

"Tell me about it." Hope drained the last of the coffee. "Do you have anything to eat? I'm starving."

"Gina's will—"

"Absolutely not!" Her eyes narrowed.

"O-kay," he said. "The Stop 'N Go is open."

"If I ever step foot in a truck stop, it will be too soon."

He resisted the urge to give her a little shake. On second thought, he was the one who needed a shake. His drive to the farm store had been rerouted down a rabbit hole—a very weird one.

"I must have missed something," Jack said. "Start at the beginning."

"The beginning of what?" She pointed at him. "And if you breathe a word of this to *anyone*—"

He grabbed her finger. She had a habit of pushing it into a guy's chest. He remembered it hurt. He remembered lots of things about her. Right now, he just needed to make sense of the last five minutes.

"Nate called you on Thursday morning. I know because we were working on the Martinez add-on. You were in Columbia."

"That's right." She rummaged through his truck's slush box. "Don't you have a candy bar in here? What sane person doesn't keep snacks in his car?"

"I pack lunch when I work. I don't keep food in my truck."

She twisted in her seat. "So where's the lunch bag? I haven't eaten since yesterday."

Jack put the truck in gear. "I'm sure your mom has food," he said, the casual suggestion masking the worry gnawing at his gut.

"I'm not going to my parents' house."

Jack stopped at the highway. "Fine. Where to?"

"Do you live with your parents?"

"Not since I was nineteen."

She opened the glove box. "Girlfriend?"

"No."

She snapped the door closed. "Roommate?"

"What is this, twenty questions? I rent an apartment near campus. But I don't have much to eat."

"Perfect." She raised her palm like a traffic cop. "I need a place to shower and grab something to eat until I can come up with a plan."

After checking for traffic, Jack pulled onto the main road toward his place. This was a terrible idea. He couldn't keep her appearance a secret, and he couldn't afford to get on Nate's wrong side. Not to mention he liked the Murphys—sometimes better than his own family. But he was working on that.

"Where's the rest of your...stuff?" he started. "Most people travel with more than a backpack. I've seen you wear five outfits in one afternoon."

She lifted her backpack. "This is it. Do you have a washer-dryer?" She sniffed her shoulder. "I smell kind of horsey."

"You actually slept in Cody's barn?"

"It wasn't that bad," Hope said. "Except Slider snores. Who knew?"

The truck jerked to a stop. "You slept with animals?"

Hope removed her braced hands from the dash and shot him a glare. "It beats sleeping with most men I know."

"Done a lot of that lately?" Jack immediately clamped down on his jaw.

"That's none of your business."

"You're right." He accelerated. It had been a cheap shot. But danged if she didn't have him spinning his wheels like a truck on ice. "You always brought out the worst in me."

"Maybe that's all there is."

"Nice, Hope. Glad to see your homeless condition hasn't changed your attitude."

Although he'd said it out of anger, he was pretty sure he was right.

"I've hit a rough spot so I might be a little snarky," Hope

said. "I need a friend. I'm not wanted by the law or anything. I'm just kind of jacked up."

Jack flexed his hands around the steering wheel. Based on her appearance, rough underestimated her situation. "Where's your ride? If you broke down somewhere, I'll take you to your car."

"I didn't break down."

The click, click, click of the truck's signal indicator broke the silence and sent a warning along his spine. She might not be in trouble with the law, but she had some seriously bad issues. Bad enough to lose her car. Crap, this wasn't the same as her old high school skirmishes. She really was homeless.

"You can clean up at my place." In the back of his mind, warning bells were blasting. He'd live to regret this. "But I'm not lying to Nate or your family. Call them. Whatever's going on, they'll help."

"I'm not a little kid anymore."

Fear more than anger edged her voice. When he glanced her way, she was picking at her nails. She'd done that since he'd first known her.

"I don't need my family to race to my rescue." Her voice had softened. "I'll manage. I just need a little time and a place to hang."

"Everyone in town knows you. You can't hide out for long. Your family is going to find out and they'll figure it out the same as I did."

"Figure out what?"

Aw man, she was going to get mad. But facts were facts. "You look homeless. Which doesn't make a lick of sense. You were a student at Carolina. What happened to your apartment, car, clothes?"

"I'm not hiding. As soon as I clean up and charge my phone, I'll call Mom. But I'm not moving home. Can you help me find a place to stay—a job would be nice too?"

Jack swallowed. This was a whole lot worse than he imagined. Nate thought she was in school and so did the rest of her family. Which was so not his business. He wasn't going to hide Hope's presence from Nate. Geez, just what he needed to wreck a new partnership.

He turned into his building's lot and stopped in front of the four-story brick structure. Each of the four apartments included a private entrance and a small patio or balcony.

An odd sound broke through his thoughts. He switched off the heater fan, and then turned off the engine.

When the noise sounded again, Hope unzipped her backpack. A fuzzy face emerged from the opening.

"It's okay Turbo," she cooed. "I'll get something for you to eat."

Jack sneezed. "Nope. Not happening."

"What?" Hope said.

Jack jerked a kerchief from his hip pocket and sneezed into it. "The cat can't come in."

"It's not a cat. Turbo is a kitten." She held the filthy creature in the air and smiled. "He was hiding on the tire of an 18-wheeler. I rescued him."

"My heart bleeds." Jack fired up the engine.

"I thought you were going to let me shower at your place."

"You." He jabbed his index finger at her. "Not the cat."

"His name is Turbo."

Jack jerked the lever to reverse the truck. "Turbo can stay at the shelter."

"Absolutely not!" Her raised voice echoed in the cab and the kitten scrambled from her grip, leaped to Jack's lap, and clawed a path to his shoulder.

"Ouch!"

"You scared him," she said, lifting the creature from his shoulder along with a few of his skin cells. "Hey, little buddy.

It's okay." She tucked the filthy animal beneath her chin. "He's hungry. Could you pick up some cat chow?"

One, two, three... welcome to the world of Hope. He gripped the steering wheel so tight, it was a wonder it didn't disintegrate. "I'll drop you and the—Turbo off at Nate's. You can work out your next move with your brother." *Because he was done.*

"Don't do this, please."

Jack averted her gaze. She was not his problem. He liked his calm, planned life. Looked forward to going to work every day. Looked forward to a well-earned partnership with Nate. Hope would wreck his life. She wouldn't mean to. But chaos followed in her wake.

He shifted to drive, his resolve wavering. "Sorry. You and Turbo need to find a different place to stay." The regret in his voice betrayed his words.

"I just want to succeed at something. Make my family proud." Her desperate grip bit into his forearm. "You know how that feels," she said, her voice cracking with vulnerability. "If Nate hadn't hired you, where would you be?"

He despised her words. Despised their truth.

His mind churned, mirroring the rough idle of his truck. Nate had given him a chance. Given him a future.

The minute he lifted his gaze to hers, defeat roared through him. Darned his sorry hide. *Look away and drive to Nate's place.*

In ten minutes she and the cat would become Nate's problem. Jack had completed his good deed today by giving her a ride.

"Jack, please," she whispered. "Don't make me beg. I need a break."

Before his sorry brain cells started firing again, he'd parked, turned off the truck and was leading her into his apartment. He pulled the door closed behind her. Talk about a cluster. What was she going to do? More importantly, what was *he* going to do?

"You could have avoided this"—he waved his arm in an arc,— "if you'd called someone last night."

"The driver let me out near Old Sunberry Road." Still cuddling the kitten, she dropped her backpack on the floor and turned in a circle. "It was late and my phone was dead so I holed up at the Crooked Creek. It was like camping out. I was safe. It just got a little cold last night."

Jack massaged his temples. Hope's family would lose... their...minds over this. "You can plug in your phone in the outlet above the kitchen counter or the one by the lamp. Why didn't you plug it in last night and call your family? I know Lil has electricity in her fancy barn. And why didn't you leave Turbo at the Crooked Creek?"

"No cable."

This fiasco just didn't stop. "Why?"

Hope grabbed his cable lying on the kitchen counter and plugged in her phone.

"Hope?"

She didn't turn. "Because I don't. Is it okay if I bathe Turbo in the sink and then shower?"

Just what he wanted: a filthy animal in his kitchen sink. He huffed out a frustrated breath. "I guess that beats a dirty kitten running all over my place. What's that stuff in his fur?"

Hope sniffed Turbo and wrinkled her nose. "Smells like a cross between motor oil and something far worse."

Not trusting his voice to betray his building annoyance, he led her down the short hall to the master bedroom. "When you finish playing cat groomer, the shower's right through there."

She peeked inside his bedroom like it might bite her. Thank goodness he'd made his bed. He wasn't a total slob. His dirty clothes were in the basket and he was pretty sure the toilet lid was down. Mom could take credit for that one.

She was studying his boots, which had to be a first. Nothing cowered Hope Murphy—until today. His arms itched to encircle her, to tell her he'd take care of it—whatever *it* was.

"Do you think—" She huffed out a breath. "Can you loan me something to wear while I wash my clothes?"

He tried not to react, really tried. But dang, he hadn't expected that one. He just figured she had a change of clothes in her backpack. Ducking his head, he pulled out a drawer, retrieving a soft new pair of sweats. Hope was only a few inches shorter than his six feet and she could cinch up the waist. Plus the sweats were warm—and he wasn't going to let his mind go down that road.

"I've got to pick up a strip of finishing nails." He shrugged, turning away from those big brown eyes that seemed to stare right into his soul. "That was the reason I went to the farm store in the first place. I'll stop at the grocery on the way back. Do you want anything special to eat?"

"I could eat the legs off your table." She grinned. "I eat anything. But I need a shower first. I'm kind of grody. Slider is a great horse, but he could use a bath. Don't worry. Once I shower and feel human again, I'll call around. One of my friends will let me crash for a while."

"What's a while?" *Just shut up, Jack!* But he couldn't. This was Hope. "You need to fess up and get some help. This is Sunberry. No one is going to judge. Well, some will. But they don't matter. I'll drop you off at your parents' home or Nate's. He'll help you work it out."

"Jack, please."

Knowing he'd never resist if he met her dark eyes, he

dropped his gaze and landed on the kitten. Turbo stared at him, its soulful gaze as haunted as Hope's.

"I need a friend," she said. "Be that friend."

Aw, dude, this was a dumb move, but he couldn't refuse. Not trusting his voice with its golf-ball sized lump in it, he nodded.

So much for getting a jump on his special project.

Dad had been right. He hadn't learned from his mistakes.

CHAPTER FIVE

Safe at last!

Hope leaned against the door, the deadbolt clicking into place with a satisfying finality. Her belly grumbled, muscles aching for a soft mattress and clean sheets she couldn't afford. The reality of her situation weighed on her like a lead blanket. However, she couldn't repay Jack's generosity by making his bed smell like Slider. She grabbed Turbo before he created a cozy nest on Jack's sofa pillows.

Inside Jack's utility area she found two raggedy towels. Turbo mewed, a tender sound melting her heart.

"We're a sorry mess," she said, running warm water into the stainless sink. "But providing your needs are simple. Mine?"

She had to come up with ideas to earn cash—quick. An image of Whit confronting Sleaze flashed in her mind. Ignoring the chill, she refocused on gently washing Turbo. The poor little guy didn't fight her gentle massage of dish soap in his fur.

"Don't worry, little one." Black oily water leaked down the

drain. "As soon as we get cleaned up, eat, and grab a nap, I'll find us a place to stay and a job."

After three shampoos and rinses, the water finally ran clear from Turbo's scrawny body. She dried and cuddled him in a clean towel and then snuggled him in the sofa cushions he'd picked out earlier. When he stretched and closed his eyes, she walked down the hall to Jack's bedroom.

Geez. The man was a neat freak, living like a monk. Not one personal photograph ornamented the walls or surfaces of the sparse dark furniture. Like she had room to judge. From barn floors to tarps, her lofty dreams of wealth and fame seemed laughable now. A cozy and quiet life near friends and family tempted—

"No. Just no." Hope turned toward the bathroom for a much-needed shower. As for a concrete plan to keep her secret safe and shake Sleaze off her trail? That would come after something to eat and a short nap.

———

HOPE BOLTED UPRIGHT, her heart pounding in her chest. She'd heard something. Someone was here. Had Sleaze sent a hit guy after her? She eased off the bed, careful to avoid disturbing Turbo, stood, and adjusted the waist of Jack's borrowed sweatpants. Easing the closet door open, she searched for something, anything to protect herself. Jack's metal baseball bat would have to do.

The floorboards in the hallway creaked. Hope tightened her grip around the cool metal and leaned back, her weight distributed, muscles tense. The bedroom door swung open.

Terror halted her breath and tensed her muscles, ready for battle. *Wait for it.*

The dim light from the kitchen fell on Jack, his eyes wide.

"Seriously?" he said, the deep timbre of his voice filling the room. "You're gonna hit me with my own bat in *my* apartment?"

She forced a grin, her lips trembling, fighting the urge to cry. A smile had gotten her through many tight spots. Except with Sleaze Bag. She'd never smile at that foul man.

Jack held out his hand.

She shrugged and handed him the bat. "A gal has to be prepared."

He returned the bat to the closet and motioned for her to follow him, but her feet had rooted to the floor. A dizzying whirl of images swirled in her thoughts, starting with Sleaze Bag, her desperate search for a ride, the wait at the truck stop—

"You're safe here."

Jack's whispered words and the warmth of his embrace stopped the horrible images. She squeezed her eyes closed and inhaled his familiar scent. His warmth eased the chill, soothed her. He'd always been around, never a real boyfriend. More a friend, a compadre in her various exploits. Thank goodness he hadn't changed his shampoo. Some things in life needed to remain unchanged.

Don't start something you can't finish! But she ignored the internal warning and let her hands glide along his chest and curl behind his neck, luxuriating in the feel of his silky hair.

"Don't let go," she whispered. *Just hold me.* But she didn't speak the last three words. She'd already lost everything. Pride was all she had left.

His hand glided up and down her back, soothing her. "Let me help you," he whispered.

"Like the time you tried to help me craft a story to my brothers and they nearly pounded you?"

His grunt brought the tiniest of grins. Despite her

attempt to lighten the mood, she didn't release her grip on him. Couldn't.

Tell him. She squeezed back a tear. Just get it off her chest. He'd always been a good listener and so had she. But not this time. She was a grown woman and needed to stand on her own two feet. She'd created the problem. It was up to her to resolve it. But how? She slid her hands to his chest, forcing herself to step away.

Jack dropped his arms but didn't step back. He'd always let her lead, trusting her when she didn't trust herself. She wouldn't disappoint him. Although she managed to force her shaky legs to step back, meeting his gaze challenged her.

Murphy up, flowed through her mind. She owed him for giving her a place to stay, clothes, and his silence. Not a hint of judgment shadowed his gaze.

"Thanks for everything you've done." Her grin wobbled and she caught her lip between her teeth to steady her chin. "Have you thought about keeping my presence a secret—just for a few days?"

While he stared at her, she silently begged him to say yes, noting how far he'd come from the gangly teenager always a step behind her. Now, she was the one trailing behind and grateful for his lead—praying he'd continue for a few days.

When he finally nodded, the breath she'd been holding whooshed from her lungs in an audible puff.

"Thought you might still be here," he said, turning away. "I picked up two of the specials from Gina's."

Still disoriented, she followed him to the kitchen, the heavenly aroma of food grounding her to the present.

Ignoring her stomach's complaints, Jack's voice softened. "Otis swears by the recipe—you know how he is about the restaurant's menu."

Tension drained from Hope's stiff neck. Whatever had

just transpired, Jack had felt it too. Thank goodness he'd possessed the fortitude to distance himself.

Hope reached for the container, suppressing the urge to tear it from his hands. Heavens, she felt like she could devour a horse. She wrinkled her nose. *Sorry, Slider.*

"I restocked while you were sleeping." He placed two paper towels and forks on the table. "And I picked up cat food and litter. Joey, the clerk at the grocery, has cats. He said we needed a Turbo toilet box. Seemed gross to me, so I stashed it beside the hot water heater in the utility area."

His thoughtfulness sent a quiver through her chin. Jack didn't even like cats.

"That was sweet," she murmured, a warmth spreading inside that had nothing to do with the cozy apartment. "I'm glad you aren't sneezing anymore."

His thoughtful actions touched a part of her she thought she'd hardened.

"It must have been something on his fur." Jack removed the food containers from the bag. "With all the muck on him there's no telling."

One more debt she owed Jack. But she didn't mind owing him. It gave her a connected feeling. Still... "Sorry about the towel. I got it from the utility area, but I don't think the motor oil will wash out."

He shrugged. "It's a towel. The thrift store features linen deals once a month. In my line of work there's no sense in buying expensive items."

Although she preferred fluffy, absorbent towels, Jack's simplified lifestyle appealed to her. Actually, everything about him appealed to her.

Off balance by her strange reaction to him, she reached for the food container, bumping his hand in the process. "I hope you bought the super-size."

She jerked back, eyes wide in surprise. Her stomach

growled, sending Turbo scurrying out of the kitchen and Jack laughing.

She glared at him, but it didn't diminish his grin. "What do you expect? Your crackers are stale and your milk is sour."

"But my clothes are comfy." He lifted a brow. "Keep them until you get on your feet. I have another pair in the drawer."

"The only drawer I opened was the kitchen drawer on the end. That and the pantry and fridge. I haven't stooped to tossing someone's place."

"Says the woman who sneaked into the Crooked Creek barn and Cody's truck."

"Even thieves have an honor code."

"Honor?"

Fine. She'd give him that one. "Perhaps I used the wrong word." She held out her hands for the food bag, hoping he'd already eaten his lunch at the diner. "Can we talk over lunch?"

His grin widened, which was starting to annoy her. Her hangry status had already hit the danger zone.

"Better check the time, babe. It's 6PM."

She hesitated, unsure if it were the use of her pet name or the loss of time that bungled her thoughts. Unwilling to test her building attraction to Jack, she turned toward the window.

No freaking way! "It can't be that late. I just took a little…nap."

Jack screwed up his mouth, an expression he'd perfected in high school. It usually preceded a comeback.

"I'd say your nap turned into a winter hibernation."

She grabbed the bag from his hands. "Give me that. We could starve waiting for you to finish criticizing my behavior."

He leaned against the counter. "You do have quite a list of … interesting qualities."

"I'm amazing with a microwave. Get the drinks." She focused on preparing the wonderful meal before she fainted from hunger or Jack. With his soft flannel shirt rolled at the elbows, his straggly dark hair, and the amusement in his gaze, he looked as good as the food.

He held up a long neck. "Cold one?"

The casual offer reminded her of simpler times, making her chest tighten with longing.

She wrinkled her nose. "It beats sour milk. But if you bought a fresh carton, I'll stick with dairy. Oh no! Where's Turbo?"

Jack pointed at a small feeder in the kitchen corner. "He's around here somewhere. I fed him and put out the litter box. But that's it for my cat duty."

"You did all that and I slept through it?"

The microwave buzzer beeped. He opened the door for her, but his mouth had softened and so had his voice. No sarcasm, no judgement, just being Jack.

"You were sound asleep," he said, his gaze holding hers for a tantalizing moment. "I didn't want to wake you."

Aggravated with herself, she shook her head. Somebody needed to wake her up. She couldn't sleep like the stinking dead and lose herself in Jack's appeal with Sleaze's debt hanging over her.

"So you stored your groceries...and left?" Her voice came out squeaky. Dratted man.

He removed the take-out box from the microwave and placed it on the table. "I had some work to do on the job site."

The rattle in her head grew louder, reminding her that her brother Nate worked in the same location. Shaken, she opened the pantry door. A fresh jar of peanut butter, bread, two packages of crackers, ramen noodles, and a variety of canned goods filled the formerly empty shelves. Two family-size boxes of Cheerios filled the right side. On the floor sat a bag of kitten food and litter.

"At least you have something besides cereal and sour milk."

He filled a glass and handed it to her. "I aim to please."

"No worries there." She lifted her glass and swallowed the lie with the sweet taste of the milk. Her life was one giant mess of worries. Jack worked with her brother. Jack had an uncanny ability to anticipate her thoughts and actions. Her traitorous body still thought Jack was special!

He wasn't. He couldn't be.

Super. Now she was even lying to herself.

She unplugged her phone and it lit up like a Christmas tree with messages from her family and—

> Good morning, Borrower!
>
> Days Left on Loan: 24
>
> Friday Payment Due: $1,415.56
>
> Cheers, Bain Vill

Her breath hitched, finger trembling over the screen.

"Problem?"

"Nope!" She needed to do something about her voice. Minnie Mouse was not a good sound for her. "Just a message from every Murphy in the Sunberry city limits." Which was true but not the reason her heart fluttered in her chest like a trapped hummingbird.

When Jack turned to place their plates on the table, she tapped the screen and Sleaze's text with the photo of Whit, Ellie, and Talley and the countdown banner disappeared. However, the number twenty-four continued to strobe in her head. Twenty-four days until Sleaze called her brother. Whit would never bow to a threat to his family. If he took matters into his own hands? Dread shivered down her spine. She had to pay off that debt. But her first payment was due tomorrow.

She didn't have fourteen cents, let alone fourteen-hundred dollars.

Hope's heart pounded as she deleted the message. She couldn't let Jack or her family find out—she had to fix this on her own.

CHAPTER SIX

SHE WAS LYING AGAIN.

Jack swallowed the urge to call her out on it. Her cheerful act might fool others, but not him. Something on her phone had caused her sudden pallor and the widening of her eyes. He'd never seen her show fear before, but she'd been shaken.

Not your problem Cline.

He waved her toward the scarred wooden table. "After you."

She checked beneath her. "What's with the seat cushion?" Her voice carried a mix of amusement and suspicion, hinting at a need for normalcy.

"I shop at a Jacksonville consignment shop," he said, glad she'd changed to a lighter topic. He lifted the lid from the steaming container, releasing a rich aroma of garlic and herbs. "Mmm. If this tastes as good as it smells—"

"It will." She grabbed the carton and served heaping spoonfuls on their plates. "That's why I'm going to be majorly ticked if my bum drops through this chair and spoils my meal."

"It'll hold. I'm saving for a big project." He hesitated, torn between respecting her privacy and wanting to help. Sharing something about his work might get her to open up about her troubles. "Chairs aren't on my priority list."

"Nate said the Martinez add-on was a financial turning point for the company."

"And a partnership for me. But the deal I mentioned is for me."

Hope narrowed her gaze. "So you're dumping my brother?"

"Expanding to two divisions." Jack blew off her suspicious look. It wasn't like he hadn't talked over his ideas with Nate. "You know Nate. He's cautious. But I think Sunberry can support remodels and new builds. Nate will continue to operate remodels and I'll open the new build division—*if* it goes through."

"Partnerships can trip you up," she said.

The edge in her voice suggested he'd hit a sore spot, but now wasn't the time to push. Instead, he explained his plan to subdivide the land he'd purchased adjacent to the Kare Center. Still, her comment nagged at him. When he wound down, her gaze hovered somewhere over his shoulder.

"Did you have a partner in Columbia?" he asked.

Turbo mewed beneath the table and Hope scooped up the kitten.

"You're excited about your ideas." Her usual fast-flowing words had slowed like she was selecting each one. "I was too when I came up with a new app. Murph-Tastic is awesome."

As she talked, her words sped up with excitement. "I got the idea when I volunteered for a kids' basketball camp and heard parents' concerns. It was perfect. Parents could track their kids' stats, games and practices, and find carpools. We even had a straightforward way to post videos and keep the kids safe. Talk about a parent solution. Do you know how many kids play basketball, especially in South Carolina? We're talking big bucks!"

"But?" He kicked himself when she immediately deflated.

She kissed the kitten and returned it to the floor, her fingers lingering like she drew comfort from the small creature. "I had the idea and the capitol. Sean had the skillset."

Although Jack anticipated how the story ended, he waited.

"The longer it took to launch, the more money we needed to fund us. I held down part-time jobs, while Sean worked on the app. When he pushed back the start date over and over again, I got suspicious." She watched Turbo leap into the bag and poke at the sides, but she didn't smile. "He was Bev's boyfriend. We'd been friends for over two years. Trusting him seemed like a no-brainer. He was a smart, geeky guy you believe in." She shrugged, an expression of defeat pulling down the corners of her mouth. "Long story short, Sean stole my idea, built the app, and left me with a huge debt."

Jack clenched his fists, anger boiling up. "Did you file a police report?"

"I tend to avoid public humiliation, especially with a he said, she said complaint. Sean and I only had a verbal agreement." She lifted her palms. "But I learned my lesson. I read every line of the last loan agreement I signed."

The delicious meal soured in Jack's stomach. "I'd be happy to help, but I'm tapped out right now," he said, regret tightening his throat. "Everything I own is tied up in the land I purchased."

"It's just money," she said.

But the slight waver in her tone made him grind his teeth. *She's trying to convince herself, not me.*

"I'll earn what I owe," she said, her voice sharpening with determination. "I just spent the last two months doing exactly that. The saddest part is, I was coming home for

Mom's party." She paused and bit her bottom lip. "Just not like this, not crawling home so defeated."

He'd been yammering on and on about his business opportunities while hers had just crashed and burned. Jack stood and dumped his container in the trash. "What's you next step?"

She waved her fork in the air. "Eat dessert with my ex high school beau."

"Is that how you think about me?" he asked, questioning if he really wanted to know where he stood with her.

"Until this morning, I hadn't thought about you."

He winced, but harsh reality had stopped wounding his pride years ago. Besides, his lack of status had nothing to do with the haunted look in her eye.

"If you need a job, Penny might have an opening."

"Chaz's Penny?"

"Yep. She's been running the restaurant since Chaz finished school and opened the salon."

The gloom and doom lifted from her expression. "Perfect. I could work at the restaurant and crash in the apartment above it."

Man, she was trying so hard to maintain her can-do attitude. He admired her resilience, even as it broke his heart. But homelessness had already drained her vitality. He didn't want to be the one to keep batting her down.

"That won't work," he said, gentling his voice. "Chaz rented the apartment to Val Reeser."

"Reeser? The name's not familiar. Is she new?"

"She moved here from Missouri. She's good people."

"I guess I'm not the only one who needs a fresh start."

Watching someone so energetic and full of life circling the drain battered his spirit as much as it did hers. Worse, he didn't have the means to help her.

He exchanged her trash for the pound cake nestled inside

the bag. "Val's around our age. You'll like her." He should've left it alone. But everything she told him about her life created more questions. "Since she doesn't have family here, everyone's tried to make her feel at home. Families help when you're in a jam."

Her eyes narrowed. "You breathe one word of this to my family and we'll pick up where we left off with your bat."

"I don't chat up the locals." He opened two small containers. "But I won't lie to your family."

"I'm not asking you to lie. I'm asking you to keep your mouth shut."

The sliced pound cake's aroma of vanilla blended with sugar couldn't sweeten her request. "There's a fine line between lying and omitting important information."

When he sat down, she placed her hand over his. "I just need a month to get back on my feet. Please. I don't want to tell my family—not like this."

He turned his palm up and she slipped her cool fingers into his, her long and elegant hand contrasting with the roughness of his.

Back off, Cline.

He wasn't going to wreck his partnership over a doomed attraction. Besides, Nate and his family were friends.

"Thirty days." He lifted his palm. "But you've got to be straight with me. No more lies."

The twitch of her mouth combined with her intense gaze didn't inspire his trust. Was she crafting a story or deciding what to reveal and what to keep hidden? He'd learned a heck of a lot about his old girlfriend from today's conversations. Most of it sketchy.

"So you sold off everything to pay off the loan?"

Hope looked away and nodded. Which verified his suspicions she was hiding something. Now, he was the one with the shakes. He didn't want to consider what she'd left out, especially when he remembered the haunted look in her eye. What happened to make a person so jumpy, especially in Sunberry?

She raised her chin toward her battered backpack on the floor near the door. "What's left is in there."

"At least you won't have to work three jobs."

"Hello?" She shoved her hair away from her face and tears formed in the corner of her eyes. "I have no clothes, no transportation, and no place to live."

"Sure you do," he said. "You're home. My sister-in-law has a closet full of clothes. I bet your friends have scads of things they don't wear. They'll help you out." He added a grin of encouragement. "I have another pair of sweats in the drawer."

"You know what I mean." Although she turned, he caught the glimmer of desperation in her dark eyes, which made him want to fall on a sword for her. "Everyone in my family is successful. I don't want to crawl home and repeat the story I just told you—not like this, not without something to show for myself."

"They love you. It won't matter to them."

She pounded her chest. "It matters to me."

"I get it," he said, remembering his own struggle. "Until this gig with Nate, I wasn't proud of my choices. But if I can work through it, anyone can."

"So you finally feel like you earned your dad's respect?"

Leave it to Hope to find his Achilles heel. "We're getting there."

"Right." Hope thumped the table. "You've got your own place, a business, and opportunities for a future, yet you still have dad doubts. Consider my situation and think how *I* feel."

Jack huffed out a breath. "Point taken. Though me and Dad don't always think alike, I think he's okay with my career choice. But you and your dad?" He shrugged. "I remember him always being there for you."

He studied her expressive features, noting the flicker of uncertainty in her eyes. People were a lot like houses. A good builder always checked what was going on inside the walls.

"Sometimes that makes coming clean harder," she murmured, pain etched in her shadowed gaze.

Her admission twisted his heart. He didn't want to question her. He wanted to take her in his arms, tell her it would be okay. But he wasn't sure her life would smooth out—especially if she hadn't given him the whole story.

"Keeping a secret in Sunberry for thirty days isn't realistic."

"It's not a choice. I don't want to tell my family about this mess until I can tell them the debt has been paid. In the meantime, I'll find a job and someplace to crash tomorrow. Then, I'll call home and get you off the hook."

He rubbed the tension in his neck, feeling like he'd fallen as low as her thieving partner. "I'll keep the details a secret. Unless Nate or someone else in your family asks me straight out. I'm not lying."

When she hugged him and his foolish heart hummed to life like a buzz saw, he knew he was in trouble. He just prayed his agreement with Hope didn't ruin his relationship with her family, especially Nate. They were perfect partners, something pretty danged rare in the building world. Hope could destroy what they had in a heartbeat.

"I've got everything I own in the land adjacent to the Kare Center." He knew he should shut up, but she needed to understand what was at stake. "That's where I want to build the new houses. It's risky buying land in these times, especially since I don't have the partnership. But once it happens, I'm set to start the new-build division."

Within moments, his concerns dissolved into excitement.

His plan was so cool. He, Jack Cline, the guy who had floundered around for freaking ever, had hammered out a great idea to grow the business and improve Sunberry.

He pulled out his wallet and placed three C-notes on the table. "I stopped at the bank this afternoon. I know it's not much, but it'll get you started. I'll help you any way I can. But I'm in a good place and it's all because of Nate and the rest of your family. They've helped me. Even buffered the issues between me and Dad. I can't jeopardize that. I don't want to lose everything I've built."

"Like I have?"

The harsh reality of her words hit him like a punch and he grunted from the emotional force. He'd given her everything he could, including his pledge to secrecy. That's all he could afford right now.

She placed her fingertips on the bills and he wished she'd place them on him. He had a few things of value. His brother had given him an old motorcycle and a hunting rifle he no longer used. He'd sell those this week and give her the money. Anything to see her smile again.

"I'm invited to your family dinner Sunday," he said, dread building in his chest. The impending meal represented the first test for his promise. But it was nothing compared to the obstacles before Hope and her mother. They'd always been close, and Hope's call would be a heartbreaker for both of them.

"I'm going to tell them I've decided to take a break from school then." She narrowed her eyes. "I am taking a break."

That started last year! But he didn't push her. Like a stable house, relationships required a solid foundation. Family affairs could be tricky, a lesson he'd learned the hard way. "And the rest of the story?"

Her eyes seemed too sparkly, but she didn't cry. "I can't tell them I've lost everything."

When he opened his palm again, she grasped it, her touch sending warmth through him. He squeezed her fingers, a silent promise of support. "You don't lose the people who love you. You may shut them out. You may hurt them, embarrass them. But you don't lose them. Talk to your family. Let them help you."

Her gaze burned into his. "When you were at your lowest point, did you ask your dad for help?"

"Dad's help had too many strings," he admitted.

She nodded. "It's hard to work with family. The lines get blurred between business and family relations."

"It's your family, your decision," he said. "What do you want me to do—other than lie by omission?"

"Put out some feelers. I'll check with Penny." She looked down at the bills still on the table. "I've lost contact with a lot of my friends. Help me determine which ones might have a place to stay. I'm not staying here."

Although mistimed, his grin popped into place along with the image in his mind. "Too hard to resist my charms?"

His stupid joke sucked the oxygen out of the room. A light flared in her gaze and every cell in his body ignited. Not a good idea.

She was shaking her head like she'd read his thoughts.

"What about the new girl? Chaz's apartment has two rooms. Any chance, I could room with her?"

Jack wrinkled his nose. "Val's pregnant and she's pretty close to popping. I think she's setting up the second room as a nursery. Your Grandma Stella and Ava were talking about it last month."

"Any other options? I need a place within walking distance of Gina's—provided Penny hires me. You don't have a bike, do you?"

"Just the old motorcycle—that doesn't run." He shrugged. "I was going to work on it. Get it going again."

"You? A mechanic?"

He welcomed the lighter talk. Drama wasn't his thing. "That's why it still doesn't run."

"I'm sure Mom has a bike or two in the garage. But if I ask, she'll want to know what happened to my car. Wait! I'll say I gave it to a friend—like Val. She was pregnant and barely making ends meet. I had to give it to her."

Jack massaged his temple. Hadn't she heard a word he'd said? "But it's not true."

She pointed a trembling finger at him. "Don't judge me!"

Aw geez. She was at the end of her rope. He stood. "Come here."

"Don't!" She grabbed the bills and moved to her backpack.

Desperation was a terrible thing to watch in someone you cared about. Someone who refused to accept help. But he understood about pride. Understood how it felt to have nothing going for you but down.

"Babe?"

When he touched her shoulder, she froze. After a pause, she dropped her backpack and turned to him. He folded her in his arms, loving the way she settled against him.

"You're not alone," he whispered. Never would be if he could help it.

The old gut-wrenching feeling clamped his chest, making him wonder if the tremor had come from his body or hers. That kind of loneliness he'd talked about never completely left—just like his memories.

Although the fire that had claimed his birth parents and little brother had occurred twenty years ago, the loss still cut. It wasn't like he'd been alone. The Clines had adopted him and given him a good home. But the old memories and emotions never went away. He pressed his feelings aside and focused on the woman in his arms.

He could help with temporary loneliness. He knew too well how it felt to be alone, even in a crowd. Unlike his birth family, hers stood nearby waiting to enfold her in their love. Too bad she couldn't see that. Something, pride or shame, was keeping her away. The reason didn't matter to him. He'd fill the void until she could face her family.

Be careful, Cline.

The warning filled his thoughts. Although he couldn't walk away, he couldn't get intimately involved with her again. Easy enough.

The familiar scent of her hair eased his tension. He liked his shampoo on her.

When he tried to release her, she sniffed and clung to his shoulders.

Was she crying? His shirt where she rested her cheek felt cool—like it was wet. Although he eased his hold, he didn't move. Didn't follow the urge to tilt her chin upward. If he kissed her, his heart would be hers again. Except this time he wasn't a high school kid worried about her older brother's threats. This time he was a man with a man's needs, a man's dreams. Dreams she could fulfill or destroy.

Focus, Cline. You're not in Fantasy Land.

He would cut off his arm rather than betray his mentor. Nate had given him a job, direction, purpose, a future. The nasty conflict caused him to grind his teeth. For him, it always came down to Hope.

Strike that word from your vocabulary, Cline.

She was a Murphy and he owed them.

CHAPTER SEVEN

Things were looking up!

Hope stopped her phone alarm and stretched, relishing the glide of fresh sheets over her flesh. After her long ride with a trucker followed by a campout in a horse stall, the comfort was almost overwhelming. Turbo rooted closer to the hollow of her neck, his faint purr humming like a miniature motor.

"You thought so too, huh?"

When she propped herself up on one elbow, her tiny furball burrowed his pink-tipped nose deeper under his paws. She sniffed his velvety fur, now a soft gray after his reluctant bath.

"Rise and shine," she murmured, nuzzling the kitten. "Jack's dish soap smells much nicer than motor oil."

Good thing she'd used the mild soap on her new pet instead of Jack's shampoo. She didn't need more reminders of Jack's presence just a room away, his nearness a constant, bittersweet ache.

The kitten tightened its curl and she slipped to her feet.

"No rest for the wicked."

With Sleaze breathing down her neck, she couldn't afford any drama. Grandma Stella would start matchmaking if she learned Hope had spent the night with Jack. A couch and a job in two days or less. How hard could that be in her hometown?

After a luxurious hot shower—she'd never take basic needs for granted again—she held up her favorite ripped knee jeans and her black trousers. Penny had been sneaking her cookies from Gina's bakery case for ten years, but a job interview called for business attire. The trousers, though, might stimulate unwanted questions.

Hope snorted. Of course, asking for a job would raise questions. *Get over yourself.*

After slipping into her white dress blouse and the trousers, she brushed her hair back into a tight ponytail. She'd run out of makeup three months ago and the stuff was expensive. As for a haircut and style? Not in the budget.

"Dang you, Sleaze Bag," she muttered. "You've made my life a mess."

Entering the galley kitchen, the first shaft of dawn filtered through the blinds, casting a hopeful glow. Jack, standing near the window overlooking the front of the apartment building, turned to greet her, his warm smile easing her anxiety.

He raised his cup. "Coffee?"

Hope rubbed her hands down her thighs. "I'm so nervous. I don't think caffeine is a good idea."

"I didn't buy eggs so if my so-called kibble for humans doesn't interest you, there's bread for toast."

"I'll pick up something—" She hesitated. No she wouldn't. She was broke, except for Jack's loan. And she wasn't going to waste his hard-earned money on food. "Toast sounds great."

When he extracted the bread from the pantry, she took the bag from him and placed two slices in the toaster. "Jelly?"

He snapped his fingers. "Are you kidding? Peanut butter and jelly are a Cline lunch staple."

The cheap meal would be her staple, too, until she paid off Sleaze. Man, she despised owing money, but Jack's reassuring high-five and grin eased her worries and sent a flicker of hope to her heavy heart. "Are you working today?"

Jack retrieved jam from the refrigerator. "I've got a few finishing touches at Art and Gracie Baker's new home. I'm meeting Nate at the Martinez Project at nine." He shrugged. "It's a late start. But when you're doing remodels and add-ons, the client sets the hours."

"So you and Nate didn't build the Bakers' new home?"

Jack shook his head. "Art's preparing to retire. We were busy completing his rental renovations so he could sell out. He hired another contractor to build his house."

When the toast popped up, Hope moved the slices to a plate. "I can't imagine Art trusting another contractor."

"That's where I came in." His grin widened and his shoulders lifted, showing his pride. "I checked the contractor's work every evening after Nate and I finished at our site."

Yearning bloomed in her chest. That's what she'd been trying to achieve—accomplish something she was proud of, something to make her family proud of her.

When a dark lock of Jack's hair dangled over his right eye, a new feeling bolted through her, and her fingers itched to push it back.

Oh heck no! But he was already staring at her, his dark eyes framed by sinful lashes narrowed in concentration. Had he said something? And why did guys always get the thick lashes? It wasn't fair. *Get your mind straight!*

His mouth did that crazy, quirky movement like he was eating sour candy—as in real sour!

She shifted her bug-eyed surprised expression to a bright smile with little hope he'd fall for her ruse. "So, you're working two jobs until the Bakers move into their new place?"

"I'm hanging fixtures today," he said. "You can drop me off and take my truck. I'll get Art to take me to the site at nine."

"Wow! You trust me with your truck?"

He did the quirky-lip thing, which she interpreted as veiled resistance. She loved it when guys played the knight.

"Thank you." She tapped the contacts button on her phone. "I accept your gracious offer. What's your number?"

As he airdropped his contact information, her finger hovered over the key. Why had he never removed her from his phone when she had removed him? What did that say about her?

It said she had enough trouble with financial problems without adding gnarly personal issues.

After stuffing her phone in her pocket, she placed her plate in the dishwasher. Jack stood, his arms crossed over his chest.

She mimicked his stance. "Problem?"

"Sunberry has a rabid grapevine. Your mom would be devastated if she learned you were in town from someone besides you."

Hope squeezed her eyes shut, battling her frustration. "Why do you always have to be right?"

"Annoying, isn't it?"

When she opened her eyes, his grin caused a little snort to erupt. The man's timing had always been good.

"I'll rearrange my tools while you're making the call." When he turned at the door, his features had softened and their gazes held. A surge of gratitude and a pang of something deeper coursed through Hope—an old connection coming to life.

"Remember she loves you," he said.

Her momentary Jack fantasy vanished. She'd never questioned Mom's love, which served to sharpen her guilt. But Mom had also taught her resilience. When Hope suffered her first bout of bronchitis, she'd been forced to drink an expectorant that tasted like something found in Lil's horse barn. She'd hated it. But Mom told her to hold her nose and swallow fast. Never hesitate when facing something bad—like hurting her mother.

When Turbo rubbed against her ankle, a gentle reminder that love prevailed, she pressed the call button.

Ava answered on the second ring and the joy in her mother's voice caused tears to sting Hope's eyes.

"Hey, Mom. I've got an appointment so I can't talk long," Hope said, her voice catching. "I just wanted you to know I'm home and I'm staying in Sunberry for a while."

"Where are you staying? Why didn't you come home? Is something wrong?"

"No, no. Nothing's wrong and I really miss you. But I'm working on some changes and I need a few days to iron out the details. I'll give you the rundown at Sunday dinner." Hope infused her tone with irony but wasn't sure she succeeded. "I know my brothers and Grandma Stella are speculating about my next move. Everything is ...well, I think you'll like it. But I'd like to give my story once to the whole family, okay?"

"Well sure, but—"

Mom wasn't buying it.

Hope swiped at her wet cheeks and forced her brightest smile, praying her voice would get the message. "I promise my news will be okay with everyone. I love you and I can't wait to have dinner with all of you."

"Aw, Honey, we're looking forward to having you with us. Always."

"Love you," Hope said, not pulling off her usual cheerful tone. "We'll talk soon."

After disconnecting, Hope blew her nose and then

splashed cold water on her face. Tears continued to hover, along with her guilt. There was nothing worse than disappointing the people you loved most.

When she closed the apartment door ten minutes later, Jack was leaning against the truck. His knowing gaze nearly brought on the floodwaters again, but she batted them back.

He tipped his chin just enough to let her know he was in her corner and then held out his keys. "You ready?"

"I was born ready." She squared her shoulders. "With a little luck I'll find a job, a place to live, and be out of your space this afternoon."

He opened the truck door for her. "And you're going to update your family?"

"Yep. Sunday dinner."

While she adjusted the seat, he walked around the front of the truck and slid in the passenger seat.

"Next year..." She adjusted the rearview. "I'll look back on this experience like it was a little bump in the road." She nodded, trying to reinforce her resolve.

"You always find the positive side to a situation," he said. "I admire that trait."

"You do?" Heck, she was delighted he believed her. Some days she didn't believe herself. "I've survived worse situations."

"Such as?"

She scrambled for something old, really old, to reference because she wasn't going to relive her night at the truck stop. Someday. Not today. Besides, she cared what he thought, and right now, she looked like a loser—which she was. But that was going to change.

The seatbelt bit into her chest. "Oops, so sorry. Your brakes are touchier than my car."

She checked the road for traffic. "I haven't driven a truck

since I drove Chad Davis's pickup into a mudhole. I had to call Dad to pull us out."

The memory lifted her spirits, a small victory that might erase Jack's look of pity, the one he thought she didn't notice.

He groaned. "So I wasn't the only one in your long line of victims. I'm still trying to live down that night we made out in Talley's driveway. It took me months of family dinners before I got over being around Whit."

"Not my smartest move." She turned onto Main Street. "After that night I always double-checked my clothes before entering the house." There was a sudden shift beside her, and she couldn't hide the grin. "I guess you missed the fallout details. You were a little handsy that night. I went into the house with my blouse buttoned cockeyed, and of course Whit noticed."

"Just when I thought it was safe around your brothers," Jack said. "It's a wonder I survived high school."

"I would've saved you." She giggled. "Besides, Whit is such a softie."

"I didn't think so. I was a shrimp until my senior year. You were even taller than me. But Whit was a beast. The size of his biceps exceeded my thighs."

"I could always handle my brothers. But Dad?" Heat blazed Hope's cheeks. "Dad pulled us out of the mud that night, but never said a word. Silence. Man that is the worst."

Her thoughts slipped to Sleaze. Too bad she couldn't silence him. He'd be blabbing his slimy mouth to Whit and everybody in town. She stiffened in the seat. Did he know where she lived? Duh. He had her car.

Hope gripped the steering wheel, her gaze narrowed on the road ahead. If she had to remove his slimy hold on her life with a potato peeler, she would succeed—once she found a job.

By the time Hope wheeled into a parking place in front of Gina's Eats and Treats, the breakfast rush had dwindled. With the most difficult step, calling Mom, behind her, the successive steps opened in front of her: job, more like jobs, lodging, and Sunday dinner. Hope swallowed. If she could face Sleaze, she could do anything.

The bell above the restaurant door tinkled with her entrance and the titillating scents of fresh pastries and frying bacon caused Hope's mouth to water. She closed her eyes for a moment, savoring the familiarity and warmth of the place she once called home. She loved Sunberry. Her friends and neighbors, the familiar haunts, and the tree-lined streets. Why had she left when everything she wanted, needed, was here?

Because she had to pay her gratitude forward and she couldn't do it until she'd paid her dues. Yeah, she'd certainly paid a few dues.

The doors between the kitchen and the dining room swung open and Penny, a full-figured woman with red hair, appeared, balancing a tray loaded with biscuits and gravy. "Be right with—Hope!"

Hope waved, her chest tightening with the familiar sights and sounds. "Hey, Penny. Finish what you're doing. I'm not going anywhere."

Penny looked back toward the kitchen. "Val!"

The doors creaked forward and a perky young woman with a pleasant smile and an equally laden tray moved toward the dining room. Hope stepped aside to let her pass, noting the shift of her hips and her baby bump. Yep, she'd give Val a job and the upstairs apartment too. Any woman who could sport that cheerful appearance in a new town of strangers deserved backup. Val had moved to the right town, and Hope would sleep on the stoop before asking for Val's apartment.

However, she wasn't above asking her to consider a roommate.

Before she could speak, warm arms and the scent of flowers mixed with bacon surrounded her.

"It's so good to see you! I didn't know you were home," Penny said, holding Hope's shoulders. "Columbia must suit you. You look awesome."

Hope maintained a frozen grin. Although she looked like the desperate woman she was, she'd gladly accept Penny's compliments with the grace Mom always preached about.

"Thanks." Hope squeezed her friend's shoulder, relishing the connection. "It's good to see you too. I blew in last night."

"So just like your brother you needed a Gina's breakfast to get your hometown juices flowing?"

"If you want to really get my juices flowing, give me a job."

Penny's overly made-up eyes widened and then a smile creased her fleshy cheeks. "You're moving home? I bet your family is over the moon. And you just made my day. A busy restaurant always needs help. Plus, I lost my greeters. Delmer broke his leg."

"Oh no!" Hope said, a wave of fear threading through her. She loved the octogenarian Ash twins. "Is he going to be okay?"

Penny added ice to beverage glasses with the diner's logo on the side. "Delmer's break required surgery, but he's going home today. Elmer covered this morning's rush and left for the hospital thirty minutes ago."

"Thank goodness the twins have a close relationship so they can help one another."

"Elmer swears he can take care of his brother, but what's he going to do at night if Delmer needs to go to the bathroom?" Penny bit her lip. "They're over eighty."

Hope filled the glasses with water and set them on a tray. "Would they be interested in a caretaker who could spend the night? I finished a Certified Nurse Assistant course last year. During my clinical rotation, I took care of a man after knee surgery."

"That would be perfect." Penny pulled her phone from her apron pocket and scrolled. "Elmer was fussing about social services sending in a stranger. But he knows you. Here's his contact information. Call him. He should be home after lunch."

Hope clenched her fist, her joy tempered by a sudden awareness—missteps that had led her away from home in the first place. That stopped now.

"Perfect." She squared her shoulders. "And a job at the restaurant? I can't replace the Ash twins, but I'd be a great hostess. Plus, it would give me a chance to see old friends."

Penny's wrinkled forehead signaled the hostess job was a bust. Hope smiled through her disappointment. At least she had the night job—if the twins agreed to hire her."

"Val's taking the hostess position. Her baby is due any time and serving tables is hard work. Trust me, my aching feet remind me of that fact every evening. April, one of our regular waitresses, quit last month to go back to school. I've been filling in for her."

Hope hefted the tray. "I've never handled a big tray of food, but I'm strong and I learn fast."

"If you handle a tray like you used to handle the basketball, you'll do fine." Penny repositioned Hope's hands to stabilize her load. "I used to love to watch you play. Sorry that didn't work out for you."

"That was a girl's dream." And Hope had buried those regrets years ago. "So can I start today?"

Penny pointed toward a family of eight seated in the

dining room. "Sweetie, you can start now. Drop off the water to that family and I'll get the paperwork and meet you back here to help take the order."

"Best news I've had today." With her hands full, Hope couldn't hug her new boss. Instead, she followed a dancing Penny to the table.

Laughing, Hope balanced the tray on one hand and pumped her index finger up and down toward the ceiling. Man, it felt good to be home again.

Ten minutes later, Hope pressed the end button to disconnect her call with Elmer Ash. Two jobs in one day and she'd scored a place to stay at night. Not her own place, but the lounge chair in the twins' apartment beat a truck stop and bunking with a horse.

Her plan was going to work—she had to believe. And then what?

An idea she'd buried the day she'd left for college surged forward. She could apply for a volunteer job with the fire department. With her coursework and job with Delmer added to her credentials, she might qualify. Of course it didn't compare to her brothers' achievements. But it was a start, and helping people had always been her goal.

The vibration against her hip halted her mental celebration. She extracted her phone, hoping the Ash twins hadn't changed their minds. The job was perfect—

> Good morning, Borrower!

> Days Left on Loan: 23

> Friday Payment Due by COB: $1,415.56

> New Loan amount if payment not received: $4,230.80

> Cheers, Bain Vill

Cheers? There was nothing cheery about Sleaze!

She sucked in a breath and focused on her anger instead of the fear. "Enjoy your short-lived power," she said, jabbing at the delete key. "I'll excise you from my life like a piece of moldy cheese soon enough."

CHAPTER EIGHT

Exhausted from a long day of work, Jack collapsed onto his comfy apartment sofa, the growing shadows mirroring his mood. He took a long swig from his beer, the cold liquid soothing his parched throat after a hot shower had washed away the day's grime.

Just as his muscles began to unwind, the familiar hum of his truck's engine amped his heart rate, a coil of dread tightening within him. Moments later, the door swished open.

"Honey I'm home!"

Despite his turbulent thoughts, Hope's cheerful greeting brought a smile to his face. He'd always loved the way she turned any day, whether calm or stormy, into an adventure. The big question: how much adventure did he need?

He held up his bottle. "Want a brewski?"

"No thanks," she said, dropping a carry-out bag on the counter and surprising him with a big hug.

Like an idiot, he stood with his arms suspended in the air. But Hope wasn't one to hug and run. Nope. She clung to him like a second skin—warm and soft.

He swallowed, trying to resist his body's response to close

her into an embrace. After a long, tortuous moment, his trai-torous arms wrapped around her. Warmth, comfort, and longing raced through his veins. How could he resist what she offered? For two days, he'd lectured her about honesty and here he was pretending he didn't want to hold her close and never let her go. Man, he was such a loser when it came to Hope.

Get a grip, his rational side shouted in his head. *Nate's sister is off-limits.*

He was going to do the right thing. To make the best decision to preserve everything he'd been working for. But with her big brown eyes looking clean through him, his resolve wavered.

What are you doing? But he couldn't look away from her.

His arms ignored his brain. He pulled her close, her heart syncing with his in a dangerous rhythm he couldn't ignore. The enticing aroma of cooked food tempted but didn't lure him from her silky hair tickling his cheek. So sweet. So warm. Just like he remembered—Holy!

He pulled back from her lush mouth and met her wide-eyed gaze.

"Where did that come from?" she whispered, her surprise echoing his.

Aw man. Hands off! But the urge to kiss her again tugged at him.

Jack forced his legs to move back and stuffed his hands in his pockets. "Not sure." Which was the truth. Shoot, his thoughts had unhinged right after she hugged him. "You started it."

"I was just excited about my day."

"Well, you can't be excited with me. This..." He moved his finger back and forth between them. "...won't work for us. Especially with your...problem."

She waved her hands like a host on a kids' program. "So

sorry if your day went awry. I had a stellar one. I got a job, actually two, and a place to stay. That's big news and very exciting. I just wanted to share it with you."

"Yeah, well that didn't go so well for us."

"Oh, it was going just fine." She turned and scooped Turbo into her arms. "But the timing sucks petunias."

Although their close encounter still had his body frozen in place, Hope returned to the kitchen with the cat. "Hey little guy. How was your day? Catch any bugs in Jack's window?"

Her insect reference jumpstarted Jack's stalled brain. "There shouldn't be bugs in my windows. I'm not that bad of a housekeeper. And I thought he was too young for a flea collar."

Hope tucked the kitten beneath her chin. "Bugs are his trigger," she said, pointing at Jack.

Turbo mewed. Now the cat was against him.

"But enough bug talk. I have dinner." Hope released the kitten and held up the bag. "Otis sent us a beta recipe. Oh my gosh, this smells so good." She clapped her hands. "Move it Cline. Our food is getting cold and I have to be at my next job by eight-thirty."

The rich tomato sauce and garlic aromas hurried him toward the cupboard for plates. Still, he used caution to avoid bumping into her. No more encounters of the close kind.

"You scored two jobs today?"

"That's the best part. I'm staying with Delmer tonight. You know, help him if he needs to go to the bathroom. They were going to hire someone, but they didn't want a stranger in the apartment and I needed a place to stay. So I volunteered and eliminated two problems."

"Great. For how long?" he said, pleased his brain had actually fired a neuron.

"A week or so. I was happy to do it for them. But Elmer

wasn't having it. So they're paying me to stay nights. When I'm not helping Delmer, I'll sleep in the easy chair in their living room."

"I'm glad they'll have someone there." Jack set two tumblers on the counter. "They're fit for their age, but they've had enough accidents. What do you want to drink?"

"Water, please."

Jack finished his beer, the bitter taste lingering as he stalled for another five seconds to corral his news. "Nate knows you stayed with me and have my truck."

"After a shift at Gina's, everyone in town knows about me."

"Your family isn't everyone," Jack said, softening his voice. "Your mom probably spread the word, but I think you owe Nate a call."

Hope took a giant bite of the pasta and closed her eyes. "This is to die for. I'm so hungry. The diner got busy and I didn't have time for lunch."

Jack focused on his plate, determined to get everything out in the open. "Nate knows you spent the night here."

"And you told him you slept on the couch," she said, like she didn't have a care in the world. But she was twirling a hair strand around her finger tighter than he tightened a screw.

"It's the truth," she said, but still didn't look away from her plate.

Why couldn't they just talk about it? It wasn't like he was blabby, but they had a sticky issue going for both of them. Even if she could blow it off, he couldn't walk the line between Hope and her family for long.

The sudden tap on his nose snapped him to the present.

"Don't look so blue." Her smile was sincere, not the fake one she used to get out of tight spots. "You know you're my hero."

Hero? Jack froze. What the heck? His bad thoughts resurfaced again, leaping to flame as hot as the fire that had claimed his family.

"I'm no hero," he said, his voice dropping to a hoarse whisper from the burden he rarely shared. "Heroes don't walk from a fire unscathed while their family members die."

"Oh, Jack," she said, her palm warm on his chest. "I wasn't trying to remind you of your family's tragedy. But you have to focus on the man you are today. You've helped so many people—me included. Forgive the five-year-old Jack. Love him. He was hurt, too."

He closed his eyes, letting her sincere words and warm touch chase away the cold memory. "Sorry. That one blindsided me. Most of the time I keep the fire in perspective. That's why I volunteer. But today?"

His appetite gone, he pushed a noodle covered in cheese and rich sauce across his plate. "I love my adopted family, but I've never forgotten my birth family. I lost them just like that." He snapped his fingers for emphasis, the sound sharp in the silent room. "That's why I'm kind of over the top about holding tight to the people you love."

"It's not over the top," she whispered, turning toward him, understanding burning in her gaze. "It's good advice and I appreciate it."

She was too close. But it wasn't just the sauce dotting the corner of her mouth—right where he'd kissed her. Right where he wanted to kiss her again. Sexual interest was one thing, but he felt a closer connection to her. One more difficult to resist.

When he lifted his gaze to hers, her dark eyes held steady.

"When you look at me like that, it's hard to breathe," she said, her hoarse whisper shredding his resolve. "Will this feeling ever go away?"

"I thought it had until I saw you climb out of Cody's truck."

"I've got to be free."

He nodded, knowing he'd never be free of his feelings. "I've got a partnership coming and the biggest project of my life."

"Okay then. We focus on getting out of this predicament." She waved her hands in front of her face and blew out a long breath. "I love helping the Ash twins. It's been a long time since I've helped someone. You know?"

He nodded, trying to regain his balance. "One more thing. Call Nate. He's worried. You don't have to give him a big explanation. Just—"

"I'll call all of them with an update tonight after I get Delmer settled. And Turbo and I still need a home base." She washed down her food with a gulp of water. "Is it ok if I still use your place for a base? You know, for me and Turbo? You won't have to do much for him. I'll feed him and clean his litter box between jobs."

He glanced at the kitten batting at his boot lace. "Turbo's okay. But I really need my truck. All of my tools—"

"I've got a bike." Excitement rushed her words and sparkled in her eyes. "The Kare Center has loaners. Elmer hooked me up with a ride with a basket."

"A bike will only work some of the time. Call me," he said, letting her enthusiasm lift his heavy thoughts. "I'll break away and pick you up. At least one way. I'll throw the bike in the back of the truck. That way you can shower and then ride to your next appointment."

"I accept." She shoveled the final bite in her mouth and ran her tongue around her lips. "If it's okay with you, I'll shower. After that, can you give me a ride to the Kare Center?"

Jack checked the time. "I've got to help the Sunberry Fire Department. We've got a fire prevention event at the library tonight. I give them a few hours a week." He shrugged. "It used to be more but the business has eaten into my spare time."

"Would they take me?" she asked. "I'd love to volunteer, and my basic life-saving accreditation is up to date."

Nate moved his food across his plate, trying to wrap his head around the way she thought.

"Hello?" he said. "Are you the woman with two jobs trying to get back on her feet?"

"Expanding my career opportunities is part of that mission."

"Sure, for people who are committed to Sunberry. It's not right to take up time and space at the department for a few months."

"Who said I was only staying in Sunberry a few months?"

"Hold your volunteer requests until *after* you pay your loan. One bite at a time," he said, ignoring the leap of longing in his heart. "That's how we build a house."

"I'm sure you and my brother build solid homes."

"Why doesn't your answer make me feel warm and fuzzy?" She beamed. "I dunno."

"Get straight with your family." He massaged his forehead. "This is Sunberry. The truth will come out one way or the other. You need to control the narrative." And he needed to control his hopes and dreams. Too bad he couldn't curb the rasp in his tone. "Don't hurt your family. They love you and would do anything for you."

Dread hitched his breath. One minute she seemed to understand and the next minute she was back to carefree Hope. She was going to hurt them just like she'd hurt him. Just like she was going to hurt him again if he didn't back up.

"It's going to be okay. I'm fixing it. Look at the tips I made." She dug into her back pocket and extracted a wad of bills. "Can you hold onto this for me? I don't have a bank account in Sunberry anymore."

With disappointment lodged in his throat, he stood and tossed the remainder of his food into the waste can. "This way."

He hesitated at his bedroom's threshold, a sanctuary he was about to share, and then walked to the closet. With a gentle, almost reverent touch, he lifted the sturdy firesafe from the shelf. Here goes. He hoped she acknowledged his trust.

"A toddler could pick the lock, but it's burn proof." He lifted his shoulders. "You know me and fire safety?"

Within minutes, he shifted his personal papers into a large envelope and handed an empty one to her. "Stash your cash in here. I keep the key under the bedside lamp."

"Perfect. I earned one hundred dollars in tips. Most of it was probably pity tips, but still."

He thumbed through the crumpled bills and halted. "You better check my truck."

Confusion lined her smooth forehead.

He counted again. "There's only seventy-five dollars and some change here. The rest must have fallen into the seat."

She waved her hand as her worry lines dissolved. "Naw, it's right. Penny was collecting donations for a baby crib for Val." Her grin was infectious. "I volunteered your truck to pick it up."

In moments like these, he didn't know if he should shake her or kiss her. Money would never be a priority for her, not when people needed something.

"Don't worry," she added. "I'll pay you back. But a kid needs a safe bed."

"You're absolutely right. You know, I can't afford a lot, but I could pay you to clean the new home," he said without thinking. However, once the words were out, he knew it was the right thing to do.

"I don't understand."

"I didn't build the Baker home, but it was one of my designs. Art and Gracie agreed to let me use it as an open house until they're ready to move in. Folks like to tour new designs so it will market my planned subdivision and single-story home designs. But if I do that, I'll need someone to keep it clean. Every time I hang a fixture or touch up paint for Miss Gracie, I make a mess."

And every time she smiled he wanted to find another way to help her out.

"The house is within walking distance of the Kare Center," she said. "I could clean it every morning after I leave Delmer and before my shift at Gina's."

He nodded because his tongue felt too thick to speak—along with his brain. She'd done it again—snuggled beside his heart in less than twenty-four hours.

"I can't pay much, maybe fifty dollars a time?"

She wrapped her arms around his neck and her scent engulfed him. He forced his arms to remain at his sides. Dang near killed him. But she didn't seem to notice.

"I'll stop by tomorrow." She shooed him out of the bedroom. "Now, let me hop in the shower or we'll both be late. Be sure to pick up cleaning supplies and leave them in the house for me."

"Got it." He pulled the door closed behind him. Picking up cleaning supplies was no problem. Picking up the pieces of his heart would be a different matter.

CHAPTER NINE

MAYBE, JUST MAYBE, HER LIFE WAS TURNING AROUND.

Feeling shower-fresh and positive about her future, Hope climbed into Jack's truck. 6:59 displayed on the dash, which would give Jack time to drop her off and pick up Elmer, who wanted to attend the safety educational event.

Hope fastened her seatbelt and smoothed her hands down her thighs, the soft material a comforting reminder of Jack's generosity. "Thanks again for the sweats."

"Keep them," he said, his calm tone soothing her. "They're just clothes. I like to help you out."

"I'll return them. Promise." And it was a promise she intended to keep. "Penny scheduled me for fifty-three hours this week, so my free time's limited. But I should be able to sneak a few hours on Monday to shop."

"Don't you have clothes at your mom's? Popping in might lift her spirits—and yours too."

His tenderness, molded by his personal loss, tugged at her heart. "You set a great example." And she was trying to emulate it. "My parents deserve time to enjoy life, travel, play with the grandkids. *Not* stress over me."

Guilt tightened her throat and she pressed her fingers against her lips to stop her chin's tremble. She wanted to stop the lies too, and she would—soon. Her phone buzzed, a reminder of Sleaze's unopened morning threat. Although she'd silenced all notifications during her work shift, his threat couldn't be silenced.

Her friends once admired her mental toughness, but the lender's warnings had shattered her confidence. With trembling fingers, she tapped her phone. The message cast a harsh glow, stark in the dim interior. She choked back a curse, fighting to keep her composure.

> Good morning, Borrower!
>
> Days Left on Loan: 23
>
> Friday Payment Due: $1,415.56
>
> New Balance: $4,230.80
>
> Can't wait to meet the big NFL star!
>
> Cheers, Bain Vill

Hope jammed the phone into her pocket, her heart racing with fear and frustration.

"Something wrong?

Really wrong. "Spam," she lied.

The lump in her throat grew, making it hard to breathe. Lying came second nature to her with Sleaze goading her on. But she was going to stop him. With her restaurant schedule, tips, Delmer's care, and now Jack's house cleaning, she'd clear around twenty-seven hundred dollars. She'd missed the payment this week, but she could make next week's—if Sleaze didn't bloat the payment with more outrageous late fees. If she failed, she'd expose her family to his threats.

"Hope?"

She blinked back hot, angry tears, her vision blurring with her struggle. Through the windshield, the Kare Center Assisted Living sign softened the night.

"Hope?" Worry edged Jack's repeated call. "Talk to me. Let me help you."

She started to explain and then halted. If he knew the depth of her debt, it might break the fragile trust they'd built. Her nails bit into her palms. Jack couldn't help. No one could. She'd made a terrible decision. She'd make it right.

"Oops." To counteract her shaky voice, she forced her brightest smile. "I don't know where my head is. Did I tell you Elmer opened an account for me at the Bistro? Isn't that sweet? They are the best. Providing a place to stay is enough and I love helping them out. I don't think I'm going to take their money. I needed a place to stay the most and I got that."

"Don't take the gift of giving away from them." Jack's lips did the quirky thing that tugged at her heart. He really was a dear man. Why had it taken her so long to notice?

"I'm not trying to do that. But I feel like I should pay them." Her speech was too bright and fast, but she couldn't stop it. "They make me happy. I love the way they bicker back and forth, when you know how much they care for one another."

When she finally turned to Jack, a weird expression crossed his face. Had he changed his mind, formed a different opinion? She'd seen his expression before. Every time it made her feel bad, like she'd missed something important. Something she couldn't recapture. Most of the time, life felt that way.

"They love paying you," he said. "Elmer has been at the hospital almost nonstop for the past week and needs a break. He'd never leave his brother with a stranger, but he needs social interaction with his Sunberry neighbors. Community is important."

"One of the reasons I came home," she said, her words flowing with relief.

Being around Jack helped her maintain perspective. She needed his solid presence to help her get through this mess—as long as she didn't panic. After a deep, steadying breath, her jitters dissolved. This was going to be a good night.

"You're staring," she said.

His smile caused the dimple in his right cheek to wink at her. "I was thinking."

"Is that dangerous?"

He didn't laugh at her joke. "You've got a good heart. Stop trying to hide it."

"Compliments make me uncomfortable." Especially, when she knew the real story, which would wipe that grin from Jack's face.

"You're home now." He winked. "Get used to them."

She turned toward the center to hide her surprise. Thankfully, Elmer stood inside the double glass doors chatting with Widow Yellon. Leashed by her side, a large dog waited.

Jack circled the hood and walked her to the entrance. "Don't plan to get to bed early tonight. The twins know everything about everybody and like to share it."

"I need someone to catch me up on Sunberry. But I'm also the professional here, and Delmer needs his rest to heal," she said, focusing on her job. "Hospitalization is stressful. His surgery compounded the wear and tear on his body."

"Delmer's accident was hard on Elmer, too," Jack said. "They depend on one another. I can't imagine one without the other."

"That's where I come in. But I'm getting back far more than I give." She unzipped her backpack to reveal a white takeout bag. "Plus, I bring gifts. Otis and Penny loaded me up with great food the twins can warm in their microwave."

Sleaze's text illuminated her backpack's interior. She'd never enjoy her community with that vile man hanging over her. And just the thought of him looking at Whit's family photo filled her with frustration. After Delmer went to bed tonight, she'd brainstorm revenue sources—flexible ones.

"Don't forget to drop off cleaning supplies and your vacuum," she said, pushing her plan to the back of her mind.

"Make a list and send me a text. I'll collect it after my talk."

When he looked at her like she was the only person on the planet, her breath rushed past her lips with awareness. Someday, if and when she unwrapped Sleaze's tentacles from her life, she wanted another chance to capture the things she'd lost with Jack. Prayed it wasn't too late.

———

AFTER SIGNING in at the front desk, Hope took the stairs to the second floor and walked the long hallway to #224. A large wreath with brightly colored eggs, a blue-feathered bird on a nest, and a massive pink, green, and yellow bow decorated the door.

Hope tapped lightly on the wood and then entered. "Night-time helper with food!"

"Come in!"

The Ash suite opened to a narrow hallway. Two bedrooms bisected by a handicap-accessible bathroom branched on the left. Straight led to a living area with a small kitchenette. Along the back wall, a sliding glass door opened onto a large deck. Pink twinkling lights blinked from the deck railing overlooking the rear of the Kare Center property.

She placed her parcel on the small dinette and walked to Delmer, seated in a large lounge chair with his casted leg elevated.

"Look at you!" She hugged the small man, taking in the scent of mint and an antiseptic odor remnant of his recent hospital stay. "You're looking pretty good considering your imprisonment. I hope my big brother kept Sunberry Memorial on its toes during your stay."

Delmer patted her hand. "He and Dana conducted a daily check." He lowered his voice to a whisper. "Good thing. It gave me an excuse to kick out my brother. I love him. But loving him in one room was a challenge."

"Jack's whisking him off to the library."

"About time," Delmer said, leaning against a pillow at his back.

Hope plumped the pillow. "Tell me what you need. If you're going to insist on paying me, don't do my job. When was your last pain pill?"

Delmer waved his hand. "I don't like taking that stuff. It muddles my head. I have enough problems without chemicals adding to it."

Hope checked the sheet resting on the kitchen counter. Elmer's legible script indicated one dose at noon. "What if you take one before bed so you can sleep?"

Delmer nodded. "We'll see. I never was one for moaning and groaning. Dad always said men shouldn't complain."

"It's just you and me now." Hope winked. "Complain away. Have you eaten?"

"Widow Yellen brought soup and sandwiches from The Bistro," Delmer said. "I swear she used it as an excuse to visit me."

"Can't blame a lady for trying," she said, emptying her bag. "Otis and Penny loaded you up with food."

"They're good people."

"Mmm, so's their desserts." She waggled her brows. "Care for some apple cobbler? I saw ice cream in the freezer. You can catch me up on the Sunberry events while we gorge."

He lifted his thumb in the air. "Miss Murphy, I like how you think."

"You talk. I'll fix dessert."

Within minutes the aroma of cinnamon, apples, and sweet pastry infused the living room. While the delicious dessert filled her belly, Delmer filled her mind with the latest stories about her friends and neighbors.

"I've missed my hometown," Hope said, collecting Delmer's spoon and bowl.

"It's a good place," Delmer said, distance in his gaze. "Did you know Elmer once got a job offer down in Texas?"

"Really? What happened?"

"He was going," Delmer said. "Wouldn't listen to anyone. Mom was still around then, but Dad had passed on."

"That must have been tough on you and your family."

"Only on Elmer. Sunberry's my home. I've always known that, but Elmer had a wandering streak." He winked. "Like you."

Until Sleaze weed whacked that streak out from under me. "So what happened?" she said, steering the conversation back to the twins.

"He showed up about six months later with nothing but his old duffel bag." Delmer shook his head, his wrinkled features lined with sadness. "Never did find out the details. He told us he got caught up in debt over a fancy car. He always liked fast wheels. When he lost his job, the bank repossessed his car. He hitchhiked home. Took him almost a week." Delmer wrinkled his face in disbelief. "Can you imagine that? Embarrassed in front of his own family. We were just glad to have him home."

"I guess he didn't want to disappoint you." A sense of ill

ease made Hope shift in her chair. The story felt too close to home.

"Did the ice cream give you indigestion?" Delmer adjusted his casted leg and winced. "Dairy does that to me once in a while. But not tonight. Otis's dessert is sitting right well in my belly. I bet it's the company."

Eager to hide her sudden blues, Hope pressed her palms together under her chin and bowed. "Thank you, Mr. Ash."

"Any time, Miss Murphy." He yawned. "I was planning to challenge you to a game of checkers. But I'm not going to make it tonight. All that moving from the hospital to home has burned up my reserves."

"No worries." She helped him transfer to the wheelchair folded in the corner. "We can play another evening."

While she helped Delmer prepare for bed, his story wormed in and out of her thoughts. At least Elmer's troubles ended after they repoed his car. She'd lost everything and still had Sleaze on her back. Instead of going away, her debt kept growing.

Once she'd positioned a pillow beneath Delmer's cast, she tucked a blanket around his bony shoulder. "The bell is right here on your nightstand. If you need anything, and I mean the tiniest request—" She wagged her index finger at him for emphasis. "Ring the bell."

"If you put that bottle where I can reach it—"

"No, sir." She shook her head. "Don't risk going back to the hospital. It's not a good place for seniors."

He searched her gaze and finally nodded. "You're right."

"Elmer needs you healthy. But it's not just him. You have a lot of friends who love you the same as I do. We need you standing on two legs."

Delmer grinned. "I appreciate your kindness. But my twin needs me to run interference for him. If something happened to me, the widow would be on him like a tick on a hound."

"The widow has had the hots for both of you."

This time he shook a bony finger at her. "Don't jinx us."

Hope grinned despite the chill racing down her spine. She'd been jinxed the moment she signed Sleaze's contract.

CHAPTER TEN

THE FOLLOWING MORNING JACK PARKED IN FRONT OF THE Baker's new home, his heart stuttering like a fading battery. Which was not only ridiculous but downright dangerous.

Hope, clueless of her appeal, waved from the home's entrance. With a grunt of frustration at his own foolishness, he exited the truck. He'd seen a lot of attractive women, but none who made his heart race just by standing there in a kerchief and men's sweats.

"Did you have everything you needed?" he said, trying to pull his thoughts to the safe side. "It took me almost thirty minutes to collect the items on the list. I thought you were running a maid service."

Despite the shadows beneath her eyes, her smile lit up his day like a beacon. He adjusted his sunglasses to shade the warmth spreading through him.

"Take a look," she said, motioning him inside the single-story home perfect for active seniors—and new families. "I overslept this morning, but I think the house looks good."

Jack followed her inside. "Let me guess. Elmer kept you up late talking."

"The twins are such characters. Delmer was the perfect patient and turned in early. But then his twin waltzed in spilling stories faster than I could keep up." She stopped by the expansive island bisecting the kitchen from the living area. "I need to write a book."

"You need a nap. Too bad you've got another shift." And he should quit thinking about brushing back the curl peeking out of her bandanna. He stepped back, letting the lemon-scented cleaner clear the remnants of Hope's scent.

"The place looks great," he said, turning in a slow circle.

"Thanks. I love the open floor plan," Hope said. "Plenty of room, but efficient use of space."

He stuffed his hands in his jean pockets to prevent them from wandering. "That was our goal when Jimmy and I worked on the blueprint. Of course, Miss Gracie helped. How'd you like the sunroom? It was her idea. She thought the extra sunlight made it more cheerful."

"The windows are a pain to clean, but the light is definitely worth it. I needed the rays this morning to keep me awake." Hope yawned. "Do you have a mini coffee maker? A cup of coffee while I'm cleaning would be nice."

"I think we can manage that."

She stopped and turned, releasing her lip from between her teeth. "This isn't a daily job, is it?"

He had wondered when she'd ask for more details, not to mention the fact that no one was looking at it yet. "It depends," he hedged, wanting to continue to help her in a way that didn't seem like a handout. "Miss Gracie has charge of the punch list. I fill her wants. I've got to add electrical outlets today."

Hope pursed her lips. "So I'll need to redo the floors tomorrow?"

Her pucker short-circuited his brain. A nod was all he could manage, which was much safer.

"The hardwoods are nice—when they're clean. But they show every speck of dust."

He moved the toe of his boot back and forth. "But check out the rich wood grain."

"Oh, the floors are gorgeous—as long as you aren't cleaning them. Can you imagine a family living here? My brothers were nonstop eaters. Even our old dog Toby couldn't keep up with the crumbs."

Jack couldn't help but grin when the image of small, grubby hands smearing crumbs and Toby gathering every lost bite flashed in his mind.

"Jack?" Hope stood in front of him, her hands on her hips. "What's going on? You ignore my question and you've got a goofy grin on your face. Are you expecting a party with lots of presents or something?"

His neck heated with frustration. What was going on with him? He wasn't used to this kind of craziness. He was just a regular guy trying to make a living—with her brother.

"I was thinking about your family," he fibbed, which was almost true. "Ellie and Sam run about a mile a minute. They make Sunday dinners with your grandmother when my parents are out of town interesting."

When her gaze returned to the floor, he silently cursed his slip. The big dinner with her family was coming too fast for her. He could offer her a small job and friendly support, but no more. Not without jeopardizing the partnership. If he and Hope got together and then blew up like they had in high school, it could ruin his relationship with Nate and her family. He'd worked too hard to risk his business. But he'd help her any way he could.

"One more day and you can come clean to them," he said, resisting his need for distance and embracing her. But darn, how could he resist when she worked so hard? The scent of his shampoo on her intoxicated him, dragging him back to memories he'd tried to bury.

"I know," she murmured. "Sometimes it feels a little heavier to shoulder than others."

He stepped back before it was too late. "If you want to shower before your next shift, we better hustle."

While Hope gave him a rundown of everything Sunberry according to the Ash twins, he drove the busy streets to his apartment. On the weekends, their sleepy town awakened. At the park, parents and kids gathered coolers and chairs for sports. Cars lined the local grocery and trucks bumped onto the rutted drive to the building supply. Sunberry was a great place, and he loved he'd had a hand in keeping it that way. Too bad he couldn't open Hope's eyes to her home.

He'd said his piece about talking to her family. With a little luck, the Murphy Sunday dinner would move his pretty roommate forward. When a snort leaked from him, the sudden crunch from his passenger seat alerted him he'd hit a nerve.

He lifted his hand from the steering wheel. "Just wondering how the Murphy family dinner would go tomorrow."

She winced. "Quit reminding me."

"I'd think you'd be anxious to get it behind you."

"Problem is..." Her voice vibrated with tension. "It's in front of me."

He pulled into the drive assigned to his unit and stopped. "You have the world's best parents."

"And the world's snoopiest brothers!"

Her pout brought another chuckle to the surface. She glared at him. "They are always into my business."

"I'd love to have more brothers at my back." Jack switched off the engine, shrugging off a sudden touch of loneliness.

Hope's exhale pulled him out of his funk. "I love my amazing brothers. I just wish they'd give me some wiggle room. I can figure things out on my own."

"I know you can." The same as he knew touching her came too easily. "I've got your back."

She studied him with the solemn-eyed stare only Hope could perform—at least for him. The slight tip of her head sent his heart tripping along a bumpy road. A solid relationship with Hope wouldn't come easily. But nothing worthwhile was ever easy.

Jack appreciated Hope's dread but looked forward to ending the Nate blackout. Without Nate's guidance, he'd still be floundering. That's why he understood Hope's situation—he'd been there. Helping her without betraying her family, however, was becoming more challenging.

Forty minutes later, Hope emerged from his bedroom dressed in her dark slacks and plain blouse. His breath stuttered in his chest. At the age of sixteen he'd labeled her gorgeous, ornery, and tougher than nails. The description still applied.

Sure, her features had matured into those of a woman, but the gleam in her eye and the tilt of her head said try me. And he'd be danged if he could avoid her siren's call.

"You washed my clothes for me."

Since it wasn't a question, he didn't respond, which eliminated the quandary if his tongue would cooperate.

She lifted her arms, emphasizing the muscular shadows beneath the filmy white shirt.

"You're staring, Jack."

"Yes, ma'am."

She placed her hands on her hips, a grateful smile softening her features. "Thank you for doing my laundry," she said, her voice tinged with appreciation and a hint of vulnerability.

"I had a few things to wash. Your clothes made it a full load. Efficiency. Besides," he added to keep the vibe light. "Your pants smelled like a dumpster. Didn't figure a foul odor would help with tips."

"Nice, Cline." The right side of her lip quirked. "You're making quite an impression."

"I never was one for impressions."

"True."

When she stepped forward, his lungs quit working and his hard self-talk circled the drain. Her cupped hands on his chin made him wish he'd shaved because he hated even the slightest distance from her touch. Of course with her dark eyes searching his, he'd lost feeling in his face. He'd swear she could see his soul. She owned it anyway. Her lips brushed his, a feathery touch that sent shockwaves through him, pulling his lids closed to relish the moment. A man could savor a kiss for a long time—even with the light touch of her mouth.

"When this is over—" She kissed him again, her hands curling behind his neck.

His breath exploded from his lungs and he tightened the embrace, listening to the race of heartbeats and the gentle rasp of their breaths.

"I'll be right here," he whispered into her hair. "Right where I've always been." *Waiting for you.* He swallowed his final words. He'd always been a coward when it came to Hope. But life had taken a lot from him. First his family, his home, and then his girlfriend. He'd reinvented himself. With Nate's help, he'd pushed to his feet. It felt good being a part of the business, having a future he loved and looked forward to. Thank goodness, the risk to his relationship with Nate would soon be over. The only thing, the real risk was opening his heart to Hope.

CHAPTER ELEVEN

ATTENDING THE SUNDAY FAMILY DINNER FELT LIKE HER last supper.

Hope gripped the armrest, anxiety tightening her chest, as Jack parked behind Nate's truck on the tree-lined lane in front of Grandma Stella's house. Memories of happier times flooded her, mixing with the dread of the impending confrontation. Although the engine stopped, she stared ahead, squinting against the setting sun's glare.

"I can't do it," she whispered. She couldn't even look at the graceful antebellum two-story, home to so many memories.

Jack's hand, gentle and reassuring, rubbed her shoulder, sending a small wave of comfort through her tense body. For a moment, she allowed herself to lean into his strength.

"Babe," he said. "It's your family. You're safe here. I'll be right beside you."

"It's too soon. They'll know something's wrong the minute I walk in."

"Of course they suspect something. They love you. When

you care about someone, you notice the little things. Let us help you."

His earnest gaze and soft tone nudged away the fear freezing her into her seat. "Maybe—"

She reached for her backpack and her phone's vibration rattled through her like a death toll, Sleaze's horrible reminder. Nineteen days. The weight of it pressed down on her, making it hard to breathe.

Pulling in a shaky breath, she scrambled for the courage that had abandoned her. With Sleaze snarling behind her, her choices had vanished. She had to find a way out, even if it meant more lies.

"Argh!" She banged her fists on the dash. "I hate playing the poor, pitiful diva."

Jack's heavy brows lifted in surprise.

"Oh, come on," she said, clinging to the flimsy excuse for her reaction. "Don't try to tell me you've forgotten how I used to act. I'm trying to shed the diva skin." *Along with the horrible new one of lies.*

His lip twitched to suppress a grimace as he glanced over her shoulder.

Her heart accelerated. "Is someone coming?"

"The front curtain just moved," Jack said.

"Dad's a retired Marine. He's probably been running recognizance since you pulled behind Nate's truck."

"It's nothing like our high school experience with Whit checking the window." Jack opened his door. "He scared the spit out of me that night."

She could certainly identify with being scared spitless. The squeak of the door sent chills down her spine.

"Get over yourself," she muttered. She could do this.

Jack met her at the right fender and held out his hand. She grabbed it, grateful for his solid presence.

"I'm always nervous at your family dinners," Jack said,

running his hand through his hair, looking distressed. "I can't keep their names straight. It's embarrassing. Every time I call one of your sisters-in-law by the wrong name, I feel like I'm digging myself deeper into a hole."

Although she questioned Jack's worry, she welcomed the distraction—even if only for a few precious moments—and hooked her arm through his. "I think I can help you with that. I often use the acronym method to help me prepare for tests. Think of it like this: Chaz is for Chef, Dana is for Doctor, Talley is for Trainer, and my mom, Ava is the Artist. Each of them has a unique trait that matches their name."

Jack halted in front of the broad steps leading to Grandma's home. "Chef, Doctor, Trainer, Artist. Got it. But how do I remember which one matches which name and which brother?"

Hope grinned. "Easy! Chaz loves to cook up hair color and owns the diner where Nate loves to eat. Dana is always patching up little Sam so imagine her bandaging knees and keeping the Murphy Dr. Kyle in line. Talley is easy because she's potty-training Ellie and Whit had trainers when he was an NFL pro. And Mom—well, she's an artist at heart. Picture her with her paintbrushes creating wonderful scenes on furniture."

"I think I can manage that," Jack said, climbing the wide stairs. "Chef Chaz, Doctor Dana, Trainer Talley, and Artist Ava. This might actually work."

"Thanks," Hope whispered. "It worked for me too."

"Was I that obvious?" he said, his cheeks flushing a bright crimson. "You looked so scared and it's not right being nervous around your own family. You could come clean about the whole issue and stop the angst today. Then we could both enjoy being with your family—without the stress of lies and betrayal."

"Don't worry." She dropped his hand. "I'm not going to jeopardize your relationship with my family."

She winced at his stricken glance. But the words were out and she'd learned apologies never eased the lash of a loose tongue. All she could do was make it up to him when she ended this mess—if she could end it.

The front door swung open before her hand touched the handle.

"Sweetheart!" Grandma Stella's arms wrapped around her, warming her ragged heart. "I've missed you so much," Grandma whispered before releasing her.

"Me too," Hope said, taking needed strength from Grandma's loving embrace.

"Jack!" Grandma pivoted to embrace him. "Always good to have you at the table. Are Bill and Connie still in Portugal?"

"Yes, ma'am. The folks are having the time of their lives."

Inside the Murphy home, Hope battled the stab of regret as familiar voices surrounded her. Every instinct in her body screamed to run, don't go in, protect her family against her failures, but a solid presence pressed against her back. Tall and steady, Jack waited by her side. No judgment. No pressure. Just support. Although she yearned to lean into his strength, she mouthed a silent thank you.

This home. This family. Maybe this man was hers—*if* she banished Sleaze from her life. Revulsion rolled through her. *Don't even think his name in Grandma's loving home.* Soon she'd pay off the debt and be free to follow her best life.

Masking her fear with her brightest smile, she moved forward, today's mantra pounding in her head.

Keep the plan simple. Deliver the story, ask Mom for a job, and sell a cheerful, positive, successful attitude for the next hour. Then, get out of Dodge and get to work.

"There's my best girl." Ryan opened his arms.

Hope inhaled Dad's evergreen scent and snuggled against his firm, broad chest.

"Missed you," she said.

"Missed you more." He stepped back, a wry grin on his lips. "You wouldn't believe how the Honey-Do List has expanded since my retirement."

"Is he complaining about my efforts to keep him busy?" A hint of cinnamon overpowered her mother's usual clean scent of cucumber. "You don't know how happy you've made me," her mother, Ava, said, hugging her.

Hope squeezed her eyes shut, trying to shield her resolve against the love and guilt overwhelming her. She would *not* allow her failures to hurt her family.

"It's good to be here," she said, dredging deep for the courage she needed. Through her peripheral vision, Dad was studying her. Her cottony dry throat struggled to swallow. She'd have to be more careful. Since the day he'd first held out his finger for her to grab, they'd formed a special bond. Although he'd always given her the choice to hold tight or release, he had a way of sensing her feelings.

"Hey, Little Sis." Whit stepped up next. "I can't wait to hear your story. Whatever it is, you know I'm here for you— just like always."

She'd loved the year she'd grown so she didn't have to look up so much to her brothers. Meeting Whit's eyes was hard. His wealth could minimize her damage, increasing her debt to him. She might pay off Sleaze but never Whit's calm acceptance.

Not this time, Big Bro. Little Sis has to prove herself.

She pointed her index and middle finger at his gorgeous blue eyes and then at hers. "In case you haven't noticed, I'm all grown up. And you have your own little munchkin to protect. Where is my niece?"

Whit puffed out his cheeks. "Busting our chops. She

never stops. It's unreal." He canted his head to the right. "The little stinker finally passed out standing by the couch. I kid you not. She stopped, dropped her head on the side of the sofa, and fell asleep. What kid does that?"

"Obviously yours." Nate gave Hope a side-armed hug. "Thanks for helping out Penny. That's a big worry off of Chaz's mind."

Chaz, Nate's best half, carried a platter of sliced beef to the table. "The restaurant is fine. If a novice like me couldn't ruin it, nothing can. Thank you so much for staying with Delmer. We've all been worried sick about him."

"He's doing great. Follows his doctor's instructions to the letter." Hope craned her neck. Grandma, Chaz, and Mom were placing the final dishes on the table. Ryan filled wine glasses. "Where are Kyle and Dana?"

Ryan set the wine bottle on the buffet behind the long family table. "New York City. Kyle had a medical convention so they decided to make it a long weekend."

"Where's Sam?"

Ava placed a plate of deviled eggs on the table. "Birthday party at Buddy Graham's house."

Hope rubbed her temple. "Remind me again. Is Buddy the vet's son or the little boy with the pony?"

"Vet's son," Ava said. "Ollie Fallon has the pony. That's where we had the fence-stringing party."

"Except Ollie and Pam moved into a place behind Hal's place. Dollars to doughnuts he'll pop the question soon." Grandma Stella said, waving toward the dinner table laden with steaming dishes of food. "Take your seats."

Relief dropped Hope into her chair like a stone. Although she loved her oldest brother, his candor always put her on edge, like a spotlight illuminating her deepest fears and failings. With Sleaze's threat breathing down her neck, she needed all the slack she could get. She also needed to stick to the plan. Her family's happiness was at risk.

Her throat thickened and she struggled to swallow. *Sorry, Mom. I'll make it up to you.* But she couldn't look up. Couldn't meet her mother's concerned, dark gaze. Mom had always been there for her, for all of them. Always. That's why she had to stay the course, one foot in front of the other.

The scrapes of chairs and low murmurs filled the silence. Hope savored each sight, each sound, each smell from her cherished family rituals, letting the stability ground her, give her the courage she needed.

This was her home. Her people. And she had to lie to them.

The heavenly aromas from the seasoned beef, roasted vegetables, and Grandma's bread battled with her conscience. Tell them the truth and shred her last bit of dignity or slog through her plan. With a wing and a prayer, she might salvage some of her pride.

Beneath the table, Jack's hand covered her bouncing knee in solidarity. She gave him a discreet nod and squared her shoulders. She could do this because of the people sitting at the table. They nurtured her, believed in her.

While her family members chatted amiably, Hope calmed her galloping heart by focusing on the simple task of passing the plates of food. She'd missed Grandma Stella's monthly dinners. Missed hearing about her family's trials and tribulation. Everyone had faced life's tests. However, her brothers' amazing successes emphasized her dismal score. Just once... She squeezed her fork. Just once she wanted to report good news, hear them congratulate her, see their smiles of approval. And there was no way that would happen today.

Grandma tapped her knife against the goblet of iced tea. "I'll say grace today."

Hope took Jack's hand and reached across the empty

space to join her mother's smooth fingers, grateful for her mother's bowed head and closed eyes. During Grandma's heartfelt blessing, Hope let her memories soothe her, take her back to happier times, give her the strength to forge through to a better future.

"And thank you for returning Hope safely home." Grandma's final words burned through Hope's veil of memories.

Beneath the table, Hope squeezed Jack's hand so hard he let out a slight grunt. She eased her grip but couldn't ease the worry about her next task.

While waiting for the round robin where her family gave updates in their lives, Hope pushed tender bites of beef around her plate, hoping no one would notice her lack of appetite. Where was Toby when she needed him? Although their old lab had made the rainbow bridge journey before she left for college, her heart squeezed for her old friend and the many times he'd snatched her uneaten food so she could earn dessert.

More tears threatened. Good gravy, she had to stop the memories and get through the meal.

Grandma Stella patted her lips with her napkin. "Shall we start with Hope? I know the family is buzzing with—"

"Excuse me!" Hope winced at her rude behavior, but dire circumstances required dire strategies. "Since my update might take longer, I'll go last. It's been a while since I've been to a family dinner and I can't wait to hear your stories."

Silence. Hope snapped her jaw shut and a bead of sweat trickled down her side. She hadn't interrupted Grandma since she'd lost her first tooth and insisted on holding it up for everyone to see.

"I guess we can do that," Grandma said, scanning her loved ones. "My news is short. Gracie Butler and some of the other ladies are taking up a donation to help Val purchase a chest for the baby. I'll take your donations to

Gracie. Just put them in the red urn on the foyer table before you leave."

"Lovely gesture," Ava said. "I'd be happy to paint a scene on it if you know her nursery theme."

"I'd give her Ellie's nursery furniture," Whit's wife, Talley said. "But we're afraid to move her from her crib."

"It's not like she stays in it!" Whit chuckled. "She's been climbing over the top since she was old enough to stand."

Hope's laugh was too loud, but the humor eased her tension.

"I've got some good news." Nate turned to his wife Chaz, who nodded.

"Do I have a new grandchild on the way?" Grandma Stella said.

Nate's eyes widened. "Uh...it's about our company."

"We're not quite ready for little ones yet," Chaz said.

The room quieted while a comical parade of expressions attacked her brother's features.

"Touché, Grandma," Hope mused. "You stumped him on that one."

Nate sipped his tea. "The Martinez family extended our contract to add a sunporch. The additional revenue puts us over our expansion mark." He nodded at Jack. "That means I need a new partner. Welcome aboard, Jack. You've earned it."

"Yes!" Jack pumped his fist in the air. "Perfect timing. Miss Gracie gave me permission to use her new build as a model home."

Nate reached across the table and shook Jack's hand. "It's all falling into place, partner. Looks like Murphy-Baker Construction will be hiring more carpenters."

"I'll check at the base," Ryan said.

Hope didn't miss the way her mom arced a brow at Dad's remark.

"I still have contacts," Ryan said. "There's always Marines who need extra cash."

"So you're creating a new branch for new-builds in addition to home renovations?" Ava asked.

"That's the plan." Jack smiled like a child on Christmas. "At least I hope my plans for the new subdivision go through. The interest rates aren't helping so I'm not building spec homes—at least not yet." He shook his head. "The land nearly drained me."

"It's a good plan," Grandma Stella said. "Sunberry needs affordable single-family homes."

"I'm interested in Sunberry ventures," Whit said. "Call me and we'll talk."

As each family gave a brief synopsis of their lives, Hope slumped against the chair, longing cutting into her spine despite its padded back. She loved helping people, but she was always on the receiving end—and she was going to change that.

When Mom's turn came and she reported business at Robey's Rewards was stable, relief dropped Hope's shoulders —until she realized her turn had arrived. Although she usually scanned her audience before speaking, today dread and guilt pinned her gaze to her empty tea glass.

Jack, like he could read her thoughts, turned and retrieved the pitcher from the buffet behind their chairs. "Anyone else need a refill?"

Hope hid her sigh of relief. How did he know she needed an extra minute? She didn't know and right now, didn't care. However tomorrow, he'd get the biggest portion of dessert from the restaurant. And maybe she'd add a kiss for the way he moved at an unusual snail's pace, carefully filling each glass, wiping the pitcher's bottom and returning it to the buffet.

By the time he reclaimed his seat, she'd bolstered her resolve.

"Okay. Here's my latest," Hope said, drawing strength from Chaz, the sister-in-law who understood life's challenges. "You've stood behind my various career decisions, and I appreciate your confidence in me. None of my classmates have the family support I get from you. I had to leave home to learn how blessed I am." She tipped her chin. "Just wanted you to know. Life gets busy and we don't always say what's in our hearts.

"Anyway, school's not taking me in the best direction. So I'm sitting out next semester and coming home—to stay."

She sipped her tea, praying the beverage would sooth her parched throat. It didn't.

"Phew!" Hope huffed out a breath. "I've been worrying about how to tell you about school for weeks. I know you have questions. First, I'm okay. There's no need for you to worry about me. Penny needed help so I'm happy to step in at Gina's. Of course, I had to help the twins. I'm honored they accepted my offer."

"If you need financial help, while you make the move—"

"No!" Hope lowered her voice. "Sorry. Thanks, Whit. You've been an awesome brother. No matter what I decide, I don't have student loans like my peers. Thank you for that. But you've been more than generous. Please give me time to work out the next phase in my life by myself."

She winced, taking in her mother's sober expression. "I loved working at Robey's Rewards, so if you've got an opening that fits around my schedule with the twins and Gina's, I'd love to fill it."

Ava smiled, and the moisture building in her mother's eyes caused Hope's throat to close. "I'd love to have you work by my side. Robey's Reward was for you." Mom's gaze panned the table. "All of you."

"Thanks, Mom." A blend of gratitude and relief shattered Hope's voice. She pressed her hand to her lips. "Excuse me. My tummy isn't used to great Murphy food."

Although she wasn't sure her family had bought her ruse, they didn't call her out on the fib. Thankfully, they limited comments to welcoming her home. With each response, her confidence grew. She'd done it. Some looks from her parents seemed to linger, but no one asked the questions she couldn't answer—yet.

"Is there something wrong with your car?" Whit said. "Kyle traded his in and Nate loaned his to a friend down on his luck. If it's still workable for you, I can take it down to Riley's and get it tuned up for you. Or we can replace it."

"Like Nate, I loaned it to a friend." Hope wanted to slap her hand over her mouth, and based on Jack's stiff posture beside her, he was going to help. But she couldn't. "Um, my friend got into a jam with a new baby and no way to get to work. Since I was coming home, I told her to use it."

A clatter of dinnerware shattered the silence beside her. Jack's tea and melting ice cubes filled her plate and soaked the linen tablecloth around it.

"Sorry." Jack's usual carefree tone sounded more like a hiss.

"No problem," Grandma said, scooting her chair back to stand.

Ava was already on her feet. "I've got it."

Within minutes, Mom returned with a dishtowel and soaked up Jack's spill. While Mom fussed near her right side, Whit and Talley exchanged glances, their foreheads lined in confusion or worry. Nate had dropped his head forward and Chaz whispered in his ear. Dad's gaze darted from her to Jack.

Hope's pent-up fear erupted in a frustrated ball of anger— at Jack. The traitor. And she was planning to bring him a yummy dessert. If he couldn't play it cool in front of her family, she'd uninvite him to the next family dinner.

The only family member who wasn't conducting nonverbal conversation with their significant others was Grandma. No doubt she and Grandpa were burning the heaven to earth lines.

Mom didn't make eye contact when she returned from the kitchen.

"I've always encouraged you to help people in need," Ava said. "So I'm sure Whit isn't concerned about the car. But how did you get from Columbia to Sunberry?"

Hope released a sore, slightly gnawed lip. "I caught a ride with a friend." And she'd racked up another lie. Except it wasn't a total lie. Bev had given her the creepy trucker's name and she'd gotten home unharmed. But friend? Yeah, that was stretching it.

Near her arm, Jack's warm presence had chilled—as in stone-cold. Geez, she couldn't even hear his breathing.

Mom, now seated in the seat beside her, touched Hope's shoulder, and an unbearable urge to snuggle against her mother overwhelmed her.

"Honey." Mom's warm, inviting voice cut through the dining room. "Let us help you. That's what families do. It's so much easier helping than it is worrying."

Unable to withstand her mother's tender gaze, Hope hugged her—hard. "That's why I came home."

Struggling to regain control so she could make her exit, Hope squeezed her mother's narrow shoulders. She'd done it. Walked through the family gauntlet.

Tucked in her backpack pocket suspended over the back of her chair, her cell vibrated with its repeated reminder.

"I'm safe," Hope said, desperate to convince them. "I'm right here in Sunberry with all of our friends. But please..." A tear escaped her hard blink. "Let me work my life out my way.

I want to show you...and myself." She tapped her chest. "I can do it."

Her mother's knowing gaze begged her to change her mind, but Hope remained resolute.

Finally, Mom dropped her stare. "How long?"

"Six months," Hope said, praying they'd accept her generous deadline—but she had to be sure she could end the lending cycle for good. She could not, would not, go through this again.

Grandma stood, attracting the family's attention to her small but mighty stature. "I'm delighted to have our family home in Sunberry. Time on Earth is short. Together, there's nothing we can't withstand."

Hope blew kisses to her silent family and forced her protesting legs to the door. *Never again would she stoop this low.*

CHAPTER TWELVE

JACK COULDN'T EXIT THE MURPHY HOME FAST ENOUGH, HIS heart thumping with a mix of anger and betrayal. How could she sit at the table and lie to the people who loved her? He yanked the truck door open, the sharp force shooting through his arm barely registering over his frustration.

Settling into the truck's safety, he peered at the Murphy home, the delicious meal he'd consumed souring in his gut. The warmth of the family dinner now felt like a distant memory. Where was Hope? Probably telling more of her so-called small lies.

Although he'd given his thanks and an excuse for a hasty departure, his spine tingled, and he imagined a wide yellow line growing down his backbone, even bigger than before. But he couldn't look at her loving family members and listen to their praise and encouragement with Hope's lies circling his brain.

His hands curled into fists, his anger simmering just beneath the surface. He'd wanted to help Hope. Wanted to love her. Wanted to fill the hole in her heart that always occupied his. But not like this. Her lies were eating him from the inside out, making him feel like he was betraying his partner and his friends. People who had always made him feel like family.

After a few moments, Hope hurried across the front lawn, her features drawn, her big eyes reddened. He powered up the engine.

"Never again!" Hope slammed the door punctuating her harsh whisper.

Exactly his thoughts, but for a whole different reason.

Jack clenched his jaw, swallowing the lecture burning on his tongue, and turned onto the road.

"You do…" Jack took a breath, willing his temper to cool. "…whatever you need to do. But leave me out of it. I'm done. Holy crap, Hope. I accept an invitation into your family home, eat their food, and participate in your…lies!"

"Do you think I enjoy lying to them?" she said, her ragged words testing his resolve.

Jack puffed out his cheeks. *This is so messed up.*

He drove through town and continued on Old Sunberry Road, letting the hum of the engine and the sound of the tires defuse his anger. When he passed the Crooked Creek entrance, the memory of her story sleeping in the barn tightened his hold on the steering wheel.

"What could possibly be worse than lying to your family?" he said.

"You don't understand."

"Try me because what I witnessed today was not the girl I knew. I thought I understood you. I know how it feels to fail your family. Every time I went home, Dad's look of disappointment cut me down. Mom was even worse. She looked at me like I was a stray kitten shivering in the corner. They took me in, gave me a home. I wanted to make them proud. You know, make them glad they gave me a chance. Show my appreciation."

"That's what I want."

At least he was right about some of her motivation. But the harsh rasp of her voice squashed his argument. She was hurting. But that didn't justify hurting her family. He turned into an unused lane and cut the engine, the silence amplifying the unresolved tension between them.

"Do you know how hurt they'll be when they learn you lied?"

"It wasn't *all* a lie. I can make this right—I have to."

All? Geez, danged if he could find an ounce of truth in what she'd said to her family. "Can't you make it right *and* tell the truth?"

"Not this time. I've crawled home with my tail between my legs over and over. I've been the stray too inept to care for itself. You pulled yourself out of that rut." Her long fingers curled around his forearm, her desperate gaze piercing his resolve. "Give me the same chance."

"You can't win their respect by lying to them." He kept his voice low, gentle. Force wouldn't work. But how did he get her to understand?

"The lies are over." Her tone strengthened, like she'd already decided. "Lying about the car was uncomfortable, but school? It was just a matter of when I stopped attending."

He leaned against the headrest and stared at the ceiling. *Stop justifying the lies.* If she didn't see her lies for what they were, how could she learn and grow? How could they have a chance?

"That doesn't work for me," he said. And if it continued to work for her? Something inside him twisted, resisted the truth.

"Twenty days," she murmured, thumbing her phone.

He rubbed the persistent pinch at the back of his neck, trying to massage away the stress that seemed to mount with every passing second. Did she have a calendar going for this cluster?

"No, that's not right." She shook her head, staring at her phone. "It's seventeen days. But with the extra hours working for Mom, I've got a chance."

"Got a chance?" He sounded like a kitten with its tail caught in a door. "What's that mean?"

A minute passed. Two. The pressure expanded inside him. If he blew up, she'd go on the defensive and they'd get nowhere. Like they were accomplishing anything in their present conversation. He was no teacher. Heck, he'd been lucky to manage a C average. That was him, average. She'd been the rock star. He'd trailed behind her, like now. If they were going to have a chance together, he needed to step up to the plate. Man, he couldn't jack this up.

He squeezed her shoulder. "Hey, you okay?"

When she turned, his heart raced. She was braced, ready for battle. For him or something else?

"I can't help you if you aren't honest with me," he said, hoping she'd finally trust him with all of her secrets.

When she looked away, he teetered between the urge to fall to his knees and plead with her or grab her shoulders and shake some sense into her. Instead, he waited—prayed.

"I told you I have to pay off the loan by the end of the month."

"Okay. That's pretty straightforward. So why did you say there's a chance? You aced math. With tips, your pay varies, but you know if you can make the payment or not?"

"I missed a payment."

What the— Jack licked his lips, trying to process her response. "Wait. How could you have a payment after six days? What kind of loan do you have?"

"It's not like I'm a great credit risk." She lifted her hands. "I don't have a full-time job."

Jack's thoughts skidded to a halt. "I'm not a high roller. Besides a car loan and a bank loan, what else is there? I mean it's not like you went to some back-alley loan shark...?"

The hairs on his forearms lifted. "Hope?"

"It's a payday lender."

"Are you...in danger?"

She shook her head, but the fist in his gut didn't recede. He rolled his shoulders but couldn't get rid of the odd feeling of panic.

Now what? He could no longer support her string of lies to her family, but he couldn't abandon her. If something bad happened, her family would never forgive him. Heck, he wouldn't be able to forgive himself. The sides of his truck seemed to move closer, trapping him inside the same horrible way he'd almost been trapped in the fire. No way out.

CHAPTER THIRTEEN

Feeling like Earth's lowest life form, Hope slogged through a busy morning helping Delmer through his routine, cleaning the model home for Jack, and riding with Jack to her first shift at Gina's—the absolute worst on her list.

While Jack kept his gaze trained on the road, guilt, along with her growing string of lies and secrets, gnawed at her empty stomach. Her failings had jeopardized everything she had and everything she thought she was. That was bad. But it wasn't right to put Jack in the same position—just for helping her. Apologizing couldn't touch the damage she'd rendered to their relationship. Her only recourse was to move forward, pay off that loathsome lender, and confess her lies and secrets to her family.

The jolt from the truck's halt across from the back entrance of the restaurant brought her to the present.

"What time do you need a ride?" Jack asked, his cold, flat tone so different than his earlier warmth.

"I get off at 1:30 and need to be at Mom's shop by 2. Can you manage it, or should I find another ride?"

"Okay."

Hope winced, wondering if okay meant drop off the planet or that he didn't mind picking her up at 1:30. At present she'd give her clean pair of socks to be independent again, not need to ask for help. But she couldn't.

"Are you picking me up or should I ask someone for a ride?" she asked, despising how small her voice sounded, despising how the small voice matched how she felt about herself.

"I'll be here at 1:30."

She closed the door and watched Jack's taillights disappear from sight, highlighting her loneliness.

Near the restaurant's rear entrance, Hope noticed a woman with long braids bending near a small boy in a clean but worn parka. The striking similarity in their features clicked—Sarina Lott, who graduated five years ahead of her. Hope hadn't heard about Sarina getting married, but she had missed a lot over the years.

"But Mom." The boy wiped his cheek. "Everybody on the team has basketball shoes."

Hope slowed her steps, not wanting to intrude but needing to get to work.

"We aren't everybody," Sarina said, tightening his hood. "Your sneakers are only a month old and perfect for basketball. We can't afford two pairs of shoes with the way you're growing."

"But Mom!"

"Benji, stop." Sarina held up one finger. "Two pairs of shoes are not in the budget. Remember? We talked about saving our money for a place of our own with a yard."

"I remember," the boy said, scuffing his shoe in the dirt.

Sarina pressed a finger to his lips. "If I have a good week, we'll check at The Sunberry Swap. They might have shoes in your size."

Another big tear slid down Benji's cheek and Hope,

waiting on the drive to give them privacy, curled her hands in her pockets.

"They never have my size," Benji said, his bottom lip trembling.

"Coach Cox will let you play in those shoes." Sarina blotted his tears with a tissue and hugged him. "Now hurry or you'll miss the bus. I love you."

Benji kicked a stone along the drive as he slowly made his way to the bus stop. Sarina turned and Hope approached her.

"Sorry, I didn't mean to intrude." Hope thrust out her hand. "Hope Murphy. I started last Friday."

"You're Nate's little sister, right?"

"That's me." Hope followed Sarina up the stairs.

"Sorry." Sarina bobbed her head back and forth, sending her long braids cascading across her face. "I had such a huge crush on your brother, I lost tabs on the rest of the family."

"I'm well aware. More girls than I could count hit me up for Nate's phone number. Your little boy is darling," Hope said, avoiding the obvious question.

Sarina's laugh sounded strained. "Benji's cuter without the attitude. He's a great kid. I just wish—" Sarina opened the door to the rattling of pots and pans and the aroma of frying bacon and baking bread. "I guess you've already gone through Gina's orientation by fire. But if you need help, send up a flare."

"Will do." But Hope couldn't shake the image of Benji's big tears, making it hard to keep an upbeat attitude. Poor little guy. He had no idea how tough the big, wide world could be. Frustration hurried her movements to stash her bag in the small office and strap a clean black apron around her waist. She loved basketball. The sport had helped her through school, providing friends and an activity. That love for the game and her desire to help others had driven her to develop the app. Now that app was generating revenue for someone else when she had someone right in her hometown who could benefit from it.

"Order up!" a cook shouted.

The bell over the front entrance jangled. Dishes clanked and pans banged. An oven timer chimed. Hope pressed through the swinging doors wondering if racehorses felt the same way when the gate opened in front of them.

After three hours of taking orders and delivering food and beverages, Hope wanted to jerk out the entry bell by its jaunty little hook and hurl it at the clocktower. And then silence. Hope's feet burned, her back ached, and her arms felt like cooked noodles. But she'd made over fifty dollars in tips. Pretty good for a breakfast and lunch rush. She patted the pocket on her apron with its cute icon of a bowl of ice cream. Chaz really needed to update the logo since the diner served excellent home-style meals in addition to their delicious desserts.

When Hope stepped through the swinging kitchen doors, Otis, the absolute best chef on the planet, held up a bag. "I hope you like egg." He winked. "I added a treat warm from the oven."

Hope placed her hands in prayer position and bowed her head. "Right now, I could win an eating contest with Nate," she said, forcing a smile as she pushed back the worry gnawing inside her.

Otis's rich laugh drowned out the clatter of pans emanating from the dishwasher station. "It's a pretty day. But if you're going to sit outside, you might need a jacket."

Hope puffed out a breath and fanned her damp bangs. "A breath of fresh air sounds fabulous. I just want to sit and chow down."

"Are you working through until the dinner rush?" Otis asked.

"Not today. I was supposed to get off at 1:30. Penny had an

errand so I stayed over. But I'll be back at 5:30," she said, trying to ignore her fatigue and generate some enthusiasm.

"That can be a long day when we're busy. You might want to soak your dogs for a bit before tonight," he said, his concern a small comfort in her hectic day. "Folks love my Monday night special. Meatloaf, garlic smashed potatoes, and collard greens. Sunberry's favorite."

Hope blotted her sweaty brow with her forearm. "Thanks. Any chance you can add too much pepper to the meatloaf?" She narrowed the space between her thumb and index finger. "Just a smidge to keep the customer load more manageable."

His smile spread wide across his face. "Don't let Chaz hear you say that."

"Can't knock a girl for trying." Hope poured a to-go cup of tea and pushed against the heavy rear door. Despite feeling like a dump truck had backed over her, she pumped her fist at the cloudless blue sky. A busy night meant more tips.

She couldn't wait to tell Jack about today's take. The second she paid off Sleaze, she'd dance up and down Main Street. The warming breeze lifted her bangs, filling her with the promise of spring and a change in her fortunes. Hungry from her busy workday, she plopped onto the picnic table and bit into her sandwich, the savory mustard and herb blend exploding in her mouth. Mmm, no wonder the dratted entry bell never stopped ringing.

The screech of hydraulic brakes turned her attention to the Sunberry school bus coming to a stop in the alley behind her. Moments later, Sarina's boy leaped from the step and skipped toward her.

"Hi!" Benji dropped his bookbag on the table with a thump. "Otis gave you that?"

Hope studied the boy over the rim of her cup. Although her appetite continued to rage, she pushed the bag toward Benji. There was no greater hunger than right after school. In the Murphy house she'd had to be quick because her brothers didn't stop until the snack box was empty.

"Coach Cox always has snacks after practice." His gaze fixed on the bag. "But it was pretzels today."

"You don't like pretzels?"

Benji dug his sneaker toe into the soft soil beneath the picnic table. "They're okay. But not as good as those rollie things."

Hope opened the package. "Looks like Otis packed a big one."

His brown eyes widened in astonishment. "I can eat them in one bite. That makes the cream gush out."

Hope bit her bottom lip, trying to suppress a smile. The kid should win a prize for his creativity. She pushed the treat toward him and before she could blink, it disappeared into his mouth, his cheeks puffed out like a chipmunk. Not one crumb fell.

"Wow!" she said. "You weren't kidding. That must have been one hard practice."

Benji's gaze dropped to the empty paper. He swallowed the pastry but didn't lift his gaze. His sneaker, a faded black with multiple scuffs on the side rubber, continued to mine the dirt beneath the table.

"Something happen at practice?" She leaned down, trying to capture his gaze. "Basketball, right?"

"Buddy and Eric got orange basketball shoes. Mine come off when I turn too fast."

"I played basketball in high school," Hope said.

Benji's frown returned. "We have two girls on our team. They aren't very good."

"I was," Hope said.

Benji didn't appear impressed. "Did your mom buy you basketball shoes?"

Guilt plunked into the pit of Hope's stomach. Jack called

her Princess. She'd never worried about basketball sneakers, clothes, boots, nothing. But she also didn't have access to endless funds—not anymore. And Sleaze?

The wad of bills created a bulge in her pocket. She'd made fifty-three dollars in tips on her first shift and Otis mentioned they'd be busy tonight. All she had to do was ratchet up the smile and work those tables. That was her talent. She'd make up the difference. Maybe she could work more shifts. And maybe she'd win the lottery. Because she couldn't expand a twenty-four-hour day.

The crisp edges of the bills teased her fingertips. She'd been so excited when she'd counted it. Benji continued to dig his sneaker into the dirt.

"Benji!" Sarina's voice broke through the silence. "Ready to head home?"

With his expression downcast, Benji slipped from the bench. "Thanks for the treat."

Hope followed them to Sarina's battered Honda.

"There's my special boy," Sarina said, hugging him, but Benji's arms hung loose at his sides.

Hope's fingers tightened on the crumpled bills, each hard-earned dollar a stark reminder of her looming debt. Just as she moved to hand Sarina the money, her phone vibrated in her apron pocket. *Sleaze*.

Her stomach churned, the weight of her debt pressing down on her. But Benji's tear-filled eyes were impossible to ignore. "Benji, would you wait in the car while I speak with your mom?"

Sarina stiffened in surprise but opened the rear door for Benji and closed it with a soft click. "Was he rude?" she whispered.

"Not at all," Hope said, her resolve solidifying with each passing moment. "He kept me company while I ate a late lunch." She paused, framing her words. "I loved to play basketball when I was a kid. Honestly, the sport kept me out of trouble, especially in my high school days."

Sarina's gaze moved from the car to Hope, probably wondering if Hope had lost her mind. Maybe she had.

"I did pretty good on tips today." Hope held out her tip money, still gripping it like a lifeline. "I think there's enough to buy Benji the orange shoes—like his friends have."

Tears moistened Sarina's eyes. "I can't take your tip money. That's too much. Benji will be fine. You know kids—"

Hope pressed the wad into Sarina's hand. "I don't know much about kids. But I know how it feels to struggle to make someone you love happy. It's a special gift when you can help out with something they need. Please. Let me do this for you and Benji."

Sarina's fingers tightened around the money, her flesh warming Hope's. For a moment, their gazes locked. When Sarina nodded, a trembling smile curving her lips, joy expanded Hope's chest, chasing away the fear and desperation.

"I don't know when I can pay you back," Sarina said, slipping the bills into her purse.

Hope shook her head, her heart too full to speak. "There's no payback. Just pay it forward."

When Sarina hugged her, peace washed over Hope, soothing her inner turmoil. She'd screwed up a lot, but this felt right.

As Sarina waved and drove toward the street, Hope's phone vibrated. Aggravated at the intrusion, she waited until the Honda disappeared from sight. She wasn't going to let Sleaze rob her of this moment.

"I hear you," she muttered. "Seventeen stinking days. You'll get yours. But not today."

She hoped her Sunberry neighbors were super generous tonight.

CHAPTER FOURTEEN

HORMONES WREAKED HAVOC ON A GAL'S JUDGMENT.

Val Reeser leaned against the restaurant's rear entrance, the touching scene between Sarina and Hope Murphy spreading guilt across her shoulders like the long shadows of the sun. She sighed, the weight of her unspoken apology pressing down on her.

Seeking comfort, she caressed her baby bump. "I love you, little one, but I'm ready for you to get here."

She wasn't, however, ready to apologize to her new colleague, an unwelcome side effect from her raging pregnancy hormones. If Mom ever found out about her unkind behavior, Val would never hear the end of it. Loneliness sharpened inside her. What she wouldn't give to hear her mother's lecture.

"It's just really hard doing this alone," she whispered.

Shame constricted Val's throat. Her negative feelings stemmed from Tate, not Hope, which only made her feel worse. She'd fallen for a guy out of her league and decided to bear his baby alone. Hope had nothing to do with her decision.

Frustrated by her hesitation, she shoved away from the doorway and approached Hope.

"I'm sorry for kind of ignoring you over the past few shifts," Val said, her heart hammering in her ears. "I thought you were a spoiled rich kid who'd take my job and apartment."

"Oo-kay, didn't expect that," Hope said, her eyes widening. "But I'm not a threat to your job or apartment. I don't operate that way and neither does Chaz, my sister-in-law."

"I knew it was wrong, but with the baby coming my worries spin out of control," Val said, relief and embarrassment twisting inside her. "Sorry I was harsh. The mean-girl streak didn't feel good, especially since I owe so much to your family."

Hope's suspicious gaze softened and she thrust her hand forward. "Apology accepted."

"Want to join me for a cookie break?" Val said, turning toward the employee break area. "I brought them out for Benji, but I didn't want to interrupt you. I figured the shoes were more important than the cookies."

"Sure." Hope glanced at the empty alley. "I'm free until my ride comes."

When a rumbling noise came from Hope's stomach, Val chuckled. "I thought only men and pregnant women's bellies produced those sounds."

"Looks like it plagues overworked wait staff too," Hope said, taking a cookie. "It was crazy busy this morning. I'm still hungry."

"Ouch! You little booger." Val pressed her hands over a spot on her belly still jiggling from the baby's kick. "Hungry is no longer in my vocabulary. With this little one, it's hangry."

Hope stared, her lips forming a tiny O as she stifled a laugh. For a moment, she seemed lost in thought, her eyes reflecting something hidden.

"You don't like Otis's cookies?" Val guessed.

Hope followed her to the staff's break table. "Your laugh is... unique. Like the front-door bell crossed with a childhood jingle."

"Those horrible bells!" Val eased her weight onto the bench seat. "Most days I want to rip them off the wall. But the weird laugh comes from my mom."

"I always wanted my mom's voice." Hope stepped over the bench like the long-legged colt on the farm near Val's Missouri home. "One minute her tone is cuddly, the next she's barking orders loud enough to cower my brothers."

Val popped a piece of her cookie in her mouth, savoring the companionship and the rich chocolate. "Mom ruled us with just a look."

"I like making new friends but mean-girl to sisters in ten seconds is a lot—even for a pregnant woman," Hope said. "I'm still a little confused."

"Not everyone does the right thing. When I see it, I try to acknowledge it."

"I played sports," Hope said. "Kids want to be good, not stand out."

But Hope had stood out, Val guessed. With her height and looks, she still did. Yet, something haunted the Murphy Princess. Despite coming from a solid Sunberry family, Hope acted more like— Val's eyes widened in surprise. Her.

Shaking off the weird vibe, she mined another chunk of chocolate. "Mmm. Chocolate calms evil hormones. Ask any pregnant woman."

"I heard my sister-in-law got weird," Hope said, still eyeing Val with suspicion.

"Pregnancy has caused all kinds of changes for me." She eyed her cookie. "Before this pregnancy I wasn't a sweet eater. Now, Otis is threatening to lock the pastry case."

Hope shoved her remaining cookie toward her, causing Val's mouth to salivate. "I thought you said you were hungry."

"It's for your little one."

"I'm not turning down the cookie." Val bit off the chocolate at the edge. "What you did for Benji was sweet. But what you did for Sarina—priceless. The pressure to provide for a child is relentless. You made it possible for her."

"I didn't do it to make friends and influence people."

"Well, your thoughtfulness spotlighted my unkind behavior. I can't believe I made assumptions based on gossip. "Val licked her fingers, hoping the rich chocolate would drown the last of her guilt. "I can imagine what's being said about me in my hometown."

"I hear you. Sunberry's grapevine runs at light speed."

"In Glen Falls the news spreads before you act!" Val held up a swollen index finger, which matched every limb on her body. "Hold that thought while I'm one with this final scrumptious bite."

Hope made a funny face. "Remind me not to get pregnant."

"Oh, trust me," Val said. "This wasn't planned." But her joke fell—flat.

Though her Sunberry neighbors had welcomed her, she'd kept much of her past hidden. The ghosts of her decisions haunted her, whispered doubts she couldn't silence. Comparing her broken life to the happy Murphy family was a bitter pill that stung each time she thought about it. Only Chaz Murphy hid a shadow in her smile—until Hope.

Hope's warm hand on her shoulder interrupted her thoughts, and tears stung her eyes.

"Sorry," she said, waving her hand in front of her face. "Hormones. I love my baby. Really. But sometimes the enormity of it scares me—a lot." She moistened her lips. "And sometimes, I feel so alone."

Hope held her gaze, and for a moment the fear twisting Val's gut eased.

"I don't know about being pregnant," Hope said. "But I understand how it feels to be scared."

The haunted look shadowing Hope's eyes halted Val's response. Her new colleague might need a friend more than she did.

"It's a heavy load to carry alone," Val whispered, turning up her palm to Hope. "Sharing my secrets with a friend helps me."

Hope's gaze darted to the vacant steps leading to the restaurant's rear entrance. "Not a word."

"Never," Val said, the unbearable weight she'd carried so long shifting.

Although Baby Reeser usually kept her warm, gooseflesh erupted with the details of Hope's secret. Val wrapped her arms around her bump, wishing she could protect her new friend like her unborn baby. She'd known lenders like the man shaking down Hope. None of the stories had ended well. However, Hope needed a nonjudgmental ear, not interference —at least not yet.

When Hope finished, she rubbed the back of her neck.

"That's a tough one," Val said, relieved the story was behind them. "I don't have the answers, but do you feel better?"

Hope nodded. "Actually, I do. I've got some thinking to do, but it's good to have a confidante. You know? Someone who doesn't know your backstory." Her voice softened, a small smile tugged at her lips, hinting at her vulnerability.

"My sister always said I was a good listener."

"Now it's your turn. Is—" Hope's gaze dropped to her baby bump. "So, are you having a boy or a girl?"

"Sorry I didn't introduce you. But I'm superstitious." The admission warmed Val's cheeks. "I've kept the gender and

name a secret. I was afraid to say it aloud in case...you know?"
Val sucked in a steadying breath, batting down her irrational
fear. "I'm naming her Liberty Reeser. Libby for short"

"I like it. So, is Libby okay?" Hope asked, her voice softening. "Or is something else bothering you?"

Val massaged her baby bump. "I left a piece of my heart in
Glen Falls."

"The baby daddy?" Hope said.

Val nodded, trying to put her thoughts into words. "I've
heard life places the right people in your path." Tears filled
her eyes and she had to pause to regain control. "I left
everyone I loved in Missouri. Now it's just me and Libby."

"I can't imagine walking away from my family," Hope said.

"But you did," Val whispered, embracing the power of
their shared pain.

Wisps of Hope's dark hair fanned her face, but she didn't
seem to notice. Her gaze grew distant, and Val shifted,
sensing the depth of her colleague's pain. Not colleague,
friend, who understood the path she'd taken.

"At first I was so eager to get away from home," Hope
said. "And then I couldn't return, couldn't face my family."

"But you came back. Maybe I can make my way back to
mine." Val swallowed the massive lump in her throat along
with the last resistance to her silence. "How did you do it? I
know you can't fix my problem, just like I can't fix yours. But
if you made it home, maybe..."

When Hope pressed her fingers against her lips and
shook her head, Val's shoulders slumped under the weight of
her own doubts and fears. Maybe there was no going back,
only forward.

Although Hope's debt didn't seem like a big deal to Val, it
obviously felt huge to Hope. Most of her Glen Falls friends
carried debt. Folks did what they had to do. But when it came
to loved ones?

"You don't want to disappoint them." Val leaned her head against Hope's.

"Letting them down keeps me up nights," Hope said, her voice rough with emotion.

After a moment, Hope drew in a ragged breath and fished a tissue from her pocket. "I only have one. Share?"

Val's croak of laughter sent a pair of bluebirds winging to higher branches. "Aaa, that's a hard no. I have limits—even to my new friends." Val lifted her face, soaking in the sun's light and the warmth of friendship. So many of Sunberry's residents had helped her, but Hope understood her.

Hope lifted her phone. "My ride's on the way."

Wadding her napkin, Val hesitated, but only for a moment. "I'm glad we talked. Chaz and Nate took me in. Gave me a job and a place to stay. Kyle and Dana helped me find a doctor. But you—" She tapped her chest. "Gave me hope."

"Thank you," Hope said, hugging Val so hard, the baby wiggled between them. "My family are good people. That's why it sucks being the worm in the Murphy apple."

"Ha!" Val pressed a hand over her mouth. She'd have to remember that expression. "You're the worm. I'm the unwed mother who left town in disgrace—except no one but my sister knows I'm pregnant."

"Secrets are killers. But there's no shame in falling in love." Hope raised her hand. "Plus, you don't strike me as a sleep-around kind of gal. Why couldn't you stay, fight for the man you love?"

Doubts crashed into Val, tripping her heart. "Long story we'll have to save."

"I'll be looking forward to lots of long talks with you," Hope said, linking arms. "I love my brothers, and their wives are cool. It's just...I needed a girl talk. I haven't had that since my roommate crapped out on me. The sharing ended after her boyfriend stole my work and left me holding the debt."

Hope halted, causing Val to stumble. Although her taller friend steadied her, her earlier cheer had faded into a grim pallor.

"Are you okay?" Val asked.

"The creep is relentless." Hope jabbed at her phone. "He sends me countdown texts all the time."

"Be careful." Val removed a worn card from the small wallet buried in her pocket. "Men like Sleaze live low on the food chain, but they're weasels and always have a back door. This is my cousin's card. He works for the Columbia police force. I don't know much about his job, but he's a solid guy. Call him. He might have tips on how to handle your problem or point you to someone who can."

"I'm careful." Hope turned over the business card. "I only meet Sleaze in busy restaurants."

"Every woman needs options." Val squeezed Hope's hand. "When you're dealing with creeps, there's always more below the surface. Don't drop your guard. My grandma's words. She's a smart lady."

"I'll keep your cousin in mind—just in case."

Hope placed the business card in her pocket and patted it.

"Full disclosure," Val said, determined to keep her new friendship on track. "Jack asked me out. I didn't go, but I thought you should know. He's a good guy. Sarina and I are hoping to get dibs on one of his new houses."

"We're not together!"

"Just like I don't still think about my baby's daddy?"

Hope froze.

"Yeah, that look," Val said. "I never went to a fancy college, but I know about feelings. There's always more below the surface. Plus, it's written all over your face."

Hope closed her gaping jaw, shock and awe written on her

pretty face. Val had never been one of the popular girls so she'd gotten pretty good at observing. She liked Hope, and they both needed a friend. A tall friend at that. Shivers raced along Val's shoulders and she pulled her sweater tighter. She hoped her new friend heeded her advice. Just talking about Sleaze had even caused her baby to rustle in her womb.

CHAPTER FIFTEEN

8:29 PM

Jack lifted Hope's borrowed bike into the truck bed, grimacing at the ache in his tired shoulder muscles. Despite their late start and the weather, he and Nate had finished the work on schedule, the pain now a welcome reminder of their achievement. However, the task required two carpenters so he'd missed taking Hope to her second job. The bike's fender rattled with his suppressed worries. He didn't know how long he could protect his business and Hope at the same time.

The flood light over the rear entrance emphasized his concerns.

"Come on," he muttered, adjusting the heater.

After two shifts at Gina's, her cleaning job and a few hours at Robey's Rewards, she had to be exhausted. Moments later, Hope stepped outside, her appearance quickening his pulse. He was dog-tired after one job, but seeing her determination renewed his sense of purpose. She waved, the wind lifting loose strands of hair around her face. Despite the shadows beneath her eyes, she trotted toward the truck with a smile.

A breath he hadn't realized he'd held whispered past his lips, his heart easing just a bit at her smile. Another day with Hope. Another day without a Hope disaster. That had to account for progress, didn't it?

She jerked open the passenger door. "Hey! Thanks for the ride."

"No problem." He held out his hand to help her with a carryout bag.

"That's for you. For the ride," she said, her eyes shining with a gratitude that tightened his chest. "I had Otis pack a lunch for you."

"Let me pay—"

"Absolutely not." She pawed through the bag. "My treat. I also brought cookies."

Before he could shift into drive, she bit into the pastry. "No arguments. You're accepting my small offering. That's my way of paying for the transportation. Biking between shifts wasn't bad, but I wasn't looking forward to the ride to the Kare Center tonight."

"It's a little nippy for night rides. Since you climbed in with a grin, I'm betting it was a good night."

"Good day and good night. I love the changes Mom has made to the shop, and I suggested a few changes she's going to incorporate. My double shift at Gina's garnered one-hundred and seventy dollars and change," she said around her cookie. "But I made a donation."

Donation? Pain shot up Jack's arm from his grip on the steering wheel. *Had she forgotten she was in a debt crisis?*

He scrambled for a soft approach. "You might want to hold off on charitable donations."

"Jack." Hope's voice took on a sharp quality. "Every kid on the team has basketball shoes except Benji. Sarina is on a tight budget."

And so was she. He struggled to get his wallet from his jean's pocket, but Hope's iron grip tightened on his arm.

"I owe over four thousand. Fifty-three dollars won't make or break me."

The sudden urge to kiss her sealed his lips. Besides, his lustful urges would not affect her business savvy. Plus, part of him wanted to cheer her big heart. Some soft mushy side he wasn't going to name.

"As long as our Sunberry neighbors keep up the tips, this is going to work!" she said.

"How long can you hold up this schedule?"

She rubbed cookie crumbs on her pants. "As long as it takes. And as long as I can mooch rides."

Trying to ignore the sharp stab of guilt, Jack turned onto Main Street. "Rides in the evening aren't a problem. I was just watching TV. Sorry I couldn't break away to take you to your mom's shop."

"Biking the few blocks between jobs is no problem. But I don't believe you lay around watching TV after working all day." Her eyes narrowed with challenge. "I remember when my brothers worked construction. Up at dawn and in bed with the chickens."

"If you can work two shifts and take care of the Ash twins at night, I can stay up past dark to give you a ride. We framed floor-to-ceiling windows today. It's a two-man job so I couldn't leave Nate."

"Grandma picked me up. It gave us time alone together."

"And Miss Stella doesn't pressure you for information?"

"She's the best, and she can give me a ride except for Tuesdays and Thursdays when she goes to her book club and master gardener class."

At the stoplight, he depressed the blinker. "So you had a good tip night. What else lifted your spirits?"

"I really like Val," Hope said. "Once she got over being mad at me."

"Val, mad?"

"Good thing I didn't ask her if she'd share the apartment," Hope said, and then gave him the rundown about her newfound friendship with Val Reeser.

"I'm glad the two of you worked it out," Jack said. "She's good people."

"I didn't know how much I missed my friend Bev. We were such good buds until she started dating Sean," Hope said, a sadness softening her voice. "Anyway, Val and I just talked, you know? I've had a lot of friends, but some people...? You feel like you've known them forever. Everything clicks, and you can share anything."

Frustration, combined with an unwelcome jealousy, contracted Jack's chest. He knew all about special friends and wanted her to consider him one. But she didn't trust him enough to share all of her secrets.

"Anyway, we had a nice girl talk in between shifts. Her story put my life in perspective. No more whining. If I screw up and miss a few meals, I'm the only one who goes hungry. Val has to worry about her baby too." The bag rattled and Hope emerged with another cookie the size of a hubcap. "Don't worry. I got two for each of us. These are so good. Plus, I need a sugar fix for my next shift."

Disappointment weighed against Jack's shoulders. Hope was missing the point. What affected her, affected the people who loved her. His family tragedy had etched the lesson on his brain, but how did he get through to Hope? Jack eyed the snack. He could eat the cookie or let Hope's problems eat him.

"I'll probably have nightmares from the sugar," he said, surrendering his battle. *And her money issues.*

"Val said you asked her out. Oh, and did you know she's a certified welder?"

Jack parked in the Kare Center parking lot, his thoughts spinning like the moths circling the sodium lights. "Missed that one."

"What a kick-butt job. They make good pay too. She just can't do it while she's pregnant. But she'll do okay once her little one is here."

"Did she tell you she wasn't all that into me?" Jack said, wanting the words back. How come he couldn't keep his mouth shut around Hope? Because they had a relationship like she'd described. The minute they were together, he over-shared. And he was an idiot!

"I don't think she's over her baby daddy, which is garbage," Hope said. "I can't believe she drove up for his graduation and there was another girl there."

The cookies churned in his gut, but he didn't know if he was upset because Hope wasn't jealous or peeved about Val's jerk of a baby daddy.

"I wanted to pound him too," Jack said. "But Val doesn't seem to be that angry at him."

"Love is blind," she said, her eyes fired with a light that sent his heart and mind into a spin.

"More like circumstances change," he said, scrambling to sort through the random thoughts firing his brain. Hope had returned from college a different person, just like Val's boyfriend.

"Val misses the lover she had—before he went to the Ivy League school," Hope said. "The man she made love to."

Her statement struck a chord. Did he miss the old Hope? No, but the question lingered, nagging at the back of his mind. They'd been kids. And he'd never been in love with her. Had he? Jack's fingers curled into fists. Man, he needed to drive a few nails—into his mushy brain.

Just shut up, dude. This was not the time to start blabbing again. If he didn't keep his crazy thoughts under wraps, she'd figure out his mind was going places it shouldn't go. Based on the way she'd narrowed her gaze, she'd already sensed his heart was on the line.

Jack sat up in his seat. So not happening. Not with his partner's little sister.

"Why are you shaking your head?"

Because he was a board short of a frame. "Just thinking about Val."

"I don't think people change much," Hope said. "At least not their core values. Val misses her home and her family."

"Did you miss yours?" Jack said, grateful to switch topics.

Hope shifted, the leather crunching beneath her weight. "I didn't leave. I went to school."

But her response was too quick, her voice too shrill, telling him he'd hit a nerve.

"My situation is entirely different," she said. "I've always wanted to do something big. But not because of pressure from my parents. They never belittled us or anyone else based on their job, clothes, or social standing."

"That's not their way," Jack said, trying to find the precise words to help her understand. "But sometimes feelings aren't based on fact. After my adoption, I wasn't sure where I belonged. I didn't understand it. Didn't know how to fix it. I just knew how it felt."

"That was a tough time. Your family's fire hit everyone in Sunberry hard," Hope said. "I remember seeing you in school and the pictures of your house. I can't imagine how you felt, but it shook me. The idea that a fire can touch someone you know without warning."

She must have noticed his shudder because she threaded her fingers through his. "I didn't experience your pain, but I often think about being alone. It's why I reach out to people, try to help ease the feeling when I can. I guess that's why I wanted to buy Benji's shoes."

Jack squeezed his eyes shut, but he couldn't shut out his heart.

"Val wasn't trying to make me jealous about you asking her out," Hope said. "But we're friends now, so she wanted to kind of clear the air, you know?"

Though the urge to pull Hope into his arms overwhelmed him, left him shaky with need and uncertainty, he didn't move.

"Val's part of my friend circle now," Hope said, unaware of how each of her heartfelt statements had wrapped around his fragile heart. "She's got a lot going on, and I'll try to help her out any way I can. Oops!" She pointed to the dash clock. "Time for my third shift."

He reached across her to open the passenger door, letting her scent and the sweet aroma of cookies fill his head. "Same time, same place tomorrow morning?"

She was staring at him again. Why couldn't he look away? His hand inched toward her.

Bad idea, Cline. But his mental warning failed to stop his movement. Her crooked eye tooth had trapped her lip. He could fix that problem.

"Jack," she whispered.

"Yeah?"

"What are you doing?"

"I wish I knew," he said, halting his progress. But he couldn't look away from the lure of her mouth. Would her lips feel like he remembered?

When he pressed his mouth to hers, an electric shock surged through him. But before he could draw her nearer, she scooted out of her seat to the ground, her eyes wide. In seconds, a tentative grin brightened her features.

"You know it will never work out," she said, her voice

tinged with a mix of regret and longing that echoed his own feeling. "But we were always good together."

He sucked in his cheeks, even bit the inside of his mouth without success. His sappy grin remained frozen on his face —even when she turned and waved from the Kare Center entry.

"Cline," he muttered. "You are in a world of trouble."

CHAPTER SIXTEEN

WHEN THIS IS OVER...

Hope thumbed through the wrinkled bills, losing count for the third time. But she couldn't focus on numbers with so many questions in her life, each one gnawing at her resolve.

"Just keep moving forward, surviving," she whispered, returning the empty envelope to Jack's safe.

Easier said than done when she was one hundred dollars short for Sleaze's weekly payment. Turbo wiggled onto her lap, purring louder than a lawnmower, his warmth offering small comfort against her rising panic. What if she couldn't make up the difference by the end of the month? What if her family didn't forgive her lies? And the thought of losing Jack —because of her connection to a shady lender—was too much to imagine.

Turbo nudged against the twenty—the paltry amount she'd held back for personal use. Her fist closed around the large wad of bills—Sleaze's payment.

"Never again," she muttered. Once this was over, she'd obtain a skill to support herself. Because she was never going to worry about money again!

A knock rattled the bedroom door and Turbo skittered beneath the bed. "Are you about ready?" Jack asked. "Nate's been flexible this week, but I don't want to be late."

Hope opened the door. "Go ahead. I'll take my bike."

"It's supposed to rain this afternoon," Jack said, a deep furrow wrinkling his brow. "Gina's is on the way."

"Go." Hope waved him forward. "It's Friday. I have to stop at Western Union."

Jack's jaw twitched. "This is making me crazy. I can take out a second loan on my truck or something."

"No," Hope said. "I appreciate the offer. But I'm not going to pull you down with my debt too. Besides, you've done plenty to support me."

"Not enough," he said ramming his hands in his jeans.

"One week closer to freedom," she said, raising the wadded bills in defiance.

When Jack's shoulders sagged, guilt twisted inside her, a sharp reminder of the burden she'd placed on him. She used to make him laugh and make his eyes sparkle with joy, not worry.

"Hey," he murmured, the low tone of his voice drawing her from her mind slump.

When he opened his arms, she stepped into his embrace, holding him too tight for too long.

His lips, firm but tender, brushed hers.

"When this is over," she whispered. *I hope you'll still be here.*

———

FORTY MINUTES LATER, raindrops splatted her cheeks and every pedal rotation brought an image of Sleaze's face beneath her tires, fueling her determination. A quick stop at the Western Union outlet and then off to Gina's—before the gray clouds billowing over her broke open. Right on cue her phone vibrated inside her pocket. Just once, she'd like to slam her phone to the ground and crush it beneath her heel.

And that was a lie. What she wanted was to smash her boot into his creepy face. If he was getting pissy about the short payment, too bad. He'd just have to get over it. She'd make up the difference this week. Her foot slipped from the wet pedal, sending a shiver through her dampened flesh. So not going to happen. She'd requested off Tuesday evening for Mom's anniversary party.

When Hope shook her fist at the sky, thunder rolled over her.

"My sentiments exactly!"

As raindrops pelted her forehead, Hope pedaled harder, her heart pounding in sync with the growing storm around her. Three blocks to go. Buffeted by the wind, the rain drops increased. Dead leaves swirled around her tires. Her phone vibrated against her hip, again.

Thunder crashed and the skies opened just as she parked her bike beneath Gina's awning. Although she usually parked it at the rear entrance, she doubted anyone would notice.

Otis burst through the swinging door, his eyes wide. "The baby's coming! Miss Val is already at the hospital and Miss Sarina is stuck at the clinic with Benji. Miss Val needs you."

"She wants me?" Hope's voice sounded more like a scared Turbo. "I know nothing about babies."

"The doctor will take care of the birthing. Miss Val needs a friend."

When her phone vibrated again, Hope answered it, her heart thudding with the fear she'd almost missed Val's message trying to avoid Sleaze's.

Val

Sorry for the inconvenience. Little Reeser is coming NOW!

Hope's finger shook, but she steadied herself and typed a firm reply.

Hope:

On my way.

Be strong.

Paralyzed by fear, Hope stared at the storm outside and the bike still dripping with rainwater beneath the awning. Seven miles separated Sunberry Memorial from the historic district and Gina's. On a sunny day the ride took twenty minutes. In the storm?

"Bad day to ride my bike," she muttered.

Otis held up his car keys. "Blue Impala parked out back. She ain't much to look at, but she'll take you to the hospital. Penny's on her way in to cover your shift."

The rest of her day crashed through Hope like a runaway train. Her wild ride to the hospital, her change into scrubs, and the birthing process faded into a terrifying whirl of chaos. But when she glanced at the ugly hospital wall clock and reviewed the photos of Val, and Libby, and the brittle smile on her face, the world seemed to right on its axis.

Exhausted but still awed at the experience, she flopped against her chair near Val's hospital bed. "Can I get you anything?"

Val pointed at a sleeping Libby parked near the window. "I've got everything I need," Val said, brushing Libby's pink cheek.

"Hey," Hope whispered, moving closer to her friend to blot the tear sparkling in her eye. "Are those happy tears?"

"I wish Mom and my sister could see her. Libby looks just like her aunt. I can't believe I said that," Val said, a chuckle blending with her sob. "Her little face is mashed like a Pekingese dog. But she still looks like my sister."

"Call home," Hope said.

Val shook her head. "I couldn't face their shame, not when I've been blessed with such a beautiful baby."

"Your mother loves you," Hope said, her fingers crossed she was right. "She'd be thrilled with her granddaughter."

"Like your mom would be thrilled with your secret?" Val said.

Hope huffed out a breath. "That is so not the same thing. But you're right. We're a mess, girlfriend."

Val squeezed her hand. "But we're a mess together."

"You know I'm here for you...and baby Reeser. Holy cow, that was scary. And I wasn't the one doing the work."

Val's melodic chuckle whispered through the room. "I couldn't have done it without you. Did I damage your hand?"

Hope flexed her fingers. "Bruised but not broken. Ha! Just like us."

"Thanks for coming. I'm sorry you missed a shift. And tips are always good on Friday afternoon."

"Don't you dare say another word," Hope said. "I have a beautiful godchild and she was worth every bone-crushing squeeze."

"I was talking about—"

Hope pressed a finger to her friend's lips. "Do NOT mention him in the presence of our precious baby."

"Oh, really!" Val laughed again and then pressed her palm to her mouth. "Did I hear a proprietary *our* from Auntie Hope?"

"You bet your buttons. Auntie Hope is locked and loaded against anyone who gives Libby a slant-eyed gaze."

"Look at her," Val whispered. "So perfect and probably exhausted after her tight squeeze."

Hope stood. "And so is her mother. You better grab a nap before she awakens. I can stop by tonight before I go to

Delmer's. Want me to bring something? One of Otis's pastries? You're feeding two now."

"A vanilla shake and one of Otis's Magnolia Mudslide cookies sound like a heavenly midnight snack. The nurse said babies tend to sleep while at the hospital, but once I take her home she'll awaken every couple of hours." Val's eyes widened. "Oh no! I didn't put the crib together. I was going to do it tomorrow."

Hope lifted her thumb. "Done."

"No!" Val slapped a hand over her mouth, glancing at her blissful babe. "You've already missed enough work for me," she whispered. "I'll put it together when I get home."

"Libby's bed will be ready and waiting tomorrow when you get home. My man has tools." Hope patted her chin to close her gaping jaw. "I don't believe those words came from my mouth."

"He's a good man," Val said. "Don't make the same mistake I did."

"Need anything else?" Hope said, refusing to take a close look at her odd thoughts.

"I'm not pressuring you to make a decision now," Val said. "Consider this a friendly reminder about possibilities once you talk to your family and Jack. Besides, today is Libby's birthday. More good things could happen."

"You're just feeling the effects of drugs," Hope said. "Crib, cookie, and milkshake. Anything else?"

"Thank you for sharing this moment with me," Val said, her voice shaky with emotion.

"I'm humbled you thought to include me." Hope swiped at the tear tickling her cheek, her heart feeling too tight in her chest. "I always wanted a sister. Now I have one."

"And I've always wanted a sister I could help," Val said. "Think about what I said."

Just as Hope nodded, her phone vibrated against her hip.

She didn't open the message until she slipped inside Otis's old
Impala.

> Good morning, Borrower!
>
> Days Left on Loan: 16
>
> Friday Payment Received: $1,215.56
>
> New Balance: $3,076.82
>
> Late fees applied for missing $200.00
>
> I'm still looking forward to meeting the big
> NFL star!
>
> Cheers, Bain Vill

As the rain battered the car roof, Hope's resolve solidi-
fied. She would not let Bain Vill ruin this precious moment or
her future.

CHAPTER SEVENTEEN

1:00 PM

Though clear overhead, dark clouds gathered over the eastern sky, mirroring Jack's thoughts. With some luck, they could lay the roof sheathing before the weather turned. He raised his hammer just as his phone vibrated against his thigh.

"It's about time," he said, scrambling to get his phone from his pocket.

> Liberty Reeser, dubbed Princess Libby, has arrived. She's gorgeous!. Mom and baby doing great.
>
> Hope

"It's a girl!" he shouted.

Balanced on a truss, Nate pumped the air with his hammer. "Fantastic. Now maybe we can get some work done."

Jack returned his phone, a blend of relief and joy expanding his chest. Healthy and happy was all he needed to know. With that worry behind him, he could focus on his job.

He hustled down the ladder, his steps lighter as he lifted the next board. With a half day in front of him, he'd be back on schedule in no time—until Hope lobbed a new development into his life.

Hours passed with the wind gathering force, the bank of clouds now dark and threatening. Jack stepped on the base of the ladder, the last sheet of plywood leaning against his shoulder. Muscles straining, he gripped the heavy board to balance its unwieldy bulk.

"Almost done," he muttered, frustrated with his inability to compartmentalize his thoughts about Hope. Step by step, he climbed, the weight pressing down on him. Physical stress, he could handle, but the mental strain kept building like the approaching storm. At the roofline, he shifted the sheet onto the trusses with practiced ease and prepared to secure it in place. His breath whistled through his teeth. Two inches off!

"Get your mind straight," he muttered, yanking the square from the opening.

The sheathing should've been done an hour ago. If he continued at this pace, the renovation would come in a month behind schedule. Meanwhile, his dreams would wither as fast as his bank account under the weight of his land loan interest. He dropped the miscut board to the ground with a thump, emphasizing his thought. Money was always the culprit. Except his new money worries were wrapped up with Hope. So he could sit back and crash his business or he could talk to Hope.

"Finished?" Nate said, frustration edging his tone. "I was hoping to get this under roof before we break for the weekend."

"Give me a second." Jack swiped the sweat tickling his ear. "My measurement was off."

"You're never off."

But he *was* off. *Way* off.

While Jack rechecked his mark and powered up the saw, he silently retraced his missteps. He should have insisted on honesty with her family. He should have loaned her his truck this morning, knowing pop-up storms were common. But he'd been aggravated—not just by losing control and kissing her, but by her rejection, which still stung. Worse, he sensed she hid her feelings as tightly as she held her secrets.

Those secrets carried a hard toll he couldn't afford to pay much longer. He'd risked his relationship with Nate, and now his work was suffering.

At four-thirty Jack stepped back, checking his work for flaws. Today had been a struggle, but he'd gotten through it—on schedule. First thing Monday morning, they'd lay the felt followed by shingles.

"Looks good." Nate held up his palm for a high five. "Chaz and I are stopping by the hospital. Do you want to ride along?"

"Nah, thanks." Jack checked his phone. "Hospitals creep me out. I'll pick up a teddy bear and drop it by the apartment once she comes home."

"Be careful, Jack."

He stiffened. Although he'd known it was coming, he didn't look forward to the discussion. When he straightened, Nate was waiting for him.

"I love my sister, but she's a heartbreaker."

Dead right on that one. "I'm keeping my distance."

Nate's laughter erupted with disbelief. "Sure you are partner. How's that thumb? You're head's so far in the clouds, I had my finger hovering over 911 most of the day."

Jack's cheeks heated. "I'm not that bad."

"I just don't want to lose my partner over my sister." Nate hefted his toolbox. "Hope's got a heart of gold. She just doesn't give it out to guys. Trust me. I've counted her wasted lovers for years. I don't want to see you added to her list."

"You think she's going to stay in Sunberry?" Jack was almost afraid to get another perspective. Afraid he'd get the wrong answer.

"Something's going on with her. Nothing new there." Nate's narrowed gaze made him uncomfortable. "I suspect you know more than you're sharing. And I get it. Hope has a way of securing loyalty from *every*body. Just take it from a man who knows and loves her. She never tells the whole story. And the part she hides?" Nate shook his head, his gaze distant. "It's always bad news. So brace yourself because in two weeks stuff will hit the fan as sure as this renovation will be completed."

"She's trying." The words rolled off Jack's tongue before he could stop them.

Nate paused, a sad smile on his face. "She always does. But it won't help the damage she leaves in her wake."

When Jack's phone buzzed, Nate paused in the doorway before heading to his truck. Resigned, Jack placed the phone to his ear.

"It was the most amazing experience!"

A grin rearranged his tired features. That was the thing about his Hope: she could make him feel like a million bucks in an instant. Propelled by her vivid description of her first birthing experience, he cleaned the worksite in record time.

"I'll pick up Val's snacks and assemble the crib as soon as I shower," he said when she finally started to wind down. "Just get in your shift. I know you're behind on hours this week."

"No way!" Hope said. "This is my goddaughter's birthday. I've got to launder the new sheets and prepare her nursery. They're coming home tomorrow."

"Make a list—" He picked up his saw and hurried toward the drive.

"Didn't you hear me?"

The thud of the tailgate reverberated with a reminder of Nate's warning.

"I'm your backup," he said, keeping his tone even despite his pounding heart. "In two weeks you'll be out of this mess and free to babysit and cuddle Val's baby all you want."

"I saw a new life begin today." Hope's tone had dropped to an urgent whisper. "Life, Jack. Compared to life, money means nothing."

Thunder rumbled overhead. Jack froze, paralyzed by his choices. Life? He'd been consumed with making a living. He wanted a life—with Hope.

When a bolt of lightning streaked across the darkening sky, he hustled into his truck, his feelings as clear as the impending storm. He'd loved Hope Murphy since third grade. He'd never stopped. Never would stop.

By the time Jack showered and drove to the diner, the wind howled through the trees, driving rain against the windows in fierce torrents. He dashed inside the restaurant and slammed the door shut, battling the gusts that threatened to rip it from his grasp. Though relentless, the outside storm paled to the simple fact that he was in love with Hope.

Love? He shook his head and turned away from the door. A flash of movement caught his eye. Hope sprang from the shadows, her dark hair wild behind her, igniting an adrenaline rush of affection through Jack. In an instant, she was upon him, leaping with an unexpected grace.

"I still can't believe what I witnessed today!"

Before he could process what was happening, her arms wrapped around his neck, and her lips pressed against his. Unstable by her weight, he stumbled backward, found his balance and pulled her closer, his lips softening beneath hers.

Somewhere in his foggy brain, voices hummed, plates rattled. But with her hands threading through his hair, her legs tightening around his waist, there was no way he'd stop.

He deepened the kiss and the sights and sounds surrounding them faded into the rapid beats of his heart.

A gust of wind buffeted him from behind. He blinked. Had he just kissed Hope in front of their Sunberry neighbors? A slow grin overshadowed his embarrassment, his heart lifting at the sound of Hope's voice. The last thing he remembered was her joy. Yep, she made him happy too. So happy he almost cried when she stepped back, a huge, delighted smile filling her face even as crimson flushed her cheeks.

"Neighbors have been dropping off baby gifts all afternoon," she said, leading him through the restaurant to the rear door. "You should see the adorable outfit Mom brought for Libby's trip home. It's precious."

Still immersed in a happy glow, he followed her out the rear entrance and raced up the stairs, its hand-forged railing rattling in protest. When he slammed the apartment door on the rain, the shudder of the wood shook him back to reality. A life with Hope was impossible with her debt looming over them.

"Friday nights at the restaurant are busy," he said, swiping off the rain from his clothes. "Was Penny okay with you leaving early?"

"Sarina needed to make up the hours she'd missed during Benji's doctor appointment," Hope said, flipping on the light and tossing him a towel.

The soft overhead lighting revealed a cozy living area cluttered with baby-themed gifts, each topped with giant pink bows. Balloons bobbed from the draft created by their entry. A bouquet of white trumpet-like flowers and stems of tiny purple blooms filled the room with a sugary and herbal scent. Jack's nose twitched. Although he wasn't a flower fan, the aroma had a calming effect—great for little humans who were up a lot.

"Wow!" he said. "When you said everyone, you meant *every* living Sunberry resident."

"People love babies." She led him down the narrow hall to a small room that looked out over Main Street. "This is the nursery and that"—she pointed at a large cardboard box— "is our assignment for the evening. I hope we can put it together before I have to leave for Delmer's."

Although he'd never constructed a baby crib, he lifted his palm. "I promise that sucker will be ready for Val's baby before I leave tonight. As for the other chores, if you leave a list, I'll take care of them."

"Stop!" Hope held up her palm, her lips set in a firm line. "I love your concern. But I'm not changing my mind. I *want* to do this for Val."

"Got it," he said. "I'm here to back you up. Whatever you and Val need."

And he was a coward. But he wasn't giving up. There was always a fix. A guy just had to be patient, check all the angles.

Despite the earlier tension about her choice, they fell into an easy rhythm. While he pawed through an array of hardware that outweighed the crib, she moved back and forth between the nursery and the tiny alcove outfitted with a stackable washer and dryer.

Tired but pleased with his work forty minutes later, Jack centered the constructed crib beneath the giant soft elephant decorating the wall.

"The kid better like elephants," he said, a smile tugging at his lips despite his worries.

When she didn't make a snarky remark, he turned and hesitated. Why was she crying? She might be the Murphy Diva, but the identity had rarely included tears. Anger usually signaled Hope's distress. It had taken him a while to work that trait out about her. His problem was determining if she were ticked or distressed.

"I'll get the sheets," she said, hurrying from the nursery before he could say something.

Satisfied the crib was precisely situated under the elephant—he'd checked with his tape measure—Jack stood and stretched his back and shoulders. Still no Hope. So should he give her a moment? Clearly she'd been trying to hide her emotions from him. The fact didn't sit well. It wasn't like he was going to say something mean or make fun of her.

Five minutes ticked by before she entered the nursery with an armful of elephant sheets. Who knew?

"Hold on," he said. "There are mattress settings. Geez, Val would break her back trying to get a baby out of there."

Hope emptied the sheets on the rocker he'd almost given up on. Man, he built houses not furniture.

Red rimmed her eyes and tipped her nose, but the tears were gone. She raised one end of the mattress frame, still keeping her face turned away while he made the final adjustments, his anxiety building with the growing silence. After he placed the mattress in the crib, he turned to her still fussing with the sheets.

"Hey," he said, running his hands down her shoulders. "Talk to me."

At first she resisted and then turned to him, fitting against him just like she always had. Like he hoped she always would.

"Why are you sad?" he whispered, holding her close, letting the beat of her heart blend with his. "It hurts me to see you like this."

Warnings rattled inside him, but he brushed them aside. There'd been too many warnings. Too many secrets. Too many assumptions. This was his chance and he wasn't going to pass it up. Succeed or fail, he was all in. Had been since the day she crept from Cody's truck bed. He'd been too pigheaded to admit it.

She stepped back, leaving a painful vacuum, her eyes shimmering with unshed tears. "I know. Me? With tears? It's pretty new and confusing to me, too." Hope raised her arms and dropped them. "It's just...all this. The baby, the nursery... I don't know. All of a sudden tears."

Disappointment twisted inside him. For once he'd like to hear the truth—all of it. Not merely the scraps she felt comfortable sharing.

He stuffed his hands in his jean pockets to keep from taking her in his arms, kissing her until she revealed every hidden piece of her. Because that's what he wanted—all of her.

"I've gone along with your secrets even when I knew it was wrong," he started, picking each word. "Your family has always supported me. Sometimes I've felt closer to them than my own. And yet, you close me out. That hurts." He studied the area rug with its smiling elephant. Nurseries were always so cheerful. He guessed parents tried to shield babies from life's realities. Its heartaches.

When he looked up, Hope's gaze locked on his. Her moist eyes stabbed him with regret. He hadn't meant to make her cry.

"I'm sorry I've dragged you into my mess." She sniffed. "I'm grateful you've stood by me. I couldn't have made it this far without you."

"I'll always be here for you," he said, holding his breath, hoping she was ready for the next step.

A fake grin captured her features before she glanced away.

"But I'll be glad when it's over," he said, burying the disappointment hollowing out his insides.

"Not near as glad as me." She bit her bottom lip. "Sometimes I feel the debt is suffocating me. Like it's a weight on my back and I'm alone in the ocean, treading water. I'm so tired. And the guilt. Geez, the guilt is eating me up inside.

But the waterworks..." She pointed at her eyes. "These are for Val."

"Why?" He hadn't meant for that to sound so defensive, but it didn't make sense to him. "She's been through a lot. But look around. She's made great friends, a home for her baby."

"But she left her family behind. Her mom and sisters weren't here to plan the shower, be with her at the hospital, cuddle her baby." Hope shook her head. "That's so sad."

"They aren't dead." The moment the words echoed in the dinky nursery, he regretted them. "Val's built a new family in Sunberry. Life happens and we lose loved ones. But we don't lose love." He glanced away, feeling foolish. "I mean, we don't have to. I love my adopted parents. And your family.... I don't know how I would've managed without them. Plus, we've got the Ash twins. Talk about a way to lift your day. Cody and Lil Barnfield are amazing friends, and there are the Grants and scores of others."

She wrapped her arms around his waist and placed her cheek against his shoulder, her breath tickling his neck, solidifying his love for her. The words 'I love you' rushed to his lips, but he held back.

He rubbed up and down her back like he'd seen Talley soothe Ellie. He didn't stop. Didn't want to do anything to spoil the moment. Life happened. Man, he knew that. Which made him appreciate the little moments because the next one might not come at all—especially with Hope.

"I missed this town so much," she said, her tone so low he had to carefully listen.

Relief eased his breathing. "I can't imagine leaving. It's big enough to support new businesses and families. Not like some of the neighboring communities struggling to support their populations."

"I'm coming home." She stepped back so they were face to face, her dark eyes boring into him.

"You are home." He swallowed. Sometimes the dumbest things rolled out of his mouth.

Her grin eased his embarrassment. "I mean for good. I knew the minute I climbed out of Cody's truck. This is where I belong—even if I had to live in a barn."

"I'll build you a house." *Put a sock in my mouth!*

"You're sweet. But the first house you need to build should go to Sarina and Val. They're kind of done with men. Together, they can raise their children."

He'd do whatever she asked, anything to make her happy. Make her his. An image of Chaz's dog Handsome flashed in his mind. Never again would he make fun of that lovestruck mutt.

"So you're not going back to U of SC?"

"One more time." Her gaze narrowed. "To settle my debt. After that, it may be a while before I return to Columbia. Except I really like the Riverbanks Zoo. Maybe I can take Libby there when she gets older."

"Are you getting close to making your payment?"

Her fingers pressed his lips. "Shh. This is my debt. I want to look that ...that... lowlife in the eye, settle, and walk away."

"You sound like you're leaving tomorrow. Don't you have until the end of the month?"

"When I held Val's baby..." Hope's gaze grew distant, like she was watching a scene he couldn't see. "My messy life seemed clearer. You know? Like I finally figured out my path."

Every hair on his body lifted. Something was up. "I'll go with you. As soon as you pay him, we'll do a happy dance." He laughed, hoping she didn't notice his nervous energy. "Nate's been taking dance lessons. I'll have him show me some moves."

Although he adored her smile, Hope hid a lot of serious stuff behind it.

"You need to stay right here and finish the Martinez job so you can start Val and Sarina's house." He grabbed her index finger to stop another jab to his breastbone. "It won't be long before they have the downpayment. Sarina is expecting a family windfall soon."

"Hold up, babe. I don't like you going alone." And based on her narrowed gaze, she didn't like his proprietary tone.

"Give me some credit," she said, her hands stiffening on her hips. "I'm twenty-five, not fifteen. And it's not like I'm a little bit of a thing."

When she puffed out her chest and got in his face, he raised his palms in surrender. "Yes, ma'am. Hope Murphy is not a gal to mess with."

She smiled and his heart took off like a runaway horse.

"I'll need your truck."

Of course she did. He nodded. "When are you going?"

"March 22nd."

He swallowed his surprise. No way. She'd be short. By a lot. And that was *if* she had given him an accurate amount. She was still holding back, and she was behind. With her charitable donations and missed work, he'd bet her loan amount was growing faster than her payments.

"Close your mouth," she whispered. "You're going to catch a bug."

He snapped his jaw closed. "I guessed it would be closer to mid-April."

When she glanced to the left, his stomach dropped.

"I'll have everything I need by the 22nd," she said.

"I've been thinking. You know that old motorbike I told you about?" He ignored her narrowed gaze. "I talked to the mechanic at Riley's Auto Repair. He said he could get it running for a few hundred. My truck is paid for—"

"No!"

"Hear me out. It would be a temporary solution. You could pay me back."

"Absolutely not! That scumbag got my car. You are not sacrificing your truck. You need it for your business."

"It's just for the summer."

"No." Hope fisted her hands on her hip. "If you sell your truck, we're done. I'm serious, Jack. I've got all the guilt I can manage for one lifetime. Understand?"

"I'm just trying to—"

Her lips closed over his, silencing his explanation, his thoughts. In seconds, only the rapid thud of their hearts and the rasp of their breaths breached the silence. By the time she pulled away, he couldn't remember his point.

"I don't need you to fix this for me," she said.

"I didn't offer because you need it," he said. "I offered because I...care about you. I want to help."

Holy, he'd almost said the L word. That would've buckled his frame. If she didn't stop studying him like that, he might have to kiss her again.

"I've got this," she said. "I mean *really* worked it out. Not a half-baked scheme, but a valid plan."

And he had fifteen days to weasel out the details. "Will you tell your family?"

"We'll see," she said. "If things go my way, I won't need to involve them anymore than they are. But like Val says, it's good to have a back door."

"I'm a good listener."

"You are."

When she closed her eyes, his heart stuttered.

Trust me, he silently prayed.

"You know I told you about Val's cousin?"

"The one in Columbia?"

She nodded. "I contacted him and he gave me some ideas. I may have a legal recourse. I also called Russ Carver, an attorney my family has used. He referred me to a Columbia lawyer who specializes in financial issues."

Jack released a sigh of relief and hugged her. With professional help, her plan could actually work out. She'd be out of debt. The lender might be out of business. At least he hoped that would be the case. They could have a future—together.

"I heard Delmer is recovering faster than expected," he said, struggling to keep his tone neutral. "Where are you going to stay when they no longer need you?"

She gave him a wry grin. "Welcome to Sunberry, where news travels fast. We talked last night. I can't believe how fast he's improved. The twins were going to keep me until the end of the month." She exhaled. "I think they worked out I needed money. But I couldn't let them do it on their limited retirement."

"When's your last night?"

"This Monday will be ten days."

He folded her hand in his. "And Tuesday night?"

"We have a Murphy Anniversary party."

When she tried to withdraw her hand, he tightened his grip, bringing her gaze to his.

"Tuesday ends the dishonesty. Besides, we're not a secret."

She canted her head to the right. "We're?"

"Nate knows I'm kind of with you."

"Translation."

The hair at the back of her head glided across his hand. He gently pressed her forward, never taking his gaze from hers. "I like where we're going," he whispered, brushing his lips against hers.

"I've had this motto." She kissed the side of his mouth. "As soon as this is over."

He resisted the urge to tighten his hold. "I hope you're talking about your financial bind and not us."

"Is there an us?"

He kissed her again, drawing it out, resisting the need to stop. "There's always been an us—at least for me."

She hesitated, biting her lip. "I've put you in a difficult situation. When I tell my family, I'll make sure they know everything is on me."

"Are you asking them for the difference?"

He couldn't wait for her answer. Not with her breath mingling with his. He cupped her chin and tasted her once, twice. Her hands slid behind his neck and he was lost. Lost in the scent of his shampoo in her hair, lost in the little sounds of pleasure she made, lost in the pound of her heart beating next to his.

After a moment, she pulled back and he rested his forehead against hers, the rasp of their breaths filling his ears. At his feet, the smiley elephant looked up from the rug. This. His chest filled with thoughts of a future with her. He wanted all of it. The cozy house. The nursery. With Hope.

Her delicate hands pushed against his chest. "Time to get the sheets on the bed, lover boy," she said, giving him a gentle push.

Lover boy? Jack grinned. He liked that nickname—a lot.

Turning back to the crib, he lifted the mattress for her. "Are you going to tell them at your grandmother's next dinner or before?"

"At Mom's anniversary party." She avoided his gaze, focusing on slipping the baby elephant sheets over the mattress edge. "I'll stay to help clean up and tell them. That way everyone can enjoy the party."

"Saving the hard news for last?"

"Pretty much."

While he fitted the mattress back inside the crib, she added the mobile with its cheery stuffed pachyderms on the crib side.

"You're part of the family." She untangled the plush

animals and balls of the mobile. "If you're there... It's okay if you are," she said, rushing her words. "Just let me tell them... in my own way."

"Sure." But that itchy feeling crept through him. Why say that, unless she was going to... "No more lies, babe." He ran his knuckles along her cheek, loving the way she nuzzled against his hand. "You admitted it's eating you up inside. So say whatever you need to say but tell them the truth."

But even after her nod, the itchy feeling persisted.

CHAPTER EIGHTEEN

MARCH 19, 5PM

Today, there would be no more secrets—only the raw truth she feared might shatter everything.

Hope's heart pounded in her ears, each beat a reminder of the confrontation awaiting her. Through the windshield of Jack's truck, the setting sun splashed the sky in shades of pink and crimson. Although the vents blew warm air, cold dread walked across her shoulders.

During the short drive to the shop, Jack had abandoned his upbeat chatter. Now, still silent, he focused on parking the big Ford behind Robey's Rewards. When he cut the engine, Hope worried he'd hear her heart pounding against her ribs. But he was out of the truck and opening her door in seconds.

She accepted his hand, the warmth of his grip calming the storm inside her. "Just poke me in the eye with a sharp stick," she whispered, her voice hoarse with fear.

"You got this, babe," Jack murmured. "I'll be right beside you."

"Confessing my litany of judgment errors doesn't occupy my list of fun things to do."

"But it will soon be behind you."

"I've carried my bad decisions long enough," she said. "But that doesn't make this easier."

He closed the door with a soft click, like he was worried she might disintegrate from a loud noise. "They'll forgive you."

"They always do," she said through gritted teeth. "That's the problem. I didn't want them to *have* to forgive me. I wanted to make them proud."

"They will be at how hard you worked to pay off the debt." He slowed his long stride to match her slow, hesitant steps. "I am."

"Thank you," she said, wishing his praise would ease her task.

The staggering amount she'd been forced to pay Sleaze wasn't the story she wanted to share with her family. But her wants didn't change the situation. Corralling her fears, she tightened her grip on Jack's hand, focusing on his calloused palm. The end of her journey was in sight.

Stay the course. The familiar mantra caused her to stumble. Hadn't Mom shared that line? Most good things had come from her family. Today's confession wasn't one of them.

"I'm just here to support you," Jack said. "Think of me as a bug on the wall—big eyes and no mouth!"

His attempt at humor brought a brief, much-needed grin to her lips. "Funny, Cline. Very funny."

He opened the back door for her. "Just trying to defuse the tension."

"The tension will be gone the minute I've ended my agreement with Toilet Man," she said, her fears momentarily subsiding with Jack's grin.

"You'll be fine," he said, squeezing her hand.

"Hey, Little Sis!" Nate met her inside the entryway. "Glad you made it."

Hope snagged her lip, narrowing her eyes on her brother, a surge of anxiety tightening her chest. His words sounded sincere. Was his hug kind of brief? Jack might have told him —not the whole story but given up clues. However, Nate wasn't the analysis brother. Brainiac Kyle held that position in the Murphy tribe.

"Are Kyle and Dana here yet?" Hope scanned the crowded shop.

"Delayed," Nate said. "Something about a last-minute test result. But the folks are greeting friends and neighbors in the front. Last time I saw Whit, he was on potty duty."

Behind Nate, Talley waved and then returned to setting up a steamer of shrimp and grits while Chaz arranged an array of pastries.

Although Hope loved the southern fare, her knotted stomach rebelled and her fingers curled with anxiety. "Need some help?"

"We've got it," Chaz said. "Go join the folks. We'll be there soon."

Although she'd prefer scrubbing floors to release her jitters, she linked her arm through Jack's, noting his stiff posture. He also had skin in the game. She had to get this right.

Pushing through her fear, she focused on the familiar faces crowding the shop. This was Sunberry, the community she loved. Her family, friends, and neighbors had gathered to celebrate Mom's success. And her mother was a success— even at raising her. She would not, could not, let Mom down again.

As she moved through Robey's Rewards, pride filled her chest. Her sisters-in-law, Talley, Chaz, and Dana had transformed the quaint gallery into a festive celebration, each detail a testament to their love and care. Fresh-cut daisies, Mom's favorite, adorned an antique parson's table. A playlist, reminiscent of their early days in Sunberry, hummed beneath the congratulations and laughter. But it was her mother's craft that touched Hope. She feathered her fingers over the surface of a 3-drawer chest, a darling child's desk, and a side table. Each piece showcased intricately painted small town scenes decorating the surface—Mom's signature craft.

"Perfect. Just like Mom," she murmured.

"I don't know how she does it," Jack whispered near her ear, loud enough for her to hear over the crowd.

Hope talked to her neighbors, each familiar face offering a small measure of comfort as she and Jack slowly made their way to the reception line. At the entrance, a woven basket held colorful brochures tracking Robey's Rewards renovation journey. Memories filled Hope's mind, displacing her fear and impending confession. Along the back wall of the room set up for addressing the audience, family photos dangled on pink ribbons suspended from a curtain rod.

Hope halted in front of an image of her at five years old, painting a wall with Kyle rolling the ceiling, Nate hunched over the baseboard, and Whit refilling roller pans.

"She was so brave," Hope murmured, heedless if anyone could hear. "We'd lost Dad and our way. But Mom led us through."

Mom had risen from the depths of loss, uniting and healing the family. The struggle had bonded them. Made her realize her brothers might harass and boss her around, but they also stood at her back. Mom had accomplished so much with four kids depending on her.

"I won't fail you," Hope whispered. "Oh!"

At Hope's waist, Sam giggled. "Aunt Hope, you promised to help me shoot baskets. I'm on a peewee team and Dad says you're the best."

"The best?" She hugged her niece, letting her innocence strengthen her. She'd assumed her brainiac brother thought she was a flake, but maybe he recognized more of her talents than she thought. Maybe it was her who had lacked confidence.

Sam flipped a braid over her shoulder, her gaze hopeful. "He said you beat him every time." Sam glanced around and her voice lowered. "He said you were even better at shooting than Uncle Whit, and Uncle Nate was the best at layups."

"You..." Hope tapped Sam's upturned nose. "...will be better than all of us because I'm going to coach you."

"Really? Keegan always beats me, and Benji told me I needed more practice."

"Maybe all you need is orange shoes and a hotshot aunt."

Sam's smile widened. "You'll coach me?"

"We'll put it on the calendar. Deal?" Hope held up her fist.

Sam bumped her knuckles and then wiggled her fingers. "Deal. I'll tell Mom as soon as she gets here. Dad will forget."

The irony of her brilliant brother's lack of focus at home inspired Hope. Too bad Val had missed the exchange. Her friend idolized Dr. Kyle. Hope checked the time. Val should be here by now. She'd never miss an opportunity to show off her new baby. Of course, while mothers made plans, babies laughed.

After an hour of strengthening old acquaintances, Hope took Sam's hand. "Time to listen to Pawpaw's big speech."

With Sam at her side and Jack at her back, Hope wove through the crowd to the dais erected for Dad's tribute. Together, they took their places beside the Murphy family while friends crowded behind them.

Surrounded by her family and community, warmth stirred and then settled deep inside her. This—her home, the people she loved—answered the questions burning inside her. The raging fire to match her brothers' achievements dwindled. All wasn't lost, nor had it ever been. Murphy competitiveness would always be part of her, but that didn't mean she was doomed. She had other talents, other values.

A screech echoed through the speakers, the crowd quieted, and her dad stepped forward, his presence strengthening her resolve. She'd make her life here with family, friends, and possibly—she rubbed her thumb over Jack's—this man. Like her, he'd struggled. But he'd found his way, and so could she. After all, she'd been named Hope for a reason.

On stage, Ryan asked Ava to join him. As the audience cheered their approval, Hope's chest lifted with pride. Although she'd always been aware of the love and respect her parents shared, never had it been so clear. Love seemed to radiate from their features, a look she'd seen elsewhere. Her breath stalled in her lungs—Jack.

As the warmth of Jack's hand around hers burned through her heart, images raced through her mind. The way Jack winked at her, his dark eyes sparkling with humor. The quick flash of his smile that emphasized the dimple in his tanned cheek. The gentle touch of his calloused fingers drifting on her flesh. The way he always leaned closer when she spoke, like he didn't want to miss a word. She sucked in a breath, noting the shift in her chest. Sleaze had stolen her money and self-respect. Jack had stolen her heart.

She glanced to her left, almost afraid to look at him. Was the love her parents shared within her reach, despite her missteps?

Like missing her father's tribute. She focused on Dad.

"I've served beside the finest and most courageous men," Ryan was saying. "However, this woman showed me the meaning of true courage. The kind of courage when every decision impacts your family and there is no backup because your partner was taken while serving his country. Ava returned to Sunberry with four children." Ryan raised four fingers. "Three adolescent boys—not the easiest age, and one wide-eyed daughter." His gaze found Hope's.

"I had the sense to know a once-in-lifetime opportunity and seized it with both hands. Once Ava and I joined ranks, we not only survived; we thrived, the same as this shop—because of Ava. She constantly demonstrates courage, resilience, and patience. That's why I'm proud and very honored to call her my partner."

He waited for the applause to subside.

"Success is rarely a solo endeavor. We have four talented and caring adult children who have picked up the traditions Ava and I started. Together with their wives and children, the Murphy family will continue."

"That's me!" Sam raised her arms in the air.

Hope raised her fist. *And me.* Beside her, each of her brothers and their wives lifted an arm, except for Kyle. Where was her oldest brother and his wife? Something must have happened to one of his patients. And where was Val?

"Jack," she whispered near his ear. "Have you seen Val and the baby?"

"No," he said, standing with the audience. "But it's too crowded to tell."

Hope typed a text and then stood on her toes to whisper near Jack's ear so Sam couldn't hear. "I can't believe Kyle missed this. I hope everything is okay."

Concern lined Jack's wrinkled brow. He turned toward Nate, standing to his left. Although the noise from the crowd drowned out his words, she recognized blooming anxiety first on Nate and then Whit's faces. Again, she checked her phone. Val hadn't responded to her text, neither had Kyle.

If Mom and Dad knew anything, they hid it well because both were smiling and talking with their many friends and neighbors.

Stay positive, she silently coached. The worries about her impending confrontation diminished as the silence from her missing brother and friend grew. Their absence didn't make sense. Kyle shared his on-call shifts with a partner so he wouldn't miss events like today. Val always responded to texts. Sure, she could be tied up with the baby. But not this long.

A change in tone sounded from the front entrance. Hope strained to listen, picking up murmurs of precious and adorable. It had to be Val and the baby. Sending up a brief prayer of gratitude, Hope hurried toward the sounds. Dana, not Val, stood in the entrance fielding questions and comments, Baby Libby snuggled in her arms. Hope froze, frantically scanning the last of the crowd for Val.

Kyle's slight head shake silenced the question on Hope's lips. While Sam wormed through the last group of well-wishers to Dana, Jack's grip stopped Hope. Her phone vibrated in her pocket.

"Kyle just sent out a group text," Jack whispered. "He'll explain after everyone leaves."

Hope's feet rooted to the ceramic floors she'd once helped install. Something had happened. But Kyle would never gloss over an emergency and though strained, his features were calm, in control.

"Babe," Jack whispered, breaking through her fears. "If you squeeze any harder, I won't be able to hold a power tool for a month."

Hope's gaze dropped to Jack's calloused hand, now pale from her vise-like grip. She forced her fingers to relax and rubbed her palms over his flesh.

"Sorry." She raised their joined hands and kissed his fingers. "Better?"

His expression heated, and thank goodness, Baby Libby held Grandma's undivided attention.

"When this is over," they said in unison.

Whit, with his booming voice and friendly smile, ushered

the last of the well-wishers from the shop and locked the door. "Mom, you need to turn down the wattage. I thought your adoring fans would *never* leave."

"Best tribute ever!" Grandma said, hugging Ryan. "Do you remember when your dad used to stand in the bleachers every time you scored?"

"No, and thank you for your restraint," Ryan deadpanned.

Grandma's grin would put the Cheshire cat to shame. "It was a struggle."

Ava held out her hands. "Let me hold that baby."

"Back room, everyone," Nate said.

"Ellie!" Talley's voice broke through the murmurs.

"Uh-oh." Whit moved Hope to the side. "I leave her for one stinking moment and—"

Chaos blooms. Any other time, Hope would've enjoyed Ellie relieving her of the Murphy chaos instigator, but not with her friend missing in action.

She tugged Kyle's sweater. "Where's Val?"

"I hope someone taped Dad's tribute," Kyle said.

Nate lifted his phone. "I got every word."

"Come on back." Chaz motioned toward the large community area located in the rear of the shop. "I saved Otis's latest creation for the family and Hope's announcement."

"What about Val?" Hope said, following her brother. "Why do you and Dana have Libby?"

Kyle stopped at the first chair seated around the large table usually reserved for Mom's drying artwork. "The baby and Val are just fine. Give your announcement and then I'll scoop you on Val."

But she didn't want to puncture a vein in front of her family. She wanted to know about her friend. Heck, she'd gladly listen to a lecture on how cotton grew rather than give her pathetic sob story to her family.

While her family took their seats, Chaz handed out dainty goblets filled with whipped cream, cake, and caramel.

"Oh my," Grandma said. "These are too pretty to eat."

Sam raised her hand. "I'll eat yours if you don't want it."

"No worries." Chaz handed a dessert to Sam. "Otis always makes extras."

Dana returned a sleeping Libby to her carrier. "I was doing so well limiting my sweets. What is this wonderful creation?"

"Otis calls it Decadent Salted Caramel Shooter." Chaz handed Dana a goblet. "I named it ambrosia. Of course, heaven works, too."

"Yummy!" Sam shouted, caramel circling her lips.

While the room quieted to the clink of spoons against glass, Hope stared at her dessert, hoping it would disappear like she wanted to do.

"Hope, honey?" Mom's voice, as silky as the whipped cream, raked along Hope's spine. "You have the floor."

Too bad the floor wouldn't open up and let her drop through. Jack's warm palm pressed against her back, but she didn't want to stand. She also didn't want to speak, but it was a little late to bail now.

Hope guzzled half of the water in her bottle, but the liquid didn't lubricate her parched throat. She tried to lick her lips. No saliva. Not a drop. She stood on trembling legs.

"First." She cleared her throat. "Congratulations, Mom. Who knew when you carted us to this place every Saturday and Sunday it would become such a stunning success. You always have an amazing way of making dreams come true. I hope someday I can experience a tenth of your success." Her voice wobbled, but she pushed past the stumble. "And Dad? Your tribute brought tears to my eyes."

Her parents graciously thanked her then waited expectantly for her news. Her news of utter and complete failure.

Jack's fingers wrapped around hers, gently removing the twisted napkin from her grip. She dipped her chin in thanks.

"I've, um...been slow at finding my career path. I'm sorry about the starts and stops. But I couldn't move forward because...because they didn't fit. Anyway, when I came home...things started to fall into place."

She nodded at Grandma. "You were right, as usual. Sunberry is where I belong. I've still got some loose ends to tie up in Columbia. But I'll be back soon with some concrete plans for my future. I just wanted to remind you to stop worrying about me. I'm okay. More than okay. I'm home."

She shot them her brightest smile to conceal the tremors permeating her body. "That's it for me. Now, please, tell us what's going on with Val."

At her back Jack's hand fell away, and her parents? Their expectant smiles had faded into...? She swallowed past the lump lodged in her throat. She'd disappointed them, again. But they would've been far more disappointed if she'd shared the entire story—which she would. Just not tonight. No way could she reveal the obscene debt she owed. Not on Mom's special night. Not with her entire family expecting some great revelation like a scholarship or award.

Each breath felt like razor blades, her heart limping along like it was on life-support. Geez, she was going to die from a system failure before she reached thirty. Tears stung her eyes as she moved from one disappointed expression to another. And every one of them was trying so hard to conceal it.

A chair screeched across the wood floors, terminating her purgatory. *Please let it be Kyle,* she prayed dropping into her seat.

For a moment, her brother's knowing gaze seemed to look right through her, before looking away.

"Dana and I hated to miss tonight's ceremony and so did Val. She sends her regards," Kyle said. "We just got Libby's test results. She has been diagnosed with a genetic disorder called MCADD. That's an acronym for Medium-Chain Acyl-CoA Dehydrogenase Deficiency. This means Libby can't break down certain fats to produce energy. However, MCADD can be managed. I've made a referral to a Duke specialist."

"Is she going to be okay?" Fear caused Hope to stutter.

"If treated early, MCADD can be managed through diet and lifestyle changes," Kyle said.

Hope froze. She'd angsted about her stupid debt, a direct result of her bad decision. Meanwhile, Val's baby had a serious illness, and Val was alone with no family nearby.

"Where's Val?" Hope asked.

"On her way to Glen Falls," Kyle said.

"Alone? Without her baby?"

"Dana and I agreed to keep Libby," Kyle said, dropping his gaze to the table. "The disorder is caused by two recessive genes. That means Val and the baby's father carry it. Val left to warn him and his fiancé. If the fiancé gets tested and doesn't carry the gene, their children will not inherit the disorder."

"But—" Air rushed from Hope's mouth like she'd been hit in the stomach. Her friend needed her. The same friend who had stood by her side and helped her through the absolute worst experience of her life. And she wasn't going to be there when Val confronted her baby daddy or her family. Because of money—the most easily replaceable item on the stinking planet!

"I need your truck," Hope said, her voice no longer riddled with fear.

"Sorry, Sis. You can't go." Kyle reached for her hand. "She told me to tell you to end it." He lifted a shoulder. "She said you'd know what that meant."

Libby whimpered from the carrier.

"Val will call you as soon as she reaches the interstate," Dana said, going to the baby.

Hope's hands curled into fists while a scream built in her throat. But she summoned the same control her mother used when she'd moved four grieving children to Sunberry. The same control Val had used to leave her precious baby and confront her baby daddy. The same control Jack used when he'd lost his home and his family and had to start a new life.

She'd end Sleaze's hold on her. But not at her family's expense. And it started right now.

Meet you on the flipside, girlfriend.

CHAPTER NINETEEN

HE'D BETRAYED THEM AGAIN, THE THOUGHT GNAWING AT him like a relentless ache.

Seated at the Murphy family, guilt flooded through Jack. He was worse than the scum on Cody's pond. Knowing the truth Hope refused to tell was bad enough, but feeling the Murphy family's suspicion made it worse.

Unlike Hope, he didn't squirm at Nate's head shake or Whit's scrutiny, but on the inside his dream to create a home with Hope shriveled and died.

Although he yearned to shout out the truth, he sat mute, waiting to make his escape. However, his silence ended today. Right along with his love for Hope.

After a long, tense hour, Jack followed Hope outside and climbed into his truck, slamming the door shut with a force echoing his frustration.

"What?" He ignored the echo reverberating in the small cab. "Was that?"

"What do you think?" Hope clicked her seatbelt into place. "You heard Dad's tribute. Did you honestly think I could ruin Mom's big night with my trash talk?"

"So the big reveal you promised at your grandma's dinner was just another lie?"

"I couldn't predict what Dad would say or what would happen to Val. She's my friend!"

He jerked the truck into reverse and suppressed the urge to tear out of the parking lot on two wheels. "And you promised her you'd end your lies tonight."

"You're worried about lies when Val's dealing with her sick baby?" Hope said, her voice rising with every word. "She's going home alone to face her family and Tate! At least I had you beside me. She has no one."

"That's rich, Hope. You finally acknowledge I honor my word." He cringed at the sound of his harsh words but couldn't stop. The hurt and frustration cut too deep. "Except we have a problem. I expected you to stand by yours and you promised to stop the lies tonight."

"I haven't broken my word," Hope said. "I've just delayed it."

Anger and disappointment ached in his chest. Total denial. How could he help her if she couldn't recognize the truth? And yet, he couldn't let it stand. Had to try.

"Bad things happen to good people. That's the way of things." Jack stopped in front of his apartment, wishing he could end the conversation before it went too far. "We need special people to get us through the rough times. But strong relationships require integrity, honesty, and respect."

"I've been honest with Val."

"But she went to Dana and Kyle for help." The minute the words crossed his lips he wanted them back. Hope had disappointed him. Let him and her family down, but harsh words couldn't be unheard. He switched off the engine. "I shouldn't have said that."

"I couldn't help Val because my life is such a mess," Hope murmured.

"Your life doesn't have to be a mess. But the more you try to hide the truth, the worse it becomes. I don't understand," he said, uncaring that his voice wobbled. "Why? What happened tonight? You worked out the script. It was honest and to the point. You practiced."

"I couldn't," she murmured, her voice muted—a stark contrast to the vibrant, gregarious woman he had grown to love. It broke his heart. "Not after Dad's praise and seeing them together, so proud, so in love."

"And the debt?" He squeezed his eyes closed and leaned against the headrest. Why couldn't he let it go, let her go?

"I know," she said, her voice trembling with the effort to hold back her emotions. "Most of the night I was practicing my speech in my head—the whole humiliating truth. How I'm a disappointment. I'll never be like my brothers, but I'll be home. I was even going to add a part about us. That you knew about my problems, but I made you keep my secret. And you let me because...I think you care about me. I'm glad. Because I think..." Her shuddering breath whistled through the cab. "I think I'm falling for you."

Her words resonated with him, making the decision harder. He grasped the failure to meet a parent's expectations and the deep desire for approval. "You say those words—and break my heart."

"I'm sorry. I couldn't tell them."

The sound of the seat rustling beside him was almost unbearable, but Jack kept his gaze forward. If he looked at her, he'd surrender to the need clamoring inside him. He couldn't afford to buckle to it.

"They were all so happy tonight," she whispered. "My confession would have splintered that happiness. Then they'd be unable to look at me, the same way you can't."

Jack stared at the front of his apartment. The curtain

moved and Turbo appeared on the windowsill, a tiny paw pressing at the glass.

"I thought we had a chance for something good," he said. "Something that lasts, like your parents have."

"They were awesome tonight," Hope said, the reverence clear in her voice. "Half of Sunberry came to congratulate Mom. Everyone knows and respects my family. My brothers. Even my sisters-in-law have become Murphys. They've lived up to the integrity of the name—except for me. I saw it in your eyes. You stopped believing in me the same way they did."

She was killing him, one word at a time. But darned his miserable hide, he couldn't shut her out. Resisting every survival instinct, he turned toward her. Tears glistened on her cheeks.

"I'm sorry I let you down," she whispered. "Blood ties my family to me. But if I don't stop this mess, their hearts will harden, too."

He curled his fingers into fists to avoid touching her, taking her into his arms. Don't drag it out. Stop here and now. They couldn't have a life together like this. At least he couldn't.

"You can still call them." He didn't recognize the flat sound of his voice. She'd done that. Sucked out his joy, his belief in her and their future. Now, he had nothing to give but pity and disappointment.

"I need your truck," she said, her voice firming.

And there it was. A soft grunt erupted before he could stop it. He'd anticipated the request and despised the part of him that had predicted her failure. Jack jerked his wallet from his pocket and extracted his truck title.

Hope squinted at the paper. "I just want to borrow it, not buy it."

"Take it. Jake fixed my bike." He removed his house and

toolbox keys from the Ford's key fob. "He found an old side car to hold my tools. I've already cleaned out the truck."

"You were prepared for...for tonight to go like this?" Her voice wavered, betraying her hurt. "Did you ever believe in me, or were you just waiting for me to fail?"

He kept his expression neutral, though inside he felt gutted. She'd nailed it. Every despicable thought. He'd known Hope since elementary school. Although he prayed she'd change, he'd prepared for the worse scenario. A ragged breath scorched his lungs, burning with the truth he'd denied too long. Deep down, the woman he loved wasn't Hope. She embodied hopelessness, a painful truth he couldn't ignore.

"Quinn thinks he has a buyer for the Ford. Sell it. With what you've saved, you might pay off your debt. Start a new life."

"Without you?"

He turned away. Turbo had disappeared from the windowsill. He guessed even the cat had figured her out. "Honesty is important to me."

"I'll need a few minutes to collect my stuff," she said after a long silence.

He shoved open the door, welcoming the stiff breeze scented with spring flowers. "Take your time. I'm going to take a walk."

"Jack?"

Just keep walking. Pretend you don't hear. But some tiny spark still wanted to believe. He stopped without turning and waited.

"I know you didn't want him, but Turbo needs a loving home. I can't give that to him, not now." She paused, her silence cutting as deeply as her words. "I can't take care of him the way he deserves." Her voice cracked on the final word, the weight of her declaration hanging heavy in the air.

"I'll make sure he's cared for," Jack said, his voice hollow with the ache in his heart.

His boots thumped on the pavement, each step echoing with his final goodbye.

———

"SHE RIPS out my heart and gives me a cat," Jack muttered to the night, just to hear a human voice. Just what he needed: something to take care of. But this mess wasn't Turbo's fault. Poor thing had stumbled into the wrong life.

But who was going to care for Hope?

As Jack moved further away from his apartment and the woman he thought he'd loved, the question haunted him. He kicked a pebble, following its easy bounce, wishing he could shake off the burden of what he'd done as easily.

The barbs of their argument shifted and switched directions like the clouds overhead, throwing his physical and emotional path in shadows. How many times would he give Hope his heart and wait for her to wreck it along with his life, especially now that his hard work and sacrifices had begun to pay off?

Although she'd have to eat some humble pie, the solution lay within reach. Ava and Ryan loved her, wanted the best for her. In honest relationships, love withstood life's disappointments. Look at him. He'd made countless mistakes finding his career path. Dad had tried to interest him in the family business. But building hadn't felt right until Nate had taken over the company and offered him a job.

Jack stumbled over the curb, his thoughts flashing through unpleasant talks with his dad, regret and shame intertwining with each memory.

"Holy crap!" Jack's hiss caused a flutter overhead. "Better try a little humble pie yourself."

Dad must have been crushed when he'd accepted a job from Nate after refusing it from his dad. And he had the brass to lecture Hope to do the right thing.

As he fished his phone from his pocket, Jack's harsh breath drowned out the night creatures. He hesitated briefly, his thumb hovering over the hotkey for his dad's number. After a moment's pause, he pressed it, the familiar dial tone echoing in his ear. It was time to confront the mess he'd left behind and clean up his own house.

CHAPTER TWENTY

WHAT MOTHER LEAVES HER BABY BEHIND? Val swiped at the tears blurring the white lines of US 17, the ache in her chest intensifying with each mile taking her away from her precious daughter. Her rational mind said Dr. Murphy and Dana would take excellent care of Libby, and they were more capable than her. Her mother's heart protested they couldn't love Libby like she did.

A car sped past her aging Honda, rattling the wheel and testing her resolve. She glanced at the rearview mirror, desperately wanting to turn around. Up ahead, a green exit sign appeared, tempting her resolve.

She rolled down her window for some cold air, and the yellow note with the words Murphy Up fluttered on the cracked dash. Hot tears streamed down Val's cheeks, but she continued past the exit and focused on last night's practice. How many times had Hope rehearsed her speech? Fifteen? Twenty? And how many times had she encouraged her friend to face her past, urging her to move toward a better life? Val swallowed, despising the memory that compelled her further away from Libby and the safety of her newfound home.

"For you, sweet girl," she whispered to the hum of the tires on the asphalt. "And for your unborn half-sister or half-brother."

Although her vow couldn't ease the ache of separation, each of the nine hundred miles to Missouri would carry her thoughts and prayers to Libby. She tapped the turn lever and changed lanes to pass a slow-moving camper, the highway stretching in an endless ribbon before her. On the Honda's center console, the digital clock rolled forward to 9PM, each tick amplifying her doubts. Thank goodness. By now Hope should be free of her unbearable burden, and her friend's voice would be a welcome change to her loneliness.

Val spoke toward her phone mounted in the left air conditioning vent. "Siri, call Hope."

Raindrops splattered against her windshield. "Great," she muttered. "Just what I need."

"Are you all right?" Hope greeted. "I'm so sorry about Libby, but Kyle assured us her M..."

"MCADD," Val provided.

"MCADD," Hope said. "Kyle swore she'd have a normal life with diet changes."

"Is she—" Val blinked back hot tears. "Is she... okay? I mean I know Kyle and Dana are reliable. It's just..." Her chin trembled and she rolled her lips to regain control of her emotions. "Leaving her felt like cutting out my heart," she sobbed. "I'm sorry. I thought I had this under control."

"I know you miss her," Hope said, her tone soothing. "But Kyle and Dana are awesome with her. My brother is the world's biggest papa bear. Trust me, nothing will happen to my precious goddaughter."

Although her friend's words were meant to comfort, they didn't quiet her fears. "My head knows that," Val choked out, her voice breaking. "But a part of me is missing."

"Rest easy. The Murphy family has eyes on your babe. You

should have seen her at the party. Don't worry." Hope's words quickened, a mix of reassurance and urgency. "Kyle and Dana didn't bring her over until everyone else had left. She made quite an entrance in her onesie with the lambs on the knees and even smiled."

A laugh coupled with a sob leaked from Val. "You're some godmother. Infants don't smile this early. She had gas."

"Hey," Hope said. "My goddaughter has superpowers!"

"Thank you." Val swiped at her tears.

"For?"

"Making this moment a little easier."

"You know I'm here for you. I also know only a tremendous force could make you leave Libby. So talk to me. Let me help."

"MCADD is inherited," Val said, the horrible words echoing in her small car. "Gabby is..., was..., my best friend. Tate and I are carriers."

"W-wait."

A shudder shook Val's shoulders as she imagined the path of her friend's thoughts. She turned up the heat to chase away the chill in her heart. Hope had to understand and support her actions. Because at present, she had serious doubts about her decision.

"Your best friend is marrying your baby daddy?"

Val pressed her knuckles against her lips, the weight of her past pressing down on her, even from a distance. Which is why she had to confront it.

"If Gabby has the same recessive gene, she and Tate could have another baby affected by MCADD," Val said, focusing on science and not the awful longing to hold her daughter. "Another family would face what Libby and I have gone through."

"But Libby's okay. Kyle said she'd live a normal life. If Gabby and Tate have a baby with MCADD—"

"It's serious, Hope. Libby is doing fine. But not all babies are." Val turned on the wipers, but the worn rubber smeared the glass. "I almost couldn't do it. I turned around twice. I'm sure everyone thinks I'm a bad mother, and that's exactly how I feel."

"No, Val. I promise no one believes that. But I'm so sorry you had to do this," Hope said, her words soothing the raw feeling surrounding Val. "You are as courageous as my mom. And trust me, she's a tiger. I just can't wrap my head around how you did it."

"Self-talk." A cross between a croak and a sob leaked from her throat. She swallowed. "I whispered to myself like I whispered my love to Libby. I miss her so much. Dana and Kyle promised they'd take good care of her. And I know they will. I just can't—"

"Hey. Breathe. The entire Murphy clan has gathered around your angel."

"I knew they would. It's so hard to leave her. But I have to do this. Glen Falls is a small community. All of my cousins live there. It's the same for my friends, including Tate and Gabby. The risk is real. I can't keep this a secret just to protect my pride—what little remains of it."

"I wish I had your courage," Hope said.

The headlights of an eighteen-wheeler illuminated the eastbound lane, the shiny glow sparking a realization in Val's mind.

"It's Libby," she said. "I had harbored hurt and betrayal for too long. But holding her in my arms, I realized I had to be better—for her."

"You've made me a better person," Hope said, her tone soft with conviction.

"Thanks. You've been a good friend too. You reminded me of what I lost with Gabby. We've been friends since second grade, until Tate and me—" Val paused. The old ache about her friends didn't seem as sharp. "I loved working and bringing home my own money," she said, her words stronger, more confident. "But Gabby always wanted to be a wife and mother. That's why I have to talk to her face to face. She'd never take a call from me. Hold on."

Val adjusted the heat and wiped at the condensation forming on her windshield. Cherry, the name she'd dubbed her 1989 red Honda, no longer received the TLC her dad had always supplied. She wiped the moisture on her jeans. Would Dad welcome her home and care for her like he'd once cared for her car? Or was the break too deep to bridge?

"I'm not as generous and understanding as you are," Hope said, her voice distant. "I wish you had talked to me. I would have come with you, helped you drive, cried with you."

"Don't get me crying again." Val sniffed. "I appreciate your offer, but this was something I had to do. And you didn't need more distractions. Think of it like talking to your folks. Jack and I could coach you, but you're the only one who could deliver the message. How did it go tonight?"

When the whisk-whisk of her wipers filled the silence for several minutes, a bad feeling squeezed Val's belly.

"I didn't come clean," Hope said in a voice so low Val could barely hear it over the hum of Cherry's tires.

Val breathed through the vise tightening her chest. If Hope couldn't deliver her well-practiced speech, how could Val succeed? Knowing her track record, she'd be lucky to stumble through the words before she started bawling like a little kid. Too bad. MCADD had forced her decision.

"Admitting your worst mistakes is a big deal," Val said. "Just saying the words scares me." Her laugh sounded more like a croak, the fear palpable. "I'm scared spitless and I'm still over eight hundred miles away. Seriously," she whispered. "My teeth are clacking."

"That might be funny if it weren't so awful," Hope said.

"Are you going to tell them...everything or just the need-to-know genetic stuff?"

That dilemma had occupied her brain for the past hour. "It feels like stepping out on the high dive," Val said. "I did it on a dare once. Nearly peed my bathing suit."

"Heights never bothered me," Hope said. "Standing up in front of my family tonight? Horrible. Their disappointed stares are lasered on my retinas. They knew I wasn't straight with them. But I still couldn't say the words. And Jack? He's done with me."

"I don't believe it!" Val cringed and lowered her voice. "I'm sorry. I didn't mean to shout. It's just... Jack loves you. Don't make the same mistake I did with Tate."

"Too late for that."

The pain in Hope's response was palpable. "What happened?"

The miles rolled by as Hope shared her own sad story. When Hope ended the miserable tale, an unladylike snort filled the Honda's silence.

"Well, girlfriend. We're a sorry pair tonight." Val lowered the window, letting the chilly breeze sharpen her senses. She'd have to make a pit stop soon. "I doubt there is anything you could do to end Jack's love."

"You didn't see the way he looked at me," Hope said. "It was awful. He didn't go inside the apartment the whole time I was collecting my stuff."

"Of course he didn't," Val said. "He's heartbroken. He wanted you to succeed. He's disappointed, but that doesn't mean he'll abandon you."

"Looks like it from this side."

Hope's words collided, turned sideways and then settled in Val's mind. And she was grateful for the distraction. "Where are you?"

"On my way to end my mess, just like you."

Val straightened so fast the seatbelt cut into her deflated baby belly. "But you said at the end of the month. What about the money?"

"What about my life?" Hope countered. "I had to take a hard look at myself. I didn't like what I saw. The consequences of my decisions have overflowed onto the people I loved. I'm stopping it."

"But you can't go back to that...that man without the money you owe him."

"Sure I can!"

Another green exit sign faded into the night. "How are you getting there?"

"You don't want to know," Hope said. "It's another heartbreaker."

"Jack's truck?"

"He gave me the title," Hope said. "I think he intended for me to sell it. Jack knew I was going to be short on cash."

"I told you he loved you," Val whispered. Oh man, this was worse than she thought—for both of them. "I should have waited until you told your family. One day wouldn't have mattered to Gabby and Tate. When Kyle told me about Libby, I panicked."

"Stop," Hope said. "You have nothing to apologize for."

Hope sounded so cavalier. Although her friend would do anything for someone else, she never thought of herself. She also underestimated the true consequences of her actions. How could she be such an optimist after twenty-five years on the planet? Jack attributed it to her protective brothers, but goodness.

"And stop worrying about me," Hope said. "I have a pissy money issue. You have a healthcare scare. Substantial difference on the priority scale."

"Of course I'll worry about you," Val said. "You're my

friend. I want you to be happy. One of us has to get the prince."

"So not true." Hope's laugh echoed the sadness churning inside of Val. "You're the reason I got the nerve to do this."

No! Val shook the steering wheel. She did not want to be responsible for something happening to Hope.

"You don't understand." Val slowed her speech, praying she'd find the words to talk Hope off the ledge. "I know people like Sleaze. He won't stop."

"Precisely my point. No matter how much I pay there will always be the fine print or a change in the interest."

"But—"

"This is going to sound crazy."

"Girl," Val said. "We have crazy down to an art form."

"Well, this is a good kind of crazy. The minute I made the decision to head back to Columbia, I felt like someone had lifted a weight off me. It was liberating! That's when I decided I would not relinquish one more day to that lowlife."

Val pushed hair away from her face. She'd gotten close enough to Hope in the past few weeks to understand her dangerous bravado. Hope had been too sheltered and didn't appreciate the dangers in the world. But talking her off the ledge long-distance was almost as impossible as facing her family.

"Why take the risk?" Val said, measuring her words. "If you wait until the end of the month, you can pay him off. It ends. When I told you to end it, I was talking about the secrets from your family."

"I'm going for the gold," Hope said. "If I have to confess to my family, I want to be able to say I ended it."

"But you have family to help you," Val said. "There's no shame in accepting their help."

"This mess has turned my life upside-down. I would give my right arm to protect them. But I didn't." Hope's voice lowered to a hoarse whisper. "I let them down and I let you all down. No more."

"No, Hope." The rest stop near Mebane, NC blazed ahead. "You didn't let me down. You gave me courage."

"Not enough," Hope said. "You didn't tell me you were leaving because I was planning to tell my folks."

The line fell silent, but she could hear Hope's breathing in the background. Her friend was just getting wound up.

"If I was riding beside you, Libby would be buckled in her car seat behind you. You wouldn't be questioning your mothering skills."

"I should have waited."

"No! I should've been there for you. You're addressing a life-or-death dilemma. I've let down a friend, lost my family's respect, and lost the man I love. Sleaze is not getting one more thing from me!"

"You have not lost Jack," Val said, wishing Tate still looked at her the way Jack looked at Hope. "He may be hurt. He may be disappointed. But he still loves you. Love like that doesn't fade. Trust me on that one. Tate is engaged to marry my best friend!" A sob leaked from her throat. "Think about that. He was unfaithful to me. His parents belittled me. I had his baby. And I'm still in love with him. I still have this terrible dream I can't rip out of my mind. Tate and I are not going to be a happy family. I know that. But my stupid heart just won't let go. Jack looks at you the way I look at Tate. He'll wait for you forever, despite everything."

A soft voice called to her, but Val couldn't hear it. Her mind was locked watching image after image of her with Tate. Tate holding Libby, a smile of love and pride on his face. And it was all smoldering dreams. Because after she told Tate and Gabby about the MCADD, she'd face the long drive home and her two best friends would carry on with their wedding plans.

"Val!"

A horn blasted behind her. Val shook her head. The speedometer registered forty-five. Too slow. She couldn't see because of her tears and the smeared windshield.

"Val! You're scaring me." Hope's voice through the cellular connection sounded tinny and distant.

Val depressed the accelerator, her heart racing in her chest. "I'm here."

"Find a safe place to pull over," Hope said, her voice soft but firm. "We've had a rough evening. Please, just pull over. I'll do the same. We'll talk this out and we'll both feel better."

"One mile." Although still shaky, the hum in Val's ears had died.

"I'm right here," Hope said. "I pulled over on the shoulder. I-95 is pretty deserted tonight."

"Great." Val's forced chuckle echoed around her. "Nothing like giving your best friend a warm, fuzzy feeling."

"Got it straight from you."

"Yeah, okay. I deserved that one."

"You did. Earned every piece of that little sucker," Hope said. "So why didn't we go through this meltdown while we were safe in your apartment last night?"

"That would be the logical course of action." Val laughed, and this time it had a little starch to it. "Got any snacks with you?"

"Are you kidding? Jack's Mr. Domestic—Oh, my word!"

"What?" Val said. "Did you hit the mother lode or something? I'm pulling into a rest stop now."

"Super. Stop at the vending machine and we'll enjoy a virtual picnic."

"I packed up my mommy snacks before I left. Vending machines are pricey and offer a crap selection."

"Maybe there's still hope for me and Jack."

"What? Hold that thought." Val parked in a space located

between the vending machines and the bathroom. "What did you find?"

"Twinkies."

"Seriously?"

"They're my favorite snack."

"Are you crying?"

Sniff. Sniff. "A little."

"Over sponge cake? I mean, it's sweet. Jack's a sweet guy."

"They're my favorite. Dad used to buy them for me when he took me fishing."

Hope fished? That was something people in Glen Falls did. Val had grown up on catfish her dad caught in the river, but Hope? She was more sophisticated, college educated.

"Dad took Jack with us." Hope blew her nose. "We sat on the bank with our grubby hands and ate Twinkies together."

Jack and Hope had grown up together just like her and Tate. Val extracted a power drink from the cooler on the floorboard. She hoped love would work out for her friends because it would never work out for her.

"Twinkies make the roof of my mouth tickle," Hope said over a mouthful of her snack. "You never did tell me how you got off that high dive."

Maybe that's because she felt like she was still on it. "My brothers and sisters kept taunting me. I couldn't turn back. But I was paralyzed." Pretty much the way she felt right now. "I couldn't move. I don't think I even breathed."

"I get the analogy now. That's how I felt standing in front of my family tonight. So how'd you get down?"

A sob sneaked out before Val could stop it.

"No crying." Hope half laughed and half sobbed. "We've got a long journey in front of us. We can't have puffy eyes botching up our night vision."

"You're crazy!" Val sniffed. "But I don't know what I'd do without you."

"You could've let me come along."

"The same way you'd let me go with you?"

"My family—"

"Has been cleaning up behind you forever," Val finished for her.

Hope chuckled. "I guess I might have repeated that line a few times around you."

"I'm glad you're taking care of the problem," Val said. "If you didn't, I'd worry Libby's first words might be clean up."

"More like free up," Hope murmured.

"That's why I picked Liberty for her name. I want her to be free to make decisions. I don't ever want her to feel forced to choose."

"It's a good name."

"I have to do this." Val gently rapped her knuckles against her forehead. "I did not leave my baby to fail."

"You won't." Hope said. "And neither will I. We've sacrificed enough."

"I wish you had taken Jack with you," Val said.

"Your cousin Zeke is helping me."

Val placed her hands in prayer position. *Thank you, thank you, thank you*, she mouthed.

"He's a good man. He won't let you down."

"Who do you have for your back door?" Hope asked, the question raising another of Val's fears.

Val gulped down her drink and then wiped her lips with the back of her hand. "Throwing my grandma's words back at me?"

"Hey, I'd never bash a grandmother. They have superpowers."

Val lifted an arm that felt like a wet noodle. She was going to need superpowers to navigate the next forty-eight hours.

CHAPTER TWENTY-ONE

Time to restore his life's foundation.

Jack's breath misted in the cool air as the click of the apartment's lock broke the quiet. At 5:00 AM, stars still glittered, though their brilliance was beginning to fade like his energy would fade at the end of the day—from lack of sleep.

An image of Hope, mussy-haired and desperate for coffee, haunted him. Was she safe this morning? Had she sold his truck and secured the funds?

When he swung his leg over his bike, birds stirred overhead. Peace settled the tension of a restless night. In the stillness he could almost hear the whispers of his past mingling with the hopes of his future. The bike's engine roared to life, reminding him of the challenge ahead—confronting his past.

Twenty minutes later Jack stood at the edge of the three-acre property, the familiar sight of the Cline family home evoking a rush of memories. Built by his father in the early 1980s, the house stood as a testament to his father's craftsmanship and pride. Bill hadn't built the home alone; Adam Staton, Jack's birth father, had been his top carpenter. Two strong men—Adam, his birth father and Bill, his adopted father and the only one Jack had really known.

Unlike his relationship with his adopted dad, the custom-designed two-story with its brick façade had weathered the years gracefully. Anxiety churned Jack's gut making him regret his decision to forego breakfast. But if Hope could travel to Columbia to pay her debts, he could walk over his parents' threshold to pay his.

At 5:30AM, Jack knew Dad would be up—retirement hadn't changed his internal clock. He walked be the sturdy porch columns and pressed the doorbell.

Within moments his dad peeked through the narrow window panel framing the solid oak door. Surprise flickered, replaced by a big smile that creased his lined features. The warmth in his gaze made Jack's chest tighten.

"Jack! Good to see you. What brings you out so early?"

"Figured I'd have a cup of coffee with you before I meet Nate at the Martinez renovation."

"I just put a pot on," Bill said, leading the way to a kitchen that had been a gourmet's delight in its heyday. But even now the oak cabinetry warmed the area.

"I'm glad you stopped by. We're leaving for Philadelphia this afternoon for Eli's first birthday. You should go with us." Bill poured two steaming cups of coffee into large ceramic mugs. "You wouldn't believe how much he's grown. Seems like yesterday that they were telling us he was sitting up. Greg said he's started to walk."

"You know how it is," Jack said, a stab of regret pinching his neck. "I can't take a vacation in the middle of a job. Maybe once it's finished."

A shadow passed his dad's gray gaze, and guilt burned Jack's thoughts just as the coffee singed his tongue. Of course Dad understood the construction business. He'd sold the company to Nate after Jack had refused to join the family business.

"Actually, that's why I stopped by." Although a nervous restlessness flooded through him, Jack forced himself to sit at the long island. "I've been talking to a friend who is trying to mend family bridges." Jack hesitated searching for the right words, unable to meet his dad's steady gaze. "You always said a man has to do more than talk the talk."

His forehead lined in confusion, Dad nodded.

"I was running my mouth giving advice. In the meantime I've been avoiding something." Jack opened and closed his hands like they held the answers to bridge the gap to his dad. "I'm doing pretty good with the business and Nate's offered me a partnership."

"That's good to hear," Dad said, his smile widening."

Jack braced. "I've always thought I disappointed you."

His dad spun his mug and Jack sensed he wanted to avoid the discussion as much as Jack did. "That was never my intent," Bill said. "Looks like we've both been avoiding things."

The refrigerator's ice machine dumped cubes into the bin with a rattle.

"I was disappointed," Bill admitted, his voice tinged with regret. "But more with myself than with you. I always dreamed of passing down the company to my son like my dad had passed it down to me. Greg never had a knack for working with his hands. He was more into numbers. Guess that's why he's an accountant. But you...?" Bill shook his head, his gaze distant like he was looking back in time. "I remember the first time I took you to the shop to build that little car for Scouts. I couldn't believe how you took to it. Man, you loved the tools and the work."

"I won," Jack said, the memory warming him. A rare, genuine smile tugged at his lips.

"You take after your dad. He was the best finisher I ever worked with. There wasn't anything he couldn't do. I was okay with the interior work, but I was better as a rough carpenter. Together, we built some fine homes." He waved his hand. "Like this one. Your dad's touch shows throughout this house from the cabinets to the mantle over the fireplace. I felt that way with you. Your mom and dad created a special son. When they died in the fire, me and Connie took over where they left off."

"I remember you telling me about him," Jack said, guilt stirring inside because he had so few memories of his birth family. "I don't really remember them. If Mom hadn't shown me the pictures of me and the Statons, I'd have no memories. I've always wished I was smarter so I'd remember them."

"The fire destroyed everything." Bill wiped up the coffee ring from his mug. "Connie spent a week digging through our photo box. We didn't have cell phone cameras then, but we always had barbecues after selling a house. Adam, your mom, you and your little brother would join us. Greg got a new camera the year of the fire and took some pictures—most were blurry, but a few were good."

Jack nodded. "I had a framed photo of my family on my dresser."

"That was one of Greg's. Connie had it enlarged for you so you could remember them. We loved you like you were our own, but we weren't trying to replace your family, just make you welcome in ours."

"As far back as I remember, you and Connie were my parents. Sometimes it felt a little weird because I didn't know what to call you to other people. Technically, you're my adopted parents, but in my heart you were my parents. I didn't want to forget my birth family, but it was too long ago."

"They were fine people and would've been proud of the man you've become."

"What about you, Dad? Are you proud of the man I've become?"

Unshed tears moistened Dad's eyes and Jack regretted his words. Although he wanted, needed, to have this talk, he hadn't meant to hurt the man who had given him so much.

"Of course I am," Bill said. "I just never understood why you wouldn't work for me. I figured it was me. I pushed too hard. But you were so good and building made you happy. I saw it every time you finished a project. I know the construction business. Few carpenters can do it all. But you can. You know your way around the rough work and have the skill to perform the fine detail too. That's rare Jack."

"I get a lot of satisfaction out of building with my hands. Most days it doesn't even feel like work."

"Love what you do and you'll never work another day in your life." Bill's chin trembled with emotion. "I just wanted to share the business with you—father and son."

"I can't explain it. I knew you loved me. But I felt like my work was never good enough."

"That's on me," Bill shook his head. "I felt the same way about raising you. I was afraid I wasn't a good father. Adam was an awesome dad. You were my second chance. Every time we'd argue I wondered if Adam was watching. If he thought I was doing a good job."

Dad sipped his coffee and Jack waited, sensing his father had something to add.

"Greg kind of blew up in high school." His father's words rushed out. "I knew it was my fault. I guess the more pressure I felt, the more I failed."

Before he had time to think, Jack hugged his dad close, feeling the shudder run across his thinning back, once broad and strong, and understanding the pain of the burden of failure.

"You didn't fail with me just like you didn't fail with

Greg," Jack whispered. Just like he hadn't failed with his dad. "We just had to find our own way. Look at us now. Greg's got a decent job and a family. And me, I'm a business partner, carrying on the company you and your father started. We couldn't have done that if you hadn't given us the foundation. We're just like a house. You laid the foundation in our child-hood, but we had to put up the frame and the sheathing."

"I'm so proud the company will have a Cline in it." Bill's voice cracked and he blinked away tears, his pride evident. "I've been meaning to tell you that. My dad didn't tell me that often enough. I swore I wouldn't make the same mistake. But I let my stupid pride take over. It's a wonder your mom didn't kick me out on my butt. I've been a grump. Kept making excuses why it was the wrong time or the wrong words to talk to you and tell you how I felt."

"I know about the wrong time and the wrong words excuse," Jack said. "I almost turned around three times on the way here."

"Thank you for being the man I couldn't be," Bill said, his grip on Jack's shoulder as solid as his love. "My vision wasn't right for you. I can see that now. Yours was much better than mine."

Jack dropped back on the counter stool, his legs wobbling beneath him with his turbulent emotions. "One thing I got from you." He laughed. "I'm just as pigheaded as you are. This has been festering inside me for too long. I didn't like feeling we were growing apart. I lost one dad. I didn't want to lose another."

"We were pretty stupid, weren't we?" Bill said, his cheeks turning a deep red. "I'm not very proud of it, but I was jealous of Nate. He had my company and you."

"Don't be too hard on yourself," Jack said. "I'm kind of honored you think that much of me."

Bill laughed, the relief and joy reflecting Jack's. "I think that's why I wanted to travel so much. I like traveling okay, but most of the time I was homesick—except when we were visiting Greg and his boy. That's the thing about grandchildren, it's like a second chance. In the early days I was busy building the company and supporting my family. I missed too many birthdays with you and Greg. I'm making that up with Eli."

"I'll keep that in mind," Jack said. "But it takes a lot of time and energy to build a successful company, especially a new division. I worry if I'm up for the task."

"I don't have a doubt in my mind." Dad gave him a sheepish grin. "You know I'm pretty good at the construction business. I wouldn't mind giving you some pointers if you want them."

"I might take you up on that."

"Are you in love with her?" Bill's sudden question pierced the air, catching Jack off guard.

"Where'd that come from?"

"I've been out of town," Bill said. "Not out of touch. This is Sunberry. I have my sources. Me and your mom were hoping to get another grandchild next year."

"It's a little early to start thinking about babies. I'm not even sure if we're a couple. Right now, I'm just doing some needed cleaning."

"Our house is in order, son. Time to work on your own."

CHAPTER TWENTY-TWO

SHE WOULD NOT LET HER FRIEND DOWN AGAIN!

Two days later Hope, wondering if the spring breeze might flatten her, walked across the asphalt to the truck and climbed inside.

Her phone vibrated at precisely 11:00 A.M.

"Where are you?" Val said as a greeting.

"Outside my hotel on Bush River Road, four miles from my target. You?"

Val's sigh resonated through the phone, a mirror of Hope's own fears. "Parked by the Welcome to Glen Falls sign. It's as worn out as I feel."

Hope closed her eyes, willing her scattered thoughts to clarify, focus. She wasn't alone. She and Val clung to the same ledge, trying to face their past.

"Why aren't you parked on your home street?" Hope said.

"I'm five minutes away."

"Are you scared?" Hope shook her head at the foolish question. Who was she kidding? They were in the same leaky boat and it was sinking fast.

"I downed twenty ounces of Diet Mountain Dew," Val whispered. "I still can't spit."

"I brushed my teeth twice. My lips are still glued to my teeth. Coffee and a continental breakfast were free, but I passed. Figured this wasn't the day for bathroom breaks." Hope huffed out a breath. "We're still doing this, right?"

"I will if you will."

A nervous chuckle escaped, reverberating off the truck's interior. "That was my go-to line with my brothers. Were you afraid I would chicken out?"

"Absolutely!" Val said. "I sure want to."

"At least we can be honest with each other in this mess."

"I almost made a U-turn in front of the welcome sign and motored home to my baby girl," Val said.

"Your cousin talked me off the ledge twice last night in between our calls," Hope admitted. "If it hadn't been for the two of you, I'd be halfway to Sunberry with my tail between my legs. You know how I hate that look."

"I do," Val said. "It doesn't look good and feels like baby poop."

"Baby poop?" Hope deadpanned.

"Right now, I'd give anything to change a poopy diaper."

"Easy, Momma Bear," Hope murmured, praying her words eased her friend's loneliness. "My goddaughter is safely sleeping, eating, and pooping without a hiccup. I roused my brainiac brother at 5:00AM. Did I tell you Kyle is not a morning person?"

"Mercy, I needed your wacky humor right now."

"Thanks." Hope rubbed her knuckles against her shoulder. Though her friend couldn't see the silly gesture, it eased the tingling in her fingers. "Sick jokes burst in my head like firecrackers when I'm under stress."

"Welcome to the Fourth of July," Val said, but her chuckle

sounded forced. "You should send a few one-liners to your brother. I don't think he got a lot of sleep last night."

An empty dump truck with an unlocked tailgate rumbled down Bush River Road, each thud amplifying her heartbeat, a reminder of the tasks before Val and herself.

"Doctors thrive on no sleep. Besides, he told me Libby was a good baby. Plus, he and Dana are tag-teaming to get up with her."

"I may have called a few times," Val said, her voice sounding small.

"Ha! Just a few?" The console screen rolled forward three minutes before Hope controlled a near hysterical laugh. The raucous sound reverberated in Jack's big truck, gaining strength and fueling her flagging confidence. If she could laugh with her body coiled like a bedspring, she could do anything.

"Thanks for making me laugh," Hope said in between lingering giggles.

"Thank you for being my friend."

"We can do this," Hope said, letting Val's heartfelt words buoy her even higher.

"We can," Val said, the crack in her voice sending a shiver of guilt down Hope's spine.

Facing a dirtbag like Sleaze paled in comparison to facing the people you loved most. Still shivering, she turned up the heat. Tomorrow, she'd be walking in Val's shoes. But she couldn't think about facing her family—not until she cut Sleaze out of her life for good.

"Is everything in place?" Val's voice had steadied.

"Locked and loaded."

"Text me when it's over and you're safe."

"I'll send you the call sign." Hope glanced at the dash clock. Fifteen minutes and counting. "The minute you arrive at your sister's, call me. We can go over the details in Sunberry. But you've got to debrief me as soon as possible. I'd lose my mind waiting three days for you to drive to Sunberry. What about your backup plan?"

"Just texted my sister," Val said. "Heading to the Carver estate now."

"It ends today." Hope's voice wobbled and she cleared her throat. "I could use one of your Mountain Dews."

"Trust me," Val said. "It wouldn't help. On the road now."

"My best thoughts are in the seat beside you." Hope swiped at a tear.

"Right back at you. Stupid postpartum hormones." Val sniffed. "No turning back."

"Merging on to I-126. Traffic is light so I should be at the restaurant on schedule."

A low-slung sports car raced around the truck, horn blaring.

"Hope?" Val's voice seemed a lot further away than seven-hundred miles.

"Right here," Hope said, her heart hammering in her chest. "Just an A-hat in a hurry. But my knees feel like mashed potatoes."

"I need to pee," Val muttered. "I'll never drink another soft drink again."

"Liar!"

"People would laugh if they could hear this conversation," Val said.

"Whatever gets us down the road. I wish I had one of those fancy ear things they always wear on TV," Hope said. "We could talk each other through the confrontations."

"Might be a little distracting with two conversations going at once."

"I like distractions. Turning on to Huger."

"Crossing the railroad tracks," Val said.

"I'm passing commercial buildings. What's it look like in rural Missouri? Cornfields?"

"It's March, city girl," Val said. "Farmers are just starting to turn the soil."

Hope turned left on Gervais, the coil in her belly twisting with each passing mile. "Here's a last bit of irony for you," she said, depressing the turn signal. "The name of the restaurant is Liberty."

Silence.

"Val?"

"Right here," Val said. "Next time, give me a heads up before you hit me with a zinger like that. I did not wear adult diapers."

"Sorry. Just thought you'd appreciate fate's sense of humor."

"Freedom," Val said. "Freedom in truth. Tate has a house on five acres south of his parents' estate. I see it at the top of the hill."

Hope wheeled into a parking space adjacent to the restaurant, her hands shaking on the wheel. "Val, are you okay? Not sure if it's the distance or nerves, but you didn't sound like yourself."

"I'm not myself," Val whispered, her soft tone edged with something new, something strong. "I'm Libby's mother and I'm on a healing mission."

"Someday she'll be proud of how strong you are," Hope said, praying she could portray the same strength. "Just as I'm proud of you, right now."

"Time for the first step in our new lives," Val said.

The resounding pop from Val's car door echoed in Hope's ears.

———

Val's closing words pulsed with each step Hope took toward the restaurant's entrance. In the doorway, she inhaled a steadying breath. Her last encounter with Sleaze had caught her off guard. Not today. Bain Vill had won round one, but she intended to take him down—all the way.

On busy weekends, the lunch rush filled the restaurant. Today, the hostess was missing in action. Hope touched the soft cotton flannel over the wire taped on her chest. Although her conscious grumbled she should have returned Jack's sweatshirt and pants, she'd been unable to leave the cuddly reminder of him. Besides, he'd given it to her— kind of.

Still, his gentle reminder helped straighten her spine and her resolve. No way would she text Val she had chickened out —again! Her friend needed encouragement and inspiration, not proof of failure.

"Sorry for the wait." The young woman dressed in signature black trousers and white shirt, probably a Carolina student, reached for menus. "How many?"

"Two!" Heat raced up Hope's neck as she lowered her voice. "Two. A seat by the window, please."

As she followed the hostess to a table facing Gervais Street, Zeke's instructions ticked in her head.

Check your surroundings.

Her gaze flicked around the room, searching for danger signs. Thursdays weren't as busy as Fridays. But it was too late for second thoughts. When the hostess stopped by a two top, Hope pointed to the right. "It's a business lunch. We'll need space for laptops."

The woman shrugged and placed two menus on Hope's preferred four-seat table. "Ralph will be your server today. I'll let him know you're waiting for another guest."

Hope checked her phone's clock for the eighth time in

ten minutes. Man, she couldn't wait to get this behind her. She could wear her big-girl panties for twenty minutes. Ten minutes to prepare and ten minutes to cut her shackles from Sleaze. Based on the live spider feeling beneath her skin, she'd be ready to spin a web around Sleaze in record time. But this time she'd be at the table first so she could watch his approach, his body language.

Another shiver raced down her back. Why hadn't she worn another layer of clothes beneath Jack's sweats?

Follow the script. Not enough people.

Over the past two days she'd imagined the meeting— every stinking minute. Every visualization, they'd met in a crowded restaurant. Two women, both older than her mother, did not constitute busy!

"And so not my backup," she muttered.

She sat with the sun at her back, placing her backpack on the chair beside her. Although she doubted the creep would try to sit beside her, she was leaving nothing to chance. With a little luck the sunlight streaming from the windows would shine in his eyes.

She shoved the table closer to the table behind them. Although Sleaze's lean form could slither into any narrow opening, she'd make his space as uncomfortable as possible. For a moment she considered adding ketchup to his seat but figured he'd notice. Worse, he might sit in the chair beside her.

Stick to the plan. Countless experts hailed a good plan's success. Somehow the odds didn't always fall in her favor. But she was working on those odds. She had a backdoor plan.

How many of her best-laid plans had sparked, fizzled, and died? She blew out a nervous breath. Most of them—but not today. This was liberation day at Liberty.

Keep cheering, girlfriend, because Sleaze is coming your way.

Sleaze, sporting a logo golf shirt and pants, might have passed for an older uncle if not for the gaudy ring on his pinky finger that sparkled like a beacon. It was probably stolen from another one of his marks.

He smiled. She narrowed her gaze.

"Miss Murphy." He frowned at the table setting and then squeezed into the seat. She suppressed the grin tugging at her lips.

"I was pleasantly surprised when I saw your text." He rested his elbows on the table and leaned toward her. "I rarely get early payments."

"This isn't a payment," she said. "I'm terminating our agreement."

When she'd first written her lines for the meeting, she imagined he might show surprise. But Sleaze seemed unfazed by her declaration. Instead of the usual manilla folder, he placed her laptop on the table. *Her laptop*. The MacAir Dana and Kyle had bought for her birthday last year.

"I love this device," he said, tapping the screen and turning it toward her. He zoomed in. "I was always good with numbers, but this—" He stroked the hard turquoise shell she'd purchased to protect the device. Too bad it hadn't protected her from people like him.

His bony forefinger tapped the screen. "Here's your loan amount, the fees, and the interest. Check my formula if you want."

She'd never understood violence. Even in her basketball days, she'd never been the player ready to mow down her opponent. She'd gone for the ball and sometimes wrecks happened, but hers had never been deliberate.

Today, the urge to smash Sleaze's face into the laptop held amazing appeal. Except she didn't want to damage her laptop. And it was *her* laptop.

"Glad to see you passed XLS 101." Instead of a sweet smile, she bared her teeth. "My seven-year-old niece can create a spreadsheet with totals. However, there's a disparity between my original document and your calculations."

Hope swallowed. Yes, it was off script. He'd strung her along. Compelled her to hide her situation from her family. She squared her shoulders. Time to call it what it was. She'd lied to her family because of the shame of getting involved with this so-called payday lender.

Jack had nailed this guy's intent. Sleaze didn't intend for her payment to end. Between his ridiculous fees and interest rate, loan applicants were more like members of a horrible debt club. She would never be able to settle this debt. His business model succeeded when customers failed to pay.

She removed the contract from her backpack and slapped it on the table beside the laptop. "My attorney highlighted the maximum legal interest rate. Your numbers don't match." She ran down the list comparing the fraudulent claims listed on his document, her voice picking up speed with her confidence. "One little teensy problem with all of this."

Sleaze's smile faded and he met her glare. "You'll pay or I'll collect from your brother."

"I owe you nothing because you are not a licensed South Carolina lender." Hope closed the laptop with a satisfying snap barely missing his fingers. "That makes you a loan shark. Which means you owe me. However, I never want to talk with you again."

"Good try, Miss Murphy." He placed his iPhone on the table, turned on the speaker feature, and initiated a call. The name Whit Murphy illuminated the screen.

Hope gripped the edge of the table, a low humming sounded in her ears. She'd gone over and over the plan with Zeke and the team, but she thought he would stop when she explained the law. Sleaze didn't care.

She moistened her lips, her fear escalating.

Don't pick up, Whit, she silently prayed. *I'll tell you everything as soon as this is over. Just don't pick up.*

Whit's voice sounded through the speaker, his confident tone deflating her last shreds of dignity and self-respect.

Sleaze smiled and shifted in his seat like he couldn't wait to start. "This is Bain Vill. I'm a fan of your NFL career. But I'm calling today about a little financial issue with your sister, Hope. She's amassed a large debt. How do you want to proceed? We can arrange to meet or I can send you an online form to arrange payment."

Hope's spine rounded in a desperate attempt to protect her vulnerable underbelly. How could she win the war after she'd lost the most important battle?

"I never discuss money over the phone," The undisguised danger in Whit's tone lifted the hairs on Hope's neck.

"Excellent. I'm based in Columbia, South Carolina." Sleaze reached for the laptop, but Hope pressed her hand over the device. Sleaze's lip curled. "I can make time this week."

"Now works for me."

Hope's eyes widened. Uh-oh. That was Whit's fight voice, only used on the gridiron. She glanced around the dining room, half expecting him to be suited up and ready to rumble. Instead, the casual restaurant atmosphere contrasted with Whit's intensity.

Across from their table, a young man wearing a Carolina jersey and a woman dressed in a navy sweater and jeans chatted. The two ladies she'd spotted earlier were—walking her way.

Sleaze shifted in his seat. With four words, Whit had reduced the cocky fraudster to a rodent, beady eyes riveting, looking for an escape. Two minutes ago, she might have cheered, but she was in the trenches now.

When Sleaze ended the call and stood up, reaching for the laptop, the weeks of frustration launched her to her feet, ready to defend what was hers. She slapped both hands on the hard shell with a smack.

"This belongs to me," she said, her firm voice fortifying her resolve.

Sleaze lifted his gaze to hers. Toe-to-toe and two inches below her five-feet-ten-inch frame, he lost his scary factor.

"Everything you own is mine!" he said, narrowing his eyes in challenge.

She jerked the device from his hands. "In your dreams."

"Bain Vill?" the plain-clothed woman held up a shield. "You're under arrest."

Although Zeke's colleagues had briefed Hope on arrest procedures, she stood like a voyeur as the officers followed the law.

"Zeke sends his regards," the officer said, forcing Hope's brain to jumpstart. "Sorry, but we'll need the laptop and you'll need to come in to make a statement."

Hope loosened her white-knuckled grip on her laptop and dropped into her chair before her legs decided to go on holiday. Her phone, still resting on the table, lit up.

> I knew you could do it!
>
> Val

A slow smile spread across her features. "Thanks, girlfriend. But I didn't do it alone." After today she'd never forget that.

She typed words of encouragement, but the undeliverable icon came up.

"My thoughts are with you," she murmured, pocketing her phone.

Too bad family problems didn't move like the police. Although the sting hadn't gone according to plan, the minute Sleaze tried to get Whit to pay, it was over—for Sleaze.

A familiar young man placed a water glass on the table. His lip twitched like he was suppressing a grin. "Do you want to order something or are you kind of done?"

The last remnants of fear, frustration, and relief bubbled up inside her and exploded with a loud laugh. "Oh, I'm done. But you know, Ralph." She removed a ten from her bag and handed it to him. "It's been a pleasure."

"Have a good day."

"I plan to." After she explained what she'd done to Whit.

But if Val could face her family, she could grovel in front of her sweet brother. She just wanted to climb out from under these terrible lies and hug him, tell him she was sorry, tell him how much she loved him.

She hesitated at the heavy restaurant door, gathering her courage.

The door whooshed behind her and she walked forward, closing her eyes. For a moment, the hum of the traffic dimmed. She tilted her head, letting the warmth of the sun reenergize her resolve. She'd faced down Sleaze. Although it wasn't a great story, she could now face her family.

She blinked, waiting for her vision to adjust to the bright sunlight. Her smile faded at the scene in front of her.

"Unfreakingbelievable!" she muttered.

Dad, Whit, Kyle, Nate, and Jack lined the sidewalk on the opposite side of the street. Arms folded, they stood shoulder to shoulder in an unyielding wall of support and strength while Zeke faced her family with his arms outstretched like he was holding back a mob.

She narrowed her gaze and crossed the street, a turbulent mix of love and frustration stirring her blood. Darn them.

She loved them more than air. But for once she wanted them to see her. Not the darling daughter. Not the little sister. Not an inept woman. See Hope Murphy. A human with flaws and talents. She'd helped remove a financial predator from Columbia. It was time they recognized her strengths the way she finally had.

CHAPTER TWENTY-THREE

Please, let her be alright!

Jack's silent prayer echoed in his mind, his fists clenching and unclenching, trying to grasp the hope slipping through his fingers. Despite the mild temperatures and gentle breeze, sweat slithered down the sides of his face while regrets flipped through him. He shouldn't have walked away from Hope. Shouldn't have given her his truck. Shouldn't have kept her secret. If anything happened to her, it would be on him. Had his brain fired one simple synapse, she wouldn't be in danger.

And he wouldn't be sweating bullets standing beside Nate and the rest of the Murphy men. Thirteen minutes! Each tick of the clock a reminder of his failure. If Hope didn't walk through that doorway in the next five minutes, he'd go in to get her—Zeke could just haul his sorry butt to jail afterward. He didn't care—as long as Hope was safe.

"Bain's in custody," Zeke said, a grin relaxing his earlier tension.

"And Hope?" Jack said, fear converting his voice into a harsh whisper.

Zeke gripped Jack's shoulder. "She's okay."

Jack's knees wobbled, relief bending him at the waist as tears pricked his eyes and his lungs refused to suck in enough air.

"She's okay," he repeated with each desperate breath.

"Hang in there, partner," Nate said.

Jack nodded and forced his body upright, his gaze unfocused at first, then sharpening on the restaurant entrance.

Sunlight flashed on the door's glass and a shadow appeared. Hope walked forward, her head high.

"It's her," Jack whispered. "Hope!"

She turned toward the sound of his voice and pinned him with a gaze. When she checked for traffic, a wisp of hair blew across her face, sending a jolt of longing through him. With his breath caught in his throat, the Gervais Street traffic faded into the background. Hope's audacious smile hit him like a hammer, her unwavering stance a stark reminder his protective instincts had underestimated her strength. He was wrecked but seeing her made it worth it.

A second or maybe a lifetime flashed by and then she was in his arms, her flesh warming his chill, the salty taste of tears ending the bitter bite of fear. She was safe. He inhaled her familiar scent. Felt the rapid beat of her heart banging close to his. Heard that weird little sound she made against his neck.

"Don't—" Something in his befuddled brain stopped his words. He changed tracks. "You bold, beautiful woman. You scare the bejesus out of me. I can't promise to keep up with you." He tightened his arms around her, silently vowing to never let her go. "But please," he whispered against her hair. "Let me try."

A sharp sting radiated from his neck, making him release the embrace to rub the site where her teeth had nipped his flesh.

"You are in a world of trouble," she whispered, digging her finger into his chest to emphasize her point. "I'll deal with you later. Right now, I'm in the thick of it."

"I've never been much of a fighter," he said, trying to soften her up with humor. "I swear if this had gone on for another minute, I might have decked Val's cousin."

When she pushed him back, her touch lingered on his skin, the warmth of her body a cruel contrast to the icy voice of her absence. He'd already endured a two-hour grilling from the Murphy men on the way to her rescue, who were now giving him the stink eye—in mass.

"The restaurant has good food." Hope's smile rivaled the sun. "My business with Bain interrupted my breakfast so I'm starving. Want to join me for lunch?"

Jack bit back the inappropriate sound building inside him, but man—Her bold approach to life never ceased to amaze him. The rest of her family, however, didn't look impressed. Not a grin, a sideway glance, nothing. Their stoic expressions made him wonder if the Murphys had a genetic factor that didn't require breathing.

"You want to eat?" Frustration and helplessness strained Kyle's voice, mirroring Jack's. Kyle opened his arms and hugged Hope. "I was scared out of my mind. Every time you push the limits, I worry you won't come back to us."

"Come on." Ryan guided her toward the restaurant. Although his baritone boomed with paternal authority, unspoken worry shadowed his gaze. "Next time, don't shut us out. We're a family. We face things together."

"I told you it would work out," Nate said, his casual tone severing the tension. "Our survival was iffy during our flight and high-speed chase to get here, but we made it. "I'm—"

"Hungry?" Hope prompted.

Jack bit his cheek, knowing a chuckle would get him in trouble.

Together, they crossed the street. With the tension subdued, Jack fell into step with Hope's long strides and casually brushed his hand against hers. Nothing. He swallowed the sting of rejection, falling behind the group while struggling to keep his perspective. Hope had to come clean with her family, which wasn't easy for her. Soon, they'd forgive her. Maybe then, she'd share the same forgiveness with him.

At the restaurant entrance, he grabbed the door and waited for the family to enter. Nate, the last man to cross the threshold, shook his head, confirming the helpless feeling tightening in Jack's chest.

He'd known the risk the minute he'd called her brother. Despite his belief that you couldn't lose those you loved, doubts shadowed his thoughts. Even in death, his family lived on in his heart. But Hope didn't forgive easily—especially a betrayal. A draft sent chill bumps along his forearms. Jack had just joined Hope's line of rejected lovers, just as Nate had predicted.

When Jack joined the Murphys at the round table for six, Hope was introducing the family to their waiter, Ralph.

"He's the best employee in the restaurant so be sure to give him a good tip," she said.

Ralph laughed nervously and sped through the order process like they'd sped to rescue her. Although Jack wasn't a big drinker, he ordered a beer. After his wild morning, he didn't need caffeine. He needed Hope.

"So." Hope folded her hands on the table. "I'm guessing after Jack broke my confidence, Whit chartered a jet. Does that sum it up?"

"I couldn't remain quiet," Jack said, his voice cracking under the weight of his confession. "Not after Quinn called and said you hadn't sold my truck. I knew you didn't have the payment."

Hope nodded, her expression cold.

"I called Whit," Nate said. "You had a full day's head start on us."

"I also had a day to work with the Columbia police. I love all of you," Hope said. "It's awesome to have a family at my back. But I wish..." Her gaze turned to Jack with a sadness and disappointment that crushed his heart. "I wish you recognized my capabilities. As you witnessed today, I'm not a reckless child. I can handle myself."

"Zeke said they made the arrest because of you," Nate said. "That's awesome, Sis."

For the next ten minutes, Hope answered questions and talked about her meeting with the SLED officers. The clinking of dishes punctuated her story, serving as a backdrop that mirrored the urgency of her tale amid the rapid service.

When a server slid Jack's plate brimming with a grilled burger and fries in front of him, his stomach rejected the notion of food. Around him, Hope's family seemed to suffer the same bout of indigestion. Only Hope bit into her burger with gusto.

She caught a drop of ketchup with her thumb. "Mmm, I swear this place has the best burgers and fries. Capturing criminals is challenging work. The team Zeke hooked me up with were amazing. It's kind of sad. They were on to Sleaze but couldn't build a case because his victims were too afraid or ashamed to come forward. But we got him."

He braced, wondering if she'd come clean. Instead, she studied him, her liquid brown eyes peering into his soul, and then addressed her family again.

"I still don't understand why you needed a loan in the first place. Why didn't you ask us? We would've helped," Ryan said. When she didn't answer, he dipped his chin. "Is this what you planned to tell us at Sunday dinner and didn't?"

Jack glanced back and forth between father and daughter. So her dad had suspected all along. After a pause Ryan folded his napkin and placed it beside his half-eaten meal. "Got it. Now comes the part where you claim it's a conversation for the entire family?"

"You always told me you addressed the entire unit after a challenging mission," Hope said, meeting her father's gaze. "I need to recognize our entire family and ensure them of my motivation."

"The Murphy women were not happy at holding down the home front on this one," Ryan added in a soft voice.

"They understand not every situation requires a call to action," Hope said, her gaze slowly moving from Ryan to each of her brothers and ending with him.

"You're right," Jack said, knowing the risk of his confession but determined to show her the honesty and respect he'd asked of her. "I should've believed in you. But I had to know you were okay. Val was the only one who had that information."

"You called Val?" Hope's shrill voice echoed in the sudden silence. "She's got enough troubles—"

"I had no idea what you were walking into," Jack said. He was talking too fast, but when she looked at him like that, all he wanted to do was fess up, make up, and hold her. He hadn't meant to disappoint her. "Val's my friend, too. I'd never do anything to hurt her, but I had to know you were okay."

"I thought you of all people would understand," she said. "Not to mention our last conversation. You were pretty much done with me."

"I wanted to be!" He tossed his napkin on top of his uneaten burger, desperation pushing his limits. "My life was a lot simpler before you came back into it, but I can't go back to that emptiness," Jack said, searching her expression for a hint of softening and finding only a steely resolve. "Problem is...I don't know why I'm trying to hide my feelings. Everybody in Sunberry knows I'm in love with you."

He raked a hand through his hair, wishing for the calm that came from holding a hammer, sawing a board, building something worthwhile with his hands. Not running at the mouth in front of the Murphy men, staring at him like he had lost his stinking mind and Hope— He blinked. She'd never looked at him like that. His heart picked up speed. So was that a good look or a bad one?

"Unfreakingbelievable," Kyle said. "Nate calls a family emergency. Whit leases a jet and a racecar to get us here. We were losing our ever-loving minds something terrible had happened to you. And now we learn you"—Kyle shook his finger at Jack— "knew what was going on the whole time and you"—he pointed at Hope— "you faced a criminal alone."

Hope slammed her palms on the table. "Excuse me. You must have missed me telling you about the sting *with* SLED. If you're unfamiliar with the acronym, it stands for South Carolina Law Enforcement Division, as in the pros." She thumbed her chest, her dark eyes blazing with anger. "I was prepared just like all of you have taught me to be. I was ready for the meeting and the cops were ready for Vill. Ding, ding, ding, gentlemen. The sting was a success."

Pride puffed out Jack's chest. Just because he'd blown his chance with her didn't mean he couldn't revel in her accomplishments. The woman was glorious!

Hope placed a hand over her heart, as if echoing Jack's silent admiration. "You can congratulate me on my success at any time. And then each of you can vow to trust me in the future. I appreciate your concern. I'm grateful for your support—When It's Needed!"

"Babe," he said, gently tugging her toward her chair, terrified by the risk he was taking but knowing he had to take it.

"Look at it from our standpoint. We didn't have all the details."

Hope stiffened and shook off his hand. "You were supposed to trust that I did."

Contrite, Jack dropped his forehead in his hand. What could he say other than he was sorry? She was right. His faith in her had faltered.

"I guess using Ivan's jet was too much," Whit said with a forced chuckle. He glanced at Hope, his usual confident demeanor cracking. "You're tougher than I give you credit for, kiddo. But don't scare us like that again."

"Ya' think?" Hope said.

"I'm sorry I overstepped. I love you." Whit's sincere words resonated with Jack. "You're the only little sister I have. I'd do anything to protect you, make you happy. That's all I've ever wanted for you. For all of my family."

Hope's features softened. She might be mad and disappointed, but she wasn't immune to Whit's heartfelt apology. Jack's heart rallied. There was hope for him.

"I love you, too," Hope said. "But you're smothering me. I have skills. I loved working with the cops. It wasn't a crucial role, but I did my part. And my day spent on library research. That's right," she added, her eyes blazing with a renewed challenge. "Unlike all of you, I honored my promise to my friend to wait while she drove to Missouri."

She glanced around the table again, but Jack wasn't sure if she was waiting for her words to sink in or a challenge. No one spoke.

"I was embarrassed because I fell for a scam. But I learned I wasn't alone. Did you know one dude was sentenced to 16 years for running a 3.5-billion-dollar illegal payday lending scheme?" She thumped her chest. "That made me feel better. Not because innocent people were swindled. But because I wasn't alone. I wasn't stupid. I just ran into a money shortage and needed help. So overall I learned a lot about money loans and myself."

"3.5 billion?" Kyle said, his voice hoarse with disbelief. "Bad things happen with that kind of money."

"Thank you, Big Brother. I'll be sure to praise Dana on your excellent training. Anyway, with my research and SLED's help, Bain Vill's days of harassing South Carolinians is over."

Jack glanced around him in the ensuing silence. Hope's family stared at her like she'd grown a wart on her nose. Now, they'd understand what he'd been living with.

Frowning, Hope clapped her hands. "Guys? I did a good thing. I even got my laptop back. Well, at least I will once they remove incriminating evidence. Would you believe Vill used my laptop for his records and didn't change the password? I watched him type it in."

"Did you have to give Vill your car as part of the payment?" Whit asked.

Hope nodded. "I'm sorry I lied to you. I loved that car, especially because you gave it to me."

"It's just a hunk of steel," Whit said. "You're what's important."

The soft clink of utensils on china mingled with a baby's cry. Outside, the wail of an ambulance siren blared and then receded.

"You guys are never this stumped for words," Hope said. "So let's hear it. I assume Jack filled you in on why I needed the loan." She turned to him and he shook his head, glad for once he'd honored part of their agreement.

"Really?" she questioned.

"I only gave them need-to-know information so they'd help," Jack said, desperate to redeem himself.

"I can't wrap my head around..." The color had drained from her dad's tanned face and his eyes had glossed over. "You were involved with a loan shark."

"Dad." She softened her voice. "It wasn't like I got his name from the internet. A so-called friend referred me. A payday lender isn't much better, but I was trying to save my app project." She thumped her chest. "It was my first business. I was so excited to tell you guys about it and then my partner stole it and left me with the debt. If it hadn't been for the Murphy posse waiting to save the day, I would have performed a happy dance in your truck bed." She clapped her hands again. "And that's the end of the story. I have to stop by the station to give a statement. After that, I'm free to go home unless they call."

"Home?" Ryan said. "So you're moving home?"

"Yep. I'm coming home to stay." She turned to Jack. "I haven't made living arrangements yet, but I'm coming home."

Jack's final glimmer of hope flickered and died. In forty-eight hours, he'd moved heaven and earth. But she didn't need saving. Didn't need him.

Ralph stopped behind him. "Does anyone have room for dessert?"

"Absolutely!" Hope's voice echoed in the restaurant, telegraphing her nervous energy. But she'd stood up to her family, told the truth. Although Jack felt like she'd torn his heart from his chest and thrown it on the floor, he was proud of her accomplishments. Heartsick but very proud.

As for her family? They never left food on their plates at Miss Stella's table. But if Liberty had a stray living off their garbage, that critter would be feasting today.

"Give me a Tollhouse Pie with vanilla ice cream," she said. "And I'm not sharing."

"Two?" Ralph said, noting Nate's raised hand.

"Add chocolate sauce to my ice cream," Hope said. "Oh! And caramel sauce too if you have it."

"It's that good?" Nate asked.

Jack studied the interaction between Hope and Nate and

understood why he'd synced with his partner, Hope's youngest brother. Nate was not only the easiest going, but he was also the fastest to forgive.

"Take a photo and share it with Otis," Hope said. "You'll need bonus points for Chaz. I've given you my story. I want something in return."

Ryan nodded, but her brothers remained very still, watchful.

"This is my story to tell, not yours. You're Murphy men, through and through. Each of you have established stable marriages so this will be a tough request." She paused to meet their gazes one by one. "Keep your lips zipped! Give me the courtesy and respect to tell Mom, Grandma, and my sisters-in-law in my own way."

Despite his misery, Jack had to bite back a grin. Every man at the table looked like she'd asked them to sit on a fire ant mound. Even Kyle's disapproval had dissolved into something akin to fear.

"Oh for goodness sakes," Hope taunted. "Man up. Tell them I asked you to let me explain."

"I don't keep secrets from your mother," Ryan said.

"If I try to keep this from Talley," Whit whined. "She'll put me on potty training for the next month!"

Jack swallowed a snarky comment, picturing Whit in shoulder pads, clutching a wiggly Ellie under his arm. What would Whit's teammates think of his new duties?

Ralph's arrival brought him to his present predicament. With a flourish, the waiter delivered two blonde chocolate-chip brownies topped with vanilla ice cream and smothered with chocolate and caramel sauce. The sweet chocolatey aroma dispersed over the table, quivering Jack's unhappy stomach, but Nate smiled and lifted his spoon.

"Wow! You didn't exaggerate about this concoction," Nate said, rotating his bowl. "But even a fancy dessert recipe won't aid my cause. Chaz always knows when I'm holding back."

"Fine," Hope said. "Tell them I helped Val's cousin with a sting operation in Columbia and you guys panicked and came down to help. Just omit the grizzly details. Then tell them I threatened your manhood if you told the good stuff before I could."

While the Murphy men commiserated how to handle Hope's request, Hope scarfed her treat and then excused herself. Jack followed, determined to plead his case one more time.

Feeling like a stalker, he waited at the end of the hall leading to the restrooms. He stuffed his hands in his trousers, wishing Turbo was around to help him soften Hope's heart.

When she returned, Jack stepped forward. "You're awesome."

Fatigue lines crinkled the corner of her mouth and eyes. "Thanks. But what I really am is exhausted and I still have to confess to the Murphy women, which is the hardest for me."

"You'll handle their meeting the same as you've handled this one," he said. "With confidence and love."

Although her eyes narrowed like she was waiting for the next shoe to fall, the glint of anger and betrayal had disappeared.

"Hope, I—"

"Don't!"

He nodded, understanding the weight of her anger, but still held her gaze—and his breath, hoping for a sign of forgiveness.

"You broke my trust," she said. "I don't know if I can forgive you. But I'll need your truck a little longer. I have to give my statement to the authorities and I have no idea how long that will take."

His heart pounded against his ribs. "Let me wait with you. Afterward, I'll drive you home."

When she didn't respond, he fisted his hands to keep from taking her into his arms. She shook her head and her gaze hardened.

"Please," he whispered, unashamed of the desperation in his voice. "Don't throw us away. I've always known you were out of my league and you've proven that point over and over again, overcoming unbelievable obstacles. This time—I didn't know what you were facing. But I know the pain of loss, and I couldn't lose you."

"That's the saddest thing about this situation," she said, her features filled with a sadness he couldn't bear to witness. "You've already lost me."

That was it. She turned and disappeared inside the dining room, but he didn't move. Couldn't. His eyes told him she'd left. His mind and his heart didn't believe it. For a moment he was back on the curb, a five-year-old watching his world burn to the ground. Alone again. But this time, he wouldn't let the flames consume him. He'd fight for Hope, no matter the cost.

CHAPTER TWENTY-FOUR

COULD SHE DO THIS?

Hope parked her bike by the sidewalk and eyed the porch steps leading to the Murphy family home. She loved the graceful lines of its structure, loved the memories she'd created with her family. Picnicking beneath the shade of the massive magnolia tree. Unwrapping presents in front of the fireplace. Listening to her family members' trials and successes at the dining table.

Hope swallowed, her throat straining with effort, but the fire continued to burn with her fear. Relief quivered with redemption, only a confession away. She drew a shaky breath, feeling the first glimmer of hope.

"Are you coming inside?"

Although Grandma's voice carried the warmth of a thousand comforting hugs, Hope had thought she was alone.

"Absolutely." Hope climbed the wide stairs, her legs only slightly shaky. She embraced Grandma, the aroma of bacon and warm bread mingling with the comfort of her loving arms, grounding her amidst the whirlwind of emotions.

Closing her eyes, she drew strength from Grandma's uncondi-
tional love.

"I'm scared, Grandma," she whispered, unable to leave the
embrace.

Grandma gently pushed her back, still holding her shoulders. Love and understanding shone in her eyes.

"There's nothing to fear in our home," Grandma said.
"This is your safe zone. It's only filled with love, understanding, and forgiveness."

"I didn't want to let you down."

"I know, dear," Grandma said, turning her toward the
door.

"You do?" Hope said, unable to hide her surprise.

Stella's melodic laugh wrapped around Hope's troubles
and lifted her heavy spirit.

"Our Murphy women are strong," Grandma said. "But
that only came through tough times like you're experiencing.
There's no judgment in these walls, only love."

Entering the house arm in arm, Grandma called. "Ladies,
our guest of honor has arrived."

As Hope stepped inside, the familiar warmth of the home
enveloped her. Within moments, her mother's arms wrapped
around her.

"It's about time," Ava said with a quaver in her voice.

"Which one of my brothers spilled the beans?" Hope
asked.

Chaz, her blonde hair highlighted with lavender and
swept into a French twist, appeared in the doorway with a
frothy beverage in her hands. "Whatever you used to tie up
Nate's tongue, I need to know. Superpowers must be shared."

Leave it to Nate's edgy wife to break down the last of her
jitters. Hope was home, the weight of her worries lifting
slightly as the familiar surroundings enveloped her.

Dana carried a platter of artfully cut fruit. "Kyle couldn't even make eye contact with me."

Hope scanned the room, her eyes stinging from unshed tears, her heart swelling with the love surrounding her. "I'm so sorry I didn't trust in you. My stupid Murphy pride really tripped me up this time."

Mom looped arms with her and led her to the cozy dining room.

"Where's Talley?"

"Bathroom," Ava said. "Her sitter canceled, and Whit had already volunteered to help your dad."

"That sounds sketchy," Hope muttered. If Dad and her brothers were converging, that could mean more drama for her in the future.

"Ahee!" Ellie streaked through the hall, colliding with Hope's knees.

"There's our girl." Hope lifted her pint-sized niece in the air, the child's innocent laughter momentarily washing away her fears and doubts.

"Aee." She pointed at the pitcher.

Dana laughed. "Mimosas. We figured we'd celebrate early. You in?"

Hope hesitated. Although she felt like she needed an IV infusion, her discussion required clear thoughts. "How strong are they?"

"Guaranteed for lightweights," Talley said, joining them with a sippy cup of ice and a bowl of strawberries. "I can't risk being an impaired mother with Ellie in tow."

Within minutes, her three sisters-in-law, her grandmother, and her mother had gathered around the table. Irish, her mother's rescue pooch, gleefully entertained Ellie with her favorite ball. Ellie launched it around the room, and Irish darted after the toy, making Ellie clap and laugh.

"I don't know how long Irish will hold her attention."

Talley raised her champagne flute. "But here's to the Murphy women."

Chaz frowned. "Hope, if you marry, you can't take the groom's name. We must continue the Murphy women trademark."

"Ah-ha," Stella said. "We've reached trademark status."

"Enough marketing," Talley said. "I want to hear every word, and I don't know how long I have before little bit decides she's bored with fetch."

"Go ahead, dear." Grandma passed her a platter of fluffy yellow eggs.

Although Grandma's voice comforted her, doubt gnawed at Hope's mind. She clenched her fists under the table, fighting to keep her composure.

"I got into a mess in Columbia because I wanted to do something big like my fabulous brothers," Hope started.

Once the first sentence escaped her lips, the dilemma that had seemed insurmountable eased into the open like the unfurling of a flower bud in spring. No one interrupted her, nor raised an eyebrow, nor gasped in surprise.

"When I walked out of that restaurant and saw Jack, Dad, and my brothers lined up across the street," Hope said. "I knew it was a lost cause. They can't help themselves. Protection comes woven in their DNA."

A tear slid down her cheek. "But if I'd come to you, none of this would have happened. Each of you have faced hard obstacles before me. I know that. But sometimes I get an idea in my head and that sucker will not budge. I just have to poke the bear on my own."

Their smiles filled the empty space in her she'd ignored too long. "It's a terrible thing when someone you love doesn't respect your trust," she whispered, comparing Jack's betrayal to hers.

"It's far worse to watch someone you love make her own

mistakes." Mom's voice cracked, along with Hope's heart. "I almost couldn't watch your struggle. But Stella helped me get through it. All of us need a strong woman to help us through the tough times."

"Thanks for letting me learn on my own," Hope said, blotting her tears with her napkin. "It wasn't my belief in all of you that wavered. I didn't believe in myself."

Grandma placed her hand on the table, palm up. "And now?"

Hope intertwined her smooth, youthful hands with Grandma's wrinkled flesh, worn and tested by life.

"I'm okay with Hope Murphy. I'm a work in progress. But I'm a Murphy. And you should have seen me take on Sleaze. I was awesome!"

"Yes!" Talley shook her fists in the air. "I'm telling you, Lil Sis. A few times there I was tempted to rattle some sense into you. Grandma had her hands filled with Ava, but I was a loose cannon. Thank goodness your niece's antics kept me occupied."

Sensing she was the center of attention, Ellie let out a delighted squeal. Irish barked, wagging his tail and spinning in a circle.

Grandma stood. "I think Hope's declaration calls for a hug."

"And refills," Chaz said.

"Yee!" filled the room.

"Uh-oh." Talley stood. "For all of ten minutes I forgot I was a mom."

"That's got to be a first," Dana murmured. "Ellie is not an easy one to forget."

"Another generation of a Murphy woman through and through," Stella said. "Now, we can enjoy this excellent chilled breakfast."

Talley returned with a wiggly Ellie in her arms. "I hope

Irish has a tough doggy stomach because he and Ellie just ate the rest of the strawberries."

"His chin whiskers are pink," Chaz said, slathering butter on a scone. "I wonder how Handsome would feel about a fresh look. After all, hair is hair."

Hope filled her plate, giving in to the hunger that followed her relief. Though her celebratory hamburger after Bain's arrest had tasted fabulous, it paled in comparison to the warmth of her grandmother's table and company. She bit into a berry, its succulence a stark reminder of the sweetness of family bonds that had sustained her through the toughest of times.

Why had she let competition and pride override common sense? These women were her people. They loved. They laughed. They counseled. She'd have to work hard to measure up to their fine examples.

After a few laughs, a few tears, and a few embarrassing stories, Hope patted her belly. "This was perfect. Perfect people. Perfect place. Perfect meal. Thank you."

"As the hostess and the Murphy matriarch, I'll accept the honors." Grandma pressed her palms together beneath her chin and bowed her head. "You're welcome. It was our plea-sure. I love preparing a meal with the people I love, for the people I love. But the pastries came from Gina's"

"Otis, once again, has outdone himself," Chaz said. "I thought about giving him another raise, but Nate thinks we should offer him a partnership."

"My grandson has marvelous ideas. Otis is a masterful baker and a lovely man," Stella said. "You couldn't ask for a better partner."

Even Ellie sensed the shift in the room and stilled on Talley's lap. Hope met her mother's wide eyes before glancing around the table at the surprised looks of her sisters-in-law.

"Grandma?" Hope hadn't meant to elongate the word, but

her brain couldn't seem to wrap around the innuendo—coupled with the look in Grandma's eyes.

"I still enjoy male companionship," Stella said. "Good thing in this family," she added, her eyes twinkling with mischief.

"Speaking of male companionship." Chaz wiped the crumbs from her lips. "What's your status with Jack?"

Hope drained the last of her drink, her mind scrambling for a response. "Jack wasn't on my agenda today."

She searched their faces, her usual practice to guard her feelings strong. Grandma's words about her Murphy safe haven surfaced. After a steadying breath she said, "I could use your feedback on my next action."

Talley stood and gathered a resistant Ellie in her arms. "I can't believe I have to bail just when we're getting to the good stuff. But I need to get her down for a nap or she'll make my life miserable this afternoon."

Dana checked her phone. "Me too. I have to get home to take the handoff for Libby. Kyle has patient appointments scheduled."

Hope stood and hugged Dana and then Talley. She sniffed the air and then patted Ellie's bottom. "You might want to make a pitstop before heading home."

Talley eyed her grinning baby. "Way to go, munchkin."

"Probably the strawberries," Ava deadpanned.

"I don't need help with the imagery," Talley said. "Reality is vivid enough."

While Talley attended to Ellie and Dana motored home, the remaining women cleared the table.

This, hummed in Hope's thoughts. She missed the easy rhythm the women fell into, each sensing the other's needs. Wanted these women and the feelings they stirred to be a constant in her life.

By the time Talley presented a clean, happy baby, the dishwasher had been loaded, the leftovers stored, and the champagne glasses refilled with lemonade for round three.

"Call me later for a recap," Talley said, giving Hope one last hug. "And welcome home. You've made your family very happy. I know Whit will sleep sounder, knowing you're nearby."

Hope nodded even as Talley's words stirred a fresh wave of guilt deep within her. She had just been searching for her path, not trying to worry her family.

"It's a lovely morning. Let's move to the patio." Grandma motioned them toward the French doors leading to the shaded backyard. "Assessing a man's strengths and weaknesses needs wide-open spaces."

While her grandmother and mother walked to the outdoor seating area, Hope lingered behind, sensing something was on Chaz's mind. Free from his baby-entertaining duties, Irish barked and romped around the lawn slowly changing from winter brown to spring green. Grandma and Mom settled in the matching wicker chaises topped with red-flowered cushions. Seemingly deep in thought, Chaz stood, her hands on her slender hips, gazing at the tree house where Hope had spent many happy hours.

Restless, Hope chose a red Adirondack chair spaced across from the chaises.

"How can I be with a man who doesn't believe in me?" Hope asked, her cracked voice exposing her pain.

Chaz turned to face them. "I'm glad you found your way home, Hope. That was a hard lesson for me, too. As for you and Jack?" She shook her head. "Ava and Stella are far more experienced with men than I am. But whatever you do, make sure you know your heart. I love Nate and I'll defend him with my dying breath."

"He's my brother," Hope said, confused by Chaz's words. "I love him too. I'm just not sure I understand—"

"Jack's been the perfect partner for Nate," Chaz said. "But that changed when you came back. Now, Nate's been working overtime picking up the slack from Jack's distractions."

"I didn't mean for that to happen." Hope turned to Grandma and Ava. "Were you aware of this?"

Ava nodded. "Ryan's helped Nate in the evenings so he wouldn't get behind."

"And they lost a day flying to Columbia." Hope rubbed her temples. "I'm so sorry."

"That's not on you," Stella said. "Nothing could stop our men. We all tried."

"I know them," Hope said. "I just wish I had known Jack better."

"I think you do know him," Ava said, her voice laced with a tenderness Hope trusted. "He's just a man—with strengths and flaws."

"But he expected me to fail!" Hope's voice broke, her frustration bitter on her tongue. "How can I trust him if he doesn't trust me?"

"Plan for the best but prepare for the worst," Grandma said. "I think he was doing everything in his power so you could succeed."

"He risked his partnership with Nate for you," Chaz said. "Do you know how hard he worked for that? Nate gave him a chance when Jack thought his dad didn't believe in him."

"I knew my secrets were eating him up inside, but I couldn't stop," Hope said, shifting beneath the weight of her guilt. "I just wanted a chance to fix my own problems. I didn't mean to put Jack in a bad position."

Chaz patted her thigh and Irish galloped to her side. "Jack gave you what you wanted right up until you left for Columbia."

Avoiding eye contact, her sister-in-law continued to

stroke the dog's head. But Hope didn't need to read Chaz's features. The truth lay in her quiet words.

"No one claimed love is easy," Ava said. "But it's been worth the struggle for me."

"Amen," Grandma said. "Murphy women are always up for a good struggle."

Chaz looked up, a cross between a smirk and a frown lining her features. "I love you dearly, Miss Stella. But I hope your struggle doesn't cause Otis to start burning his pastries."

Their laughter eased the tension inside Hope and opened her eyes to her relationship with Jack.

"I let him down," she murmured. "He was doing his best to help me, but I was so wrapped up in my shame I couldn't see it."

"Sometimes we wear bifocals and sometimes we see 20/20," Grandma said with a chuckle.

"You probably both had a hand in the letdown," Ava said, giving Hope an encouraging smile. "That means you both have some groveling to endure."

Hope leaned back in her chair, the afternoon sun high above the trees, warming the patio just as her family warmed her heart. "Jack said the people you love deserve honesty and respect."

"So." Mom's gaze felt like it could see into Hope's soul. "I'd say Jack's a man worth keeping in the Murphy family. However, it's your decision. Is he a keeper, or do you need help disposing of the body?"

"The jury's still out on the verdict," Hope said, raising her hands. "But don't put your shovel away until after I talk to him."

Although their laughter enveloped her in acceptance and joy, the guilt continued to gnaw at her.

"Jack and I have some harsh words between us. But my heart is ready to forgive him." The heavy feeling she'd been carrying shifted. "Regardless of how our relationship goes, I owe him a lot. Thanks, Chaz, for making me see that." She followed a sugar ant's progress through the rough grass. Though tiny, the insect journeyed forward. "I want to do something meaningful to support MBC, but I need your help to figure out how," she said, her voice breaking with sincerity.

"I don't know anything about apps," Stella said. "But when you talked about your basketball design, it sounded like it was perfect for parents. Can you design something for the company? You know like the symbol Chaz has on the napkins at Gina's?"

"Not just a logo," Chaz said. "You mentioned the parents and coaches could communicate on the sports app. What if you designed something to streamline client communications and tied it into project management?"

"That could so work," Hope said, brightening with the sudden onslaught of ideas stirring her thoughts.

"When Ryan helped me with Robey's Rewards," Ava said. "It showed me he cared about my success. I felt the same way when you asked to work at the shop."

"Thanks, Mom," Hope said, her top suddenly tight with the expansion of her chest. "I loved doing it. Love being a part of something important to all of us."

"They need a website, too," Chaz said. "When Sarina built mine for Gina's and the salon, I tried to get Nate to hire her. She's been taking classes when she can afford them. Her prices are reasonable because she's trying to grow a side business."

"Are you kidding me?" Hope said. Stopping Sleaze had been awesome, but this? Doing something she loved and was good at, helping people she loved... "I have to admit I was anxious about coming here today. But talking with you, brainstorming a new business..."

Hope laughed—a deep cleansing laughter—until tears of

relief streamed down her cheeks. "Why was I so stupid for so long?"

"By ourselves," Grandma said. "A force to be reckoned with. Together? We rock!"

Chaz shook her finger at Hope. "Go easy on me. I can't lose three of my best waitresses in one month. That said, if you cure my exhausted man and create an avenue for Sarina to move up in the world, I'm all in. Just give me time to rehire and tell me what I can do to help."

Together, they stood, giving out hugs and congratulations. As Hope stepped into their loving embrace, a memory of Jack's fallen expression filled her mind. "Designing the app, logos, and website is a no-brainer. But what if Jack can't forgive me?"

"Then you show him the error of his ways," Chaz said.

Hope relished the loving embrace, praying her newfound Murphy strength wouldn't desert her. Not wanting to end the moment with her sister-in-law, she ignored the vibration in her hip pocket.

Chaz stepped back, a perfectly sculpted brow raised. "Better answer that. It could be my future brother-in-law."

Hope excused herself to the foyer and touched her screen.

> Good morning, Borrower!
>
> Days Left on Loan: 16
>
> Friday Payment Due: $1,415.56
>
> If not received, New Balance: $3,066.88
>
> I love rubbing shoulders with NFL stars!
>
> Cheers, Bain Vill

Hope laughed. She'd taken on Sleaze. With her family's encouragement, her next steps unfolded before her.

"Hold on tight, Jack," she murmured. "You're not going to recognize Hope 2.0!

CHAPTER TWENTY-FIVE

SHE'D SACRIFICED PRECIOUS MOMENTS WITH HER daughter. And still, they didn't believe her.

Val circled the small guestroom, arms aching to hold Libby, senses longing for her fragrant baby scent. Unable to endure the crushing weight of her guilt and the tiny room, she rushed to the back door. It creaked, resisting her escape. She shook the knob, the urgent shudders matching the frantic beat of her heart. A scream built in her throat with her futile escape efforts.

With a wrenching shudder, the door burst open and she tumbled onto the hard Missouri earth, discarded like yesterday's wash water. The chilled air, fragrant with the first blooms of wildflowers, cooled the sweat on her brow but didn't ease the memories. Born and raised in southern Missouri, she, along with her daughter, now felt rejected by her childhood home.

With a heavy heart, Val picked herself up and followed the beaten path to the tire swing suspended in the pecan tree, the memory of her mother's hands pushing her toward the clouds. She pressed her denim-covered hips against the frayed rubber, yearning for the wind's freedom against her skin.

The cool air washed across her, lashing her noble intentions to warn Tate and Gabby about the dangers of MCADD. Her lost friends' expressions of surprise followed by loathing were forever etched in her brain.

The rope squeaked with each pump of her legs, its rough friction against the tree bark echoing the way Tate had shattered her newfound confidence. Only her younger sister, Hannah, had offered her refuge, a nonjudgmental ear, and belief. The one redeeming result of her efforts: Hannah had scheduled genetic testing.

When her legs tired and the swing didn't bring answers, she stopped and pressed the number to the one person who would understand.

"I pray you fared better with your family," Val said, her voice a fragile whisper almost lost in the birdsong. "One of us has to succeed."

For a moment, the clear song notes lured her from the present, a needed reminder that somewhere peace existed.

"Val!"

Val winced at her friend's squeal and pulled the phone away, then forced a chuckle. "I hope your enthusiasm means you nailed it."

"Better than I'd hoped for and better than you predicted! Sorry." Hope's voice dropped. "I didn't mean to give you a hearing deficit. I'm on my bike riding back to your apartment."

"Should I call back?"

"Nope. Dad bought me a phone holder that mounts on my handlebars." Hope's gleeful laugh brought a grin to Val's lips despite her misery.

"You talk. I'll peddle," Hope said. "Just tell me if I'm too loud. The wind causes a lot of white noise."

"You must be pedaling fast."

"Relief does that to a person." Something rattled on the line before Hope said, "How'd it go with Tate?"

"You first," Val said, freezing her smile into place. Mom always swore if you forced a smile, your words would sound cheerful too. Emptiness hollowed out the last of Val's determination. She had never questioned her mother's belief and now she didn't even have that.

Thankfully, her friend was so giddy with success, she didn't notice Val's blues. Besides, her battered psyche needed a lift even if she couldn't focus on Hope's details. Fifteen minutes later, her friend's words slowed, indicating the end of her tale. Val pushed hard against the moist mulch spread beneath the tire. The wind ruffled her bangs, providing a momentary false sense of freedom. At least Hope had broken the scars restraining her.

"Any negative impacts you didn't anticipate?" Val asked, hoping to keep her friend talking and the subject away from her results.

After two swings of silence, Val drug her grayed sneakers to slow the swing. "What's wrong?"

"It's Jack. Hold on. I just rode up to your place."

The familiar vibration of the iron railing clattered over the line. Moments later, silence.

"Okay. I'm back," Hope said, sounding winded.

"I warned you about losing Jack," Val said.

"I know," Hope said. "But you know how it is. When we talked about our plan, I had no clue how much bravado it would take to pull off."

That makes two of us. Val swallowed her comment while Hope, on her usual high-energy roll, continued to relay her latest dilemma with Jack.

"So you're going to fix it with him, right?" Val pressed. "I can't have my two best friends in the world at odds with each other."

"Working on it," Hope said. "Val?"

Catching the change in her friend's tone, Val stood. "Right here."

"What's wrong?"

Val forced a smile, despite the way everything felt so wrong. "Just enjoying your news," she said, hoping her voice didn't betray her.

"You haven't asked about Libby," Hope said in a whisper-like quiet. "I've been chatting you up like life's all lollipops and roses. I don't think the sun is shining in Missouri, is it?"

"They didn't believe me." Val blurted out, unable to hold back.

"Wait, none of them? Tate, your family?"

Val dropped back into the swing, no longer trusting her legs to support her weight. "Dad told me I wasn't welcome in his home."

"Oh Val, I'm so sorry," Hope said.

"Stop," Val said in a sob. She clenched the rough rope fibers, struggling for control. "Right now..." She sucked in a breath. "I need a fight song, not a ballad."

A breeze rustled the bare tree limbs.

"You can do this, girlfriend." Hope's voice was a lifeline, steady and unyielding. "I'm right here. Just tell me what happened and then we'll produce a plan. You went to Tate's. What happened?"

Val gripped the phone, her knuckles white, clinging to Hope's unwavering support. "They must have been expecting someone else, because he and Gabby came to the door."

"Did you tell them?"

"I didn't get a chance. They slammed the door in my face. I guess I sort of lost it," Val said, her cheeks hot with embarrassment. "All I remember was going from window to window, shouting my story." Val stopped talking and slowed her rapid breathing.

"Yesterday evening, I ambushed Tate outside his firm. When I told him about Libby and MCADD, he accused me of making up a phantom baby to destroy his and Gabby's happiness."

"Oh Val," Hope said, the empathy in her voice too much for Val to bear. "That must have been awful for you."

"I know things have changed. But Gabby, Tate, and I were friends first. The three of us did everything together. They know me. Even after all that's happened, how can they believe I would make up such a terrible story?"

"We may never have those answers," Hope said. "But we know it's the truth. You did the right thing. It's up to them to verify the information and decide an action. So tell me what happened with your parents."

"Mom was so excited to see me," Val said, remembering the moment of joy and safety in her mother's arms. "Mom, Dad, and I sat at the kitchen table like we've done a million times while I was growing up. Dad's stoic and hard to read. Mom's like an open book, love and kindness on every line. Anyway, they listened, and I knew they were sad and disappointed. I expected that."

"I can be there tomorrow." Hope's voice broke through Val's sobs. "I've already checked flights. I can fly to Memphis or St. Louis and rent a car to drive to Glen Falls."

"No, I'm okay," Val said, swiping at her eyes, determined to regain control. "I'm at Hannah's place now. It's just—Dad looked right through me like I wasn't there. I think his reaction surprised Mom too, but she didn't say anything when Dad pointed to the door."

"Tell me what I can do," Hope said. "Would it help if Kyle verified the science? What if he sends you a copy of the test results?"

"Libby needs me, and I need her," Val said, the words renewing her flagging self-esteem. "I'm driving back to Sunberry as soon as Hannah comes home from work."

"That's dangerous," Hope said. "I'm afraid for you to drive alone this upset."

"I'll be careful," Val said, recalling the velvety flesh of Libby's cheek. "I have a very special child to raise."

"Call me when you leave," Hope said. "I'll talk you home."

"I'm only coming back to pick up Libby," Val said. "I've got to show Tate Libby is real. And I hope..." Val inhaled a steadying breath. She had to regain control. Libby depended on her to be strong. "Libby gives me courage, makes me want to be a better person. I thought she could help Mom and Dad too. Anyway, give Kyle and Dana a heads up. Maybe you could talk Jack into helping you pack for me. I'm not sure how long I'll be gone so if Chaz wants to find another hostess and rent out the apartment, I'll understand."

"Don't worry about the details," Hope said. "Just stay safe. My family will be here for you. But please promise to call me when you leave?"

"I will. And when you get around to apologizing to Jack, put me on speaker." Val paused, smiling at the image of her friends as a happy couple. "I'll referee as needed."

"Bless your generous spirit," Hope whispered. "Jack and I will weather this so we can help you make your family understand."

Unable to trust her voice, Val nodded and ended the call. At least one of them had made it.

CHAPTER TWENTY-SIX

HOLY SMOKES, HE'D SURVIVED A WEEK FROM THE DARK side!

Jack glanced at his battered left hand, a painful reminder of his distraction over Hope, then swung his leg over his bike, ready to head home. The slam of Nate's truck door echoed behind him, verifying how far down Jack had slipped, even frustrating easygoing Nate.

When he pulled on his helmet, a raindrop splatted the visor, mirroring the tears he refused to shed.

"Bring it on," Jack muttered, too exhausted to care about the looming thunderstorm.

"I am—" He revved the engine, frustrated he couldn't clear Hope's laugh, her passion, and her loyalty from his mind —even for a second! "Remedial!"

His shout challenged the roar of the cycle's engine but didn't ease his frustration any more than the loneliness. Riding faster than usual, he sped out of the Martinez neighborhood toward the main road, his thoughts racing past the blurred homes.

Life with Hope would be a continuous emotional roller-coaster. He shifted gears. It couldn't be worse than the desolation without her. Managing the family-business connection was bound to be messy. Not that it was new, but he was glad to have a family at his back, regardless of the fallout. With Hope, they could start their own. And if he had a little girl just like Hope? He'd have a firm understanding of why Ryan's hair had grayed.

"Man up, Cline," he muttered, cutting a corner so sharply his boot scraped the pavement. "You're in for the ride of your life."

As he rolled into his apartment's parking lot, the heavens unleashed a torrential downpour, soaking his clothes through until they clung uncomfortably to his skin, droplets streaming from his helmet. With water-soaked fingers, he popped the lockable lid and Turbo's tiny head emerged, eyes wide with curiosity.

"Sorry, little buddy," Jack murmured, gently scooping up the kitten and nestling its warm, furry body beneath his jacket, welcoming the soft purr against his chest. "It wasn't supposed to rain today. Had I known a storm was brewing, you could have stayed at home."

Except the creature had a mind of its own, much like his missing girlfriend. If Jack abandoned the kitty for more than two hours, Turbo unrolled the toilet paper, the paper towels, and scattered trash throughout the three rooms. Of course he could confine the little booger in the carrier—if he'd been made of stouter stuff.

Jack locked the lid, securing his tools, and hustled inside. While Turbo scampered to his food bowl and crunched kitten kibble, Jack stripped down in the laundry room and headed for a much-needed shower, the snarl of his loneliness fixed in his mind.

The pelt of hot water soothed his tired, aching muscles

that made him feel a century old, but did nothing to resolve his problem. Two whole days had passed since she'd kicked him to the curb. How long would it take for her to get over his shortcomings? Geez, she knew he wasn't perfect. But didn't trying account for something?

Fifteen minutes later, he wrapped a towel around his waist and stepped into his adjacent bedroom. He paused, his ears straining for the smallest sound. Turbo usually had a quick snack and then napped until Jack started dinner. However, the kitten was as unpredictable as Hope. He raked a frustrated hand through his damp hair. Every thought in his sketchy brain held a Hope reference. This couldn't continue.

Tomorrow, he'd find her and make her talk—just as soon as he hung Miss Gracie's swing. When he didn't hear additional sounds coming from the living room, he collected clean underwear and retreated to the master bath. Five minutes later, he turned off the tap and wiped the toothpaste foam from his lips. Turbo was definitely up to something and he was in no mood to clean up after his kitty.

"Okay, buddy. I don't know what you're up to but—"

A tangled mess of hair reminding him of the bird's nest he'd removed from Miss Gracie's tree appeared at the crack in the bedroom door followed by Hope's squinty-eyed expression.

"About time you got home," she said, sassy as ever. "Turbo looks like he weathered my absence just fine."

Jack blinked, his mind a chaotic swirl of questions and emotions.

"Do you have anything to eat?" She turned and walked toward his kitchen. "I'm starving. I've been working at Val's place all afternoon and didn't take time for lunch."

Man, he had to get more sleep. The exhaustion weighed on him, making it hard to think straight.

He pulled a clean t-shirt over his head and hurried to the kitchen. "We need to talk."

She opened the fridge, the cool light spilling out and casting a soft glow on her tousled hair. She looked gorgeous.

"After we eat." She gathered eggs, orange juice, Canadian bacon, and deposited them on the counter. "Have you fed Turbo? His bowl is empty."

"Snack," he managed to say. But swear to heavens he felt like she had smacked him over the head with a two-by-four.

Oblivious to his cognitive impairment, she rummaged through his pantry and tossed a loaf of bread on the counter beside the eggs.

"Your milk better be fresh," she said. "I've got a taste for scrambled eggs. Too bad you don't have a red pepper or onions. An omelet sounds wonderful."

He thumped the heel of his hand against his forehead. *Don't go there, Cline.*

"I was thinking about hot chocolate all the way home," Hope said, her voice muffled by the rattle of pans. She emerged from beneath his cabinet holding a skillet. The sudden memory of her preparing to swing a bat at him muddled his thoughts.

"Val needs our help."

Jack shook his head, unable to make her continuous leap of topics. But regardless of what was going on with him and Hope, he'd never leave a friend hanging. More focused, he snatched the carton and poured milk in the kettle to warm. "I'll do whatever I can for her."

"You know you gave me your truck," Hope said, cracking six eggs, one at a time with the smack, smack, smack of his breaths.

Technically, he'd given her the truck to pay off her debt, which was no longer needed with Vill's arrest. Before he could point out that important detail, Turbo leaped onto the counter, his small pink nose sniffing at the Canadian bacon, scattering Jack's thoughts once more. He scooped up his kitty. Meanwhile, Hope went about preparing their meal like she hadn't just launched a grenade in his head.

"Okay," Jack said. "I surrender. What do you want me to do?"

She blinded him with a bright smile. "Have dinner with me."

He held Turbo in front of his face. "She's crazy," he said, fixed on its inquisitive blue stare. The kitten cocked its head like it understood. "But we love her anyway."

His eyes widened when his words echoed in his ears, which operated on a more rationale level than his brain and mouth. Turbo meowed. Even the cat recognized his blunder.

Hope, however, whipped the eggs like she'd scrambled his brains.

"In a minute," she said. "I'm going to say something you need to hear."

His heart revved up. "Considered me warned and spill the news." Before he said or did something dumb like fall to his sore knees and beg her to forgive him.

"I can't."

Jack's head tilted up. Neither could he, but what else could he do? A cobweb stretched from his kitchen fixture toward the living room.

"Jack?"

He should remain single. He was a simple guy. As long as he stuck to tasks like hanging Miss Gracie's swing and pounding nails, he'd be okay. Because his future with Hope— was going nowhere, except the loony bin. Besides, his battered heart couldn't take a replay like he'd suffered in Columbia.

"I get it." He lowered his raised hands and removed two mugs from the cupboard. "You were clear in Columbia. I know I let you down. I'm sorry. I panicked when I thought someone I loved might be in danger. But I did it. It's over. I can't change my actions."

Steam lifted from the filled cups. Did she even like hot chocolate? She had him so messed up he couldn't remember. Best to close his mouth—tight. With his feelings and words jumbled up inside him, he'd say something dumb and end up in more trouble than he was already in.

"Val's on her way back to Sunberry," Hope said. "But as soon as she picks up Libby, she's heading back to Missouri and she doesn't know how long she'll be gone. There's no way she can get all of her baby stuff in her little car. Good grief, she'll need a car seat, and bassinet, and her stroller, plus diapers and her clothes. You need to trade vehicles with her so she can transport her stuff."

"I lay my heart on the line," he whispered, devastated that once again she'd stomped on it. "And you want my truck… again."

She smiled and patted his cheek, but he was too numb to feel her flesh against his.

"I knew you'd agree, especially since you already have your motorcycle." She served a steaming plate of eggs on a plate and added Canadian bacon and two slices of toast. "You can add your own jelly."

He stared at his plate.

She sat at the counter and picked up a fork. "Eat your eggs. I know how you get when you're hungry. I promise I didn't poison it."

He'd worked all day, his stomach growling on the way home, but now he didn't think he could swallow one bite, which made perfect sense. It was hard to feel hunger while watching his hopes and dreams circle the drain. Sorry thing was he wanted to believe in a future with her. He'd never wanted anything more than to make a life with her. But he couldn't change the past.

His fingers twitched. Purring like a lawnmower, Turbo bumped his chin with her tiny nose. At least the cat loved him.

The metallic sound of metal against glass interrupted Turbo's purr. Jack blinked at Hope's empty plate and then slowly lifted his gaze, his breath trapped in his lungs. Hope sat with her chin propped on one graceful hand, her gaze steady—on him.

"Don't like my cooking?" she said, the soft hum of her voice reminding him of Turbo's purr.

Dazed, he stared down at his plate while his cat, with dainty precision, pawed at a chunk of ham.

"I'm not upset because you didn't believe in me," Hope said, her playful tone now serious. "Truth is, I didn't believe in me either."

She stood and walked around the counter to stand behind him, launching his heart like a rocket and blurring his vision. To make matters worse, her hands traveled across his shoulders and moved down his chest. He swallowed, which was a small miracle considering his mouth felt cottony dry. When her breath tickled his ear, an involuntary shiver shook his shoulders. Confused, terrified to break the moment, he froze, praying he could survive his erratic heartbeat while an old dream about feeling her hands on his body erupted behind his eyes.

"I believed in us." She kissed his cheek. "I believed you'd always stand by me and listen," she whispered, kissing him again. "Even when my ideas were a bit...unique."

The word unique broke through his brain fog, making him grin. When she wormed beneath his arm, he turned and she climbed on his lap. Face to face with her, his lungs struggled to suck in air.

"I love you, Jack Cline. I think we should make an official announcement that we are a couple. All of my earthly belongings are piled on the porch."

"I thought you were only with me for my truck," he said, his voice feeling rusty and overloaded from his fluttering heart.

She ran her tongue along the seam of his lips and his body launched into autopilot. His head canted, deepening the kiss, his heart pounding.

When fire raged in his lungs, threatening to explode from lack of oxygen, he released her, blinking at the mischievous glint sparking her gaze.

"That was a pretty good kiss from a starving man," she said. "Anything else?"

His growl of frustration filled the silence. "I've been in love with you since you made fun of me because I couldn't bait a hook."

She made the funny face that always made him laugh. "Thank your lucky stars I didn't clobber you. I was furious that day. My brothers were away at camp and I had Dad all to myself—and you show up." Her playful look turned sultry and she nibbled his lip. "You destroyed three perfectly good night crawlers."

"I always figured I couldn't keep up with you."

"You weren't trying hard enough."

He brushed the side of her mouth with his lips. "I'm a little slow on the uptake. But I got it now."

"I don't need rescuing," she said.

"I do."

For once, he'd said something to halt her quick wit.

"Full disclosure." She dropped his gaze. "My debt predicament is over. But I attract drama like nuts attract squirrels. You said you're a simple man. Can you be happy with a complex woman?"

Leave it to the woman he loved to ask the tough questions. Based on the way she had squeezed her eyes closed, she held doubts about his answer.

He tapped the tip of her nose. "Hey?"

She squinted at him like she was afraid to read his expression.

"We'll just have to see if I can man up." He winked. "Just promise to give me a breather every now and then. By the way, are we going for the traditional path or do we live in sin?"

She slid from his lap. "Nice, Jack. That sounded like something your father would say. Or better yet, your grandfather."

"I'm a simple, small-town guy who could use a fresh plate of eggs. I like my life." He scraped his eggs into Turbo's bowl. "You do have three brothers and a former Marine father."

"And you're not much of a fighter?"

"Not a secret." He grinned. "But I'm a good lover."

"Is this the part where I get a roller skate to support your expanding head? Not sure if you can lift it with that big ego."

"Ouch! Harsh. So what? You want to date? Get to know me?" He tried to hide his frustration. "Because I already know you. I know what I want."

She jerked open the refrigerator door and removed eggs and bacon. "Make yourself useful and get your own bread."

He might as well get used to it. She was always going to mess with him. But two could play this game, and he'd already committed to upping his game. He nuzzled the back of her neck, making her wiggle away.

"And?" He followed her to the range.

She glanced over her shoulder, her eyes bright, her cheeks flushed. "We'll have to take some breathing time because I've got a hot new project."

Refusing to consider what she meant, he kissed beneath

her ear, his pulse quickening with the sound of her gasp. "Any chance that I'm your hot project?"

"You aren't the project, but it's for you."

He suppressed the molten lava surging through his veins and focused on her words, every fiber in his body jangling with a warning.

"But." She held up her palm like the safety officer at the school crossing. "Hold that thought."

"Welcome to my world on Hope," he muttered while she dug through her backpack and carried a sheaf of papers to the counter.

When she made a production of smoothing the sheets, he got the feeling she was stalling for time. His heart rate revved up again. In the land of Hope, anything could happen.

She smoothed out the first page with a drawing on it. "Keep in mind this is just a preliminary workup. Sarina and I only had a few hours to work on it today."

Jack squinted at the title, MCB Logo Design Brief, his thoughts colliding in his head like a nail gun on steroids.

"You...designed this...for me?"

"This is my draft. In a few days, we'll have a presentation ready to give you a visual preview of the design. I still need to research your target audience." She flipped to the second group of documents. "This might look a little confusing, but it's a diagram. Houses have blueprints and so do apps. This shows how your clients can connect with you with questions. And this is a project management component. I've designed an app with places for task lists, timelines, and milestones. This one." She tapped at a box. "These are the tabs for budget and costs, resource management—I remembered you told me materials can be a problem—"

"You did this for me?" Embarrassment heated his cheeks. He must have sounded like a dope repeating the same questions but— "It's amazing."

The shy smile on her face and the way she glanced away—
"You crazy, wonderful woman."

"Does that mean you like it? I mean, it'll be much better
in a few days. I'll create a PowerPoint and walk you through
the flow so we get it just right."

He wrapped his arms around her waist, relishing the way
her hands slipped around his neck, skyrocketing his heart rate
and quickening his breaths. "It'll be perfect, just like you are.
Now, can we revisit that talk about taking a breather?"

She grinned. "We could do that."

"So remind me what I'm taking a breather from."

"Stress." Her shoulders lifted. "I want to enjoy just being
with you. You know? Without worrying about a huge debt
and lies."

The past few weeks had taken a toll on her, hollowing her
cheeks and carving fine lines around her mouth and eyes.

"I was kind of hoping to enjoy being with you for the rest
of my life." He brushed his lips against hers. "How long did
you plan to torture me?"

When she caught her lip with her teeth, he swallowed a
groan.

"I was thinking a month or two, maybe the summer." She
smiled. "No torture involved unless you call meeting with me
about the app torture. I remembered how much fun we had
after high school graduation."

He tightened his hold. "This would be an adult summer."

She wiggled from his grasp and returned to the range.
"The timing has to be right. We need to make sure our families will be around."

"Full disclosure." He dropped his arms, embarrassment
surging through him. "Your finances might be solid again, but
mine are a little shaky. Until there are new homes with sold
signs in the window, I'm going to be strapped."

She straightened. "I'm not a bought woman."

Her comeback didn't even rate a grin.

"I want it all," he whispered, his voice trembling with vulnerability. "A partner, a house, kids, and a dog."

"We have a kitten."

She spooned his meal onto a clean plate and handed it to him. Holding her gaze, he set it aside and took her into his arms. "I want you and me together. From now on. Drama and all."

"Fall wedding?"

"If that's what you want."

"Nothing expensive. Something small. I think at Kyle's place. I always loved that old barn."

"Hope?"

"Hmmm?"

"You talk too much."

Holding Hope close, Jack felt the storm outside fade away, replaced by the promise of their future together.

––––––

Loved Hope and Jack's story? Start at the beginning of the Murphy Family Saga!

AN INDEPENDENT WIDOW. Four fatherless children. The Marine officer who ordered her deceased husband's last patrol. Will she risk her family's future for a second chance at love?

Download your copy of

HOME TO STAY
NOW!

Do you love being first ? Like getting all the information

so you can make the best decisions? **Turner Town News**, my monthly newsletter, gives you the inside scoop. Plus, if you subscribe now, you'll get a FREE download of the **Clocktower Romance Character Map.**

With my character map you can track your favorite character to help you decide which book to read next! I've made it super easy. Just click I WANT TO STAY IN TOUCH for your free character map.

A CLOCKTOWER ROMANCE

HOME TO STAY

BECKE TURNER

ABOUT HOME TO STAY

Try dating when you have teen sons. That's a challenge—even when the man is not your neighbor or the kid's soccer coach. No, no, no! The man in question is a marine officer who led my deceased husband in his final campaign. Got your attention, now?

It gets worse. He's competing against me and my sons for the *only* available lease in the historic district. Yep, the one with the best foot traffic for our new shop. The shop my children and I want to build to honor their father.

Wish me luck because the gloves are off. We're going to kick Ryan Murphy to the curb. So much for a gal's love life. But family always comes first.

You're going to fall as hard as Ryan does for this struggling family.

———

If you love a military romance with a single mom struggling to raise four children, you'll love award-winning this heartfelt love Ava and Ryan's romance.

Click the link to start the Murphy family saga today!

HOME TO STAY

PLEASE LEAVE A REVIEW

If you enjoyed **Murphy's Rescue**, please leave me a review on, Goodreads, Amazon, and Bookbub.

Reviews help readers find books from people who have enjoyed a story and help me improve my craft. Yes, your opinion matters. If you can spare just five minutes to leave even a one or two line review, it would be so helpful in this book's success.

- **Goodreads Review:**
- Click on the link: Goodreads, click on **Murphy's Rescue** cover and rate and write your review.
- Or go to Goodreads.com, type **Murphy's Rescue** in the search field. Click on the title, scroll down and click on the Write a review button.

- **Amazon Review:**
- Click on the link: Write an Amazon review, scroll down to the write a customer review button on the left side of the screen, and fill in the box with your review.

- Or go to Amazon.com, select Kindle Books from the Amazon menu at the top of the page and type **Murphy's Rescue** in the search field. Click on the title, scroll down the left side of the page, and click write a customer review button.

- **BookBub Review:**
- Click on the link: Bookbub, scroll down to the review button, click and leave your review.
- Or go to Bookbub.com, sign on, type **Murphy's Rescue** in the search field. Scroll down to the red Write a Review box. Click the box and write a review.

One or two sentences to say I liked a character, it was a page-turner, or I laughed at the child is all it takes for a review. Plus, you can copy the same review for each site. I'm into easy. Thanks so much!

———

BOOKS BY BECKE TURNER

Clocktower Romances are set in fictitious Sunberry, NC and the characters throughout the series are friends or relatives. There are no cliffhangers and each book can be read as a stand alone and in any order of publication.

———

AWARD-WINNING MURPHY CLAN

- *HOME TO STAY* (The beginning, Ava and Ryan Murphy)

- *MURPHY'S SECRET* (Whit Murphy's romance)

- *MURPHY'S CINDERELLA (Kyle Murphy's romance)*

- *MURPHY'S CHOICE (Nate Murphy's romance)*

- *MURPHY'S STANDOFF (Marriage in crisis, Ava and Ryan Murphy*

- *MURPHY'S RESCUE (Hope Murphy's romance)*

SUNBERRY FRIENDS & NEIGHBORS

- *CAROLINA COWBOY*

- *LOVING TROUBLE (companion novella to CAROLINA COWBOY)*

- *THE PUPPY BARTER*

- *A SUNBERRY CHRISTMAS*

- FLIGHT WITHOUT WINGS

Want a bigger bang for your buck? Choose a 3-book collection!

THE CLOCKTOWER ROMANCE COLLECTION

- *HOME TO STAY*
- *CAROLINA COWBOY*
- *MURPHY'S SECRET*

THE MURPHY MEN COLLECTION

- *HOME TO STAY*
- *MURPHY'S SECRET*
- *MURPHY'S CINDERELLA*

THE MURPHY BROTHERS COLLECTION

- *MURPHY'S SECRET*
- *MURPHY'S CINDERELLA*
- *MURPHY'S CHOICE*

THE FEEL GOOD COLLECTION

- *HOME TO STAY*
- *THE PUPPY BARTER*
- *MURPHY'S CINDERELLA*

DECADENT SALTED CARAMEL SHOOTER RECIPE

Dear Reader,

In "Murphy's Rescue," the Murphy family is known for their love of home-cooked meals and heartwarming desserts that bring everyone together. One of their all-time favorite treats is the Decadent Salted Caramel Shooter—a perfect blend of sweet and salty that leaves everyone wanting more. This delightful dessert not only satisfies your sweet tooth but also creates cherished moments with loved ones, just like the Murphy family does.

Whether you're reading about Hope's journey of resilience or Jack's quest for redemption, you can enjoy this delicious recipe inspired by the warmth and love that the Murphy family shares. Gather your ingredients and follow the steps below to create a dessert that's sure to become a favorite in your own home.

Enjoy this treat as you dive deeper into the world of Sunberry and the heartfelt story of "Murphy's Rescue." Here's to love, family, and a touch of sweetness in every chapter of life!

DECADENT SALTED CARAMEL SHOOTERS

Ingredients:

For the Salted Caramel Sauce:

- 1 cup granulated sugar
- 6 tablespoons unsalted butter, cut into pieces
- 1/2 cup heavy cream
- 1 teaspoon sea salt

For the Chocolate Layer:

- 1/2 cup heavy cream
- 1 cup semisweet chocolate chips

For the Whipped Cream:

- 1 cup heavy cream
- 2 tablespoons powdered sugar
- 1 teaspoon vanilla extract

For Garnish:

- Sea salt flakes
- Caramel candies or chocolate shavings (optional)

Instructions:

Prepare the Salted Caramel Sauce:

1. In a medium saucepan over medium heat, melt the sugar, stirring constantly until it turns into a deep amber color.

2. Add the butter and stir until melted and combined.
3. Carefully pour in the heavy cream (it will bubble up) and whisk until smooth.
4. Remove from heat and stir in the sea salt.
5. Let the caramel sauce cool slightly before using.

Prepare the Chocolate Layer:

1. In a small saucepan, heat the heavy cream until it just begins to simmer.
2. Remove from heat and add the chocolate chips.
3. Let sit for a minute, then stir until smooth and melted.
4. Allow the chocolate mixture to cool slightly.

Prepare the Whipped Cream:

1. In a chilled mixing bowl, beat the heavy cream, powdered sugar, and vanilla extract until soft peaks form.
2. Set aside.

Assemble the Shooters:

1. In small shooter glasses, layer the salted caramel sauce first, followed by the chocolate layer.
2. Top each shooter with a dollop of whipped cream.
3. Sprinkle sea salt flakes on top for garnish and add a caramel candy or chocolate shavings if desired.

Chill and Serve:

1. Refrigerate the shooters for at least 30 minutes to let the layers set.
2. Serve chilled and enjoy the decadent flavors!

ABOUT THE AUTHOR
Updated 3/15/24

Becke Turner, award-winning author, grew up in Salem, Illinois. Her path to becoming a writer began at the University of Miami, where she ran a successful writing business to finance taxi rides to her horse. Inspired by authors like Zane Gray and Julie Garwood, Becke wrote her first manuscript while raising her son.

With a background in nursing and healthcare policy, Becke has worked at prestigious institutions like Barnes-Jewish Hospital and Ohio State University Wexner Medical Center. She developed programs to enhance molecular diagnostics and prevent Medicare fraud before retiring in 2017 to write full-time.

Now living in Blythewood, SC, with her husband of over fifty years, Becke writes sweet romances about strong women and their adventures. She is the proud mother of two and grandmother of five.

Her stories appeal to readers who love family, home, and

the joy of nurturing relationships. Connect with Becke and get a FREE BOOK by signing up for her newsletter at

Becke@becketurner.com

ACKNOWLEDGMENTS

Medium-chain acyl-CoA dehydrogenase deficiency (MCADD) is a rare genetic disorder that impairs the body's ability to convert certain fats into energy, especially during fasting periods. Approximately 1 in every 10,000 to 20,000 infants in the United States is born with MCADD each year. Without proper management, MCADD can lead to severe health issues such as hypoglycemia, seizures, and sudden death, significantly affecting life expectancy. However, with early diagnosis and appropriate treatment, individuals with MCADD can lead healthy lives.

Children inherit MCADD in an autosomal recessive pattern, meaning that if both parents are carriers of the gene, there is a high risk their child will inherit two copies of the gene and develop MCADD. Infants who inherit only one copy of the affected gene typically do not develop the disorder but will carry the trait.

MCADD came to my attention when I learned about a new friend's grandson who was diagnosed with the disorder. Despite my lifelong career in healthcare, specifically in genetic testing, I was not familiar with MCADD. This underscores the importance of early diagnosis for the survival of infants with this disorder. Fortunately, MCADD is included in the Recommended Uniform Screening Panel (RUSP) for newborn screening.

For more information on this disorder, please visit:

- National Institutes of Health (NIH)
- Parental Experiences of Raising a Child With Medium Chain Acyl-CoA Dehydrogenase Deficiency - PMC (NIH)
- Newborn Screening HRSA website.

Murphy's Rescue

Written by Becke Turner

Cover Design by Special-T Publishing

Edited by By the Book Editing, Beth Belmanno

Copyright @ 2024 Becke Turner

This book is a work of fiction. Names, characters, places, and incidents either are products of the author's imagination or are used fictitiously. Any resemblance to actual persons, living or dead, events, or locales is entirely coincident.

Published by Special-T Publishing, LLC

ISBN - 978-1-953651-30-03

Library of Congress Control Number:

First Edition

First Printing --

Made in the USA
Columbia, SC
25 September 2024

42382766R00167